A Body in the Forest

ALSO BY P.F. FORD

THE WEST WALES MURDER MYSTERIES
Prequel: A Date with Death
Book 1: A Body on the Beach
Book 2: A Body out at Sea
Book 3: A Body down the Lane
Book 4: A Body at the Farmhouse
Book 5: A Body in the Cottage
Book 6: A Body under the Bridge
Book 7: A Body in the Forest

SLATER AND NORMAN MYSTERIES
Book 1: Death by Carpet
Book 2: Death by Plane
Book 3: Death by Night
Book 4: Death by Kitchen Sink
Book 5: Death by Telephone Box
Book 6: Death in Wild Boar Woods
Book 7: Death in the River
Book 8: Death in a Skip
Book 9: Death of a Pensioner
Book 10: Death of a Long-Lost Son
Book 11: Death by Takeaway
Book 12: Death by Caravan
Book 13: Death by Jogging
Book 14: Death by Sports Car

A Body in the Forest

P.F. Ford

JOFFE BOOKS

Joffe Books, London
www.joffebooks.com

First published in Great Britain in 2025

Cover art by Dee Dee Book Covers

ISBN: 978-1-80573-304-1

To my amazing wife, Mary — sometimes we need someone else to believe in us before we really believe in ourselves. None of this would have happened without your unfailing belief and support.

PROLOGUE

Friday, 1 November

The driver slowed his car and peered along the beam of the headlights into the gloom ahead. It was pitch dark and there were no streetlights to help him out, but then that was exactly why he had chosen this time of night to be here. He knew the car park was along here somewhere; he'd checked out the suitability of the site just a couple of days ago.

At last, he saw the faded wording on the sign ahead. He couldn't read Welsh, but he'd heard the locals refer to this place as the "Dragon Forest", so he guessed that must be what the sign said. He turned into the tiny car park and drew up in a space that wouldn't be visible from the road, and killed the engine. The chances of anyone driving past at this time of night were almost zero, but it made no sense to take chances.

He grabbed a torch from the glove box, stepped from the car and went round to the boot. He opened it and shone the torch onto her face. He contemplated her for a moment. Just hours ago, her features would probably have been distorted in terror, but now, with her eyes closed in death, she looked to be at peace. He thought she would have been beautiful

1

when she was alive, and it saddened him to think she was an innocent victim in the grand scheme of things.

The last thing he had wanted to do was violate her by putting his hands on her naked body, so he'd managed to cover her in an old bedsheet before placing her in the boot. Now, he gathered the corners together and hefted the bundle over his shoulder. He reached inside to grab a spade, and as he quietly closed the boot lid, he realised she weighed almost nothing.

'Come on, little beauty,' he muttered quietly. 'Let's get this done.'

* * *

Forty minutes later, he set the spade down and stood on the rim of the hole he had dug. It was too dark to see much, but he felt he must have gone deep enough by now. He reached for his torch, making sure to keep the beam low, and shone it down into the grave just long enough to see if the hole would accommodate the body.

The victim was so small she could have comfortably worn kids' clothes, so he thought the grave would serve its purpose.

Not for the first time, he wondered idly who she was. Going by her diminutive stature and skin colour he guessed she was from the Middle East or possibly Asia. She had probably come here seeking a better life. She certainly would have had no idea why she had been selected to die.

He reached over and carefully manoeuvred her body into the hole. Gently, he arranged her arms and adjusted the sheet to cover her modesty, leaving her face until last. Finally, he covered that too, and as he reached for his spade, he realised he was weeping.

'Jesus, man, pull yourself together,' he muttered, wiping his eyes with a fold of the sheet.

He was just about to begin covering the body with soil when he thought he heard the faint sound of approaching voices. He stopped and listened, but all was silent. *Of course not, you idiot,* he thought. *Who's going to be out here in the forest at midnight?*

But then he heard the sound again, and this time there was no mistaking it. It was definitely voices. He turned towards the sound and caught the faint beam of a torch flicker between the trees. Whoever it was, they were still some distance away, but they were definitely heading in this direction.

Quietly cursing his luck, he wondered what to do. He hated to leave a job unfinished. If he stayed here, would they see him? Of course they would; he was in the middle of a clearing! So that was it then. He had no choice. He would have to run.

CHAPTER ONE

Monday, 4 November, 07.30

If you had been out at sea looking towards the small coastal town of Llangwelli, you would have noticed a hill rising to the west of the town. If you had a pair of binoculars, you might also have spotted the figure of a man. Dressed in bright yellow waterproofs, hunched against the wind and the fine drizzle, he was making his way along the path that ran up the hill.

A short distance ahead of the man, a small dog in a bright red waterproof coat galloped joyfully up the path, then back to the man, who bent down to pat her.

The man was Detective Sergeant Norman Norman. The dog was called Trudy, adopted by Norman after a recent case in which her owner had been murdered.

'Jeez, Trudy, I wish I could have as much fun in this crappy weather as you do,' he said as he gently took a ball from the dog's mouth.

Before he threw it again, he raised a hand to his brow to shield his eyes from the wind, and turned to peer out to sea through the mist. As always, the sight made him smile. 'There again, I see your point,' he said. 'If we didn't enjoy living out here, there'd have to be something wrong with us, right?'

The dog barked, which he took for agreement — or more likely impatience — so Norman threw the ball back up the hill. Trudy turned and galloped after it.

His phone began to play a distorted version of something that could have been a Led Zeppelin track.

'Crap,' muttered Norman, patting at his coat. 'Why do these things have so many pockets?'

It took the best part of a minute to pat his way through a dozen pockets before he located the phone. He glanced down at the screen, saw who was calling and then turned his back on the wind, his phone at his ear.

'Hi, Sarah, what's up?' DI Sarah Southall was Norman's immediate boss.

'Wow!' she said. 'What's that noise? I can barely hear you. Are you in a wind tunnel?'

'One of the obligations of being a dog owner is making sure the dog gets enough exercise. So I'm out on the hill with Trudy.' He adjusted his hood to keep the phone from getting wet. 'Is that better?'

'You're out on the hill in this weather? Are you mad?'

'You should try it,' said Norman. 'When it's not actually pouring with rain it's quite exhilarating. Trudy loves it. Anyway, I'm sure you didn't call me to discuss my walking habits. What's up?'

'I've been called in to see the chief constable.'

'Over the boss's head?'

'I'm assuming he's going to be there too,' said Southall.

'So, basically, what you mean is, I'm in charge this morning.'

'Yes. I'm sorry to spring it on you so suddenly.'

'Don't worry about that,' said Norman. 'But you do remember I've got an appointment to attend first thing. I'm not going to get to the office until about ten.'

'Oh, damn. I'd forgotten about that,' said Southall.

'Don't worry. I'm sure they can cope without us for a couple of hours. It's not as if there's much on,' said Norman. 'Have you any idea why you've been called in?'

'Not a clue,' said Southall. 'I'll fill you in as soon as I get back from the meeting.'

'Okay. I'll catch you later,' said Norman.

* * *

It was now nine fifteen and DI Sarah Southall stopped outside the door to the office, took a deep breath and did her best to make herself look neat and tidy. If the chief constable had seen fit to ask her to a meeting, she wanted to appear competent and businesslike. She knocked and poked her head around the door.

The CC's secretary looked up from her computer and smiled.

'DI Southall?'

'That's right,' said Southall. 'The CC is expecting me.'

'He won't expect you to be hiding behind a door.'

'What? Oh, of course not.' Southall stepped into the office, her cheeks feeling distinctly warm.

'I thought Superintendent Bain would be here too,' she said.

The secretary placed a finger on a large desk diary in front of her and ran it across the page. 'His name's not down here.'

'Oh,' said Southall, surprised. 'Do you know what this is about?'

'It's a short notice thing, so I know as much as you.'

'And you wouldn't tell me anyway,' said Southall.

The secretary smiled again. 'Loyalty and discretion are my middle names.' She pointed to two chairs opposite her desk. 'Take a seat. He's on the phone, but he said to tell you he'll only be a couple of minutes.'

Southall walked across and settled nervously into one of the chairs. The secretary leaned towards her.

'I can tell you that you can relax and stop worrying,' she said, keeping her voice low. 'You're not in any trouble, and he's in a good mood.'

Before Southall could speak again, a phone on the desk buzzed. The secretary pressed a button and an authoritative voice boomed out across the room.

'Is DI Southall here?'

'She's sitting right in front of me.'

'Good. Please ask her to come through.'

The secretary pointed to a door to the left.

'Despite what the grapevine might have said, he's a nice man. He doesn't like arse-lickers, but he does like what he's heard about you,' she assured Southall with a wink.

Southall gulped. 'No pressure then.'

'Just be yourself. Trust me, you'll be fine.'

Southall marched to the door, paused for a moment and knocked.

'Come in,' called the chief constable.

* * *

At 09.45, Norman made his way up the stairs and backed through the double doors into the main office at Llangwelli police station.

He expected to see Detective Constable Judy Lane, but her chair was pushed under her desk, which was bare. The only other person in the room was DC Catren Morgan, who looked up from her desk and frowned at him. She raised her eyebrows and nodded towards the far corner where DI Sarah Southall's office was situated.

'Hi, Catren, what's up?'

'We've got a pro—'

'Ah, at last,' cried an unfamiliar voice. 'I suppose you must be Detective Sergeant Norman.'

Norman looked back at the office, where a uniformed officer was standing in the doorway. He was lean and tall, just like their boss, Superintendent Bain, and wore a similar uniform, but that's where the similarity ended. Bain was close to retirement age and usually had an air of calmness about him. The newcomer was in his forties, with a fearsome frown on his face. Anger seemed to radiate from every part of his body.

'Well, Norman. What time do you call this?' he demanded.

Norman slowly and deliberately looked down at his wrist. 'That'll be nine forty-eight by my watch.'

'Is this how you run this place?' demanded the man. 'This . . . this—' he pointed at Morgan — 'officer is hardly of high enough rank to be in charge of an incident room.'

Norman had no idea who this man was, but he was clearly outranked, so he counted slowly to ten before he spoke.

'I can assure you that DC Morgan is in line for promotion and is more than capable of holding the fort,' he said. 'I'm sure you are also aware that detectives don't always work set hours, so we must sometimes fit personal stuff in where we can. I can't recall a senior officer ever complaining when it's been the other way around and I've worked through the night.'

The man's face had begun to turn a deep shade of red, but before he could respond, Norman walked towards him, still speaking.

'Can I ask who you are?'

'Never mind that—'

'I'm sorry, but I can't ignore the fact that you appear to have taken over DI Southall's office, yet I have no idea who you are. I wouldn't be doing my job if I didn't ask for some form of ID.'

'DC Morgan knows who I am, but if you insist, I have a warrant card I can show you.'

'It's okay, Norm,' said Morgan. 'This is Acting Superintendent Evans.'

'Acting Superintendent?' echoed Norman. 'What's happened to Nathan?'

'If you mean Superintendent Bain, he's going to be away for a few weeks.'

'Well, yeah, we know that,' said Norman. 'He's getting a new hip, but he'll be back in a couple of weeks. I'm sure we can manage just fine without him.'

'I hate to disillusion you, but the chief constable doesn't share your optimism about the timing of Superintendent Bain's return, nor does he share your opinion regarding the running of this department in the interim. So he's asked me to fill the position temporarily.'

Norman remained unimpressed.

'Well, whatever, this is still DI Southall's office,' he said. 'Nathan's office is upstairs. He likes to let us get on with our jobs.'

Evans sniffed disapprovingly. 'I think you'll find I'm a bit more hands-on than Superintendent Bain.' He picked up a sheet of paper from Southall's desk and held it out for Norman. 'And, just to prove it, here's a job for you.'

'What is this?' Norman quickly scanned through the page. 'This is a job for a DC. It doesn't need me.'

Evans's face was dangerously red by now.

'Yes, I might even agree with you if there was a spare bloody DC to send. I understood there were three of them, but it seems two are currently missing.'

Norman couldn't argue with that, and he wondered where the other two were. Only now did he realise that he hadn't seen their cars in the car park, which meant they weren't even in the building. He turned to Morgan for inspiration.

She shrugged. 'Car broke down.'

Norman turned to Evans.

'Well, there you go,' he said. 'Shit happens. Unfortunately, this morning it's happened at a time when I had an early appointment, and DI Southall has been called to see the chief constable at short notice. Now you wouldn't expect her to tell the CC she couldn't make it, would you? Besides, DC Morgan is here.'

'DC Morgan is doing something for me,' snapped Evans. 'And if I had sent her out, there would have been no one here at all. Don't think I'm going to tolerate slackness, or casual informality. You will cut out the flippant attitude, show some respect for my rank and address me as "sir". Is that clear?'

Norman nodded. 'Crystal—' deliberate pause — 'sir.'

'Good. Where have you been anyway?'

'Who, me?' asked Norman. 'I've been for my annual medical assessment.'

Evans glowered.

'Sir,' added Norman.

'I have to say I'm disappointed,' said Evans. 'This is not the start I was expecting. I can see I'm going to have my work cut out improving standards around here.'

Norman immediately thought of a smart-arse retort, but decided silence was probably the better option.

'Well, don't just stand there, man,' snapped Evans. 'Go and do your job!'

Norman turned on his heel and made for the door. As he passed her desk, he raised his eyebrows at Morgan, who mouthed "sorry".

* * *

It had taken Norman a good twenty minutes to reach the address Evans had given him. He had spent the journey imagining various scenarios featuring himself and Evans, a man who seemed to encompass everything Norman disliked. None of the scenarios ended well — for Evans.

'Maybe this is a bad dream and when I wake up, he'll never have happened,' he muttered hopefully as he found a parking space a few yards down from the house he was visiting.

He was just about to open his car door when his mobile phone began to ring.

It was the office. 'Jeez, now what?' he muttered. 'Yo, Catren, what's up?'

'I beg your pardon?'

It wasn't Catren Morgan, it was Evans. 'Sorry. I saw it was the office calling, so I assumed it was Catren,' said Norman.

10

Silence.

'Sir,' added Norman.

'Buck up, Sergeant,' said Evans. 'We're supposed to be professionals. At least try to sound like one even if you can't act that way.'

Norman bit his tongue.

'Where are you?' asked Evans. 'We've got a shout on here, and you're nowhere to be found.'

'I'm out here doing the job you asked me to do,' said Norman.

'Job? What job?'

'Mrs Cooper. I was just about to interview her, sir.'

'Mrs Cooper?'

'Mrs Cooper. The name and address on the job you sent me to about half an hour ago. I've just got to her house, and I was about to go and knock on her door.'

'Forget that. It's too trivial to worry about now. It looks as if someone has found a body.'

'But I'm here now,' said Norman. 'I might as well speak to the lady. The rest of the team can start without me, and I'll catch up.'

'You seem to be forgetting that at the moment, you are the team. And right now, I don't care about the lady. Understand?' hissed Evans. 'Just stop whining, will you, and do your job.'

Norman stared at the phone, put his hand over it, swore quietly and brought it back to his ear.

'Where's the body?' asked Norman, reluctantly adding, 'sir.'

'Some place called the Dragon Forest. I'll meet you there.'

Norman ended the call, tossed the phone onto the passenger seat and started his car.

'Oh, great,' he muttered. 'Just what we need at a potential crime scene.'

* * *

At ten thirty, Southall made her way up the stairs and stopped in front of the door marked *Superintendent Nathan Bain*. Normally the door would be open when she arrived, and he would be waiting for her, but not today. Southall knocked on the door.

'Come in,' called an unfamiliar voice.

Southall opened the door and stepped inside.

'Ah, you must be DI Southall. Do come in.'

The man stepped forward, smiled, and shook her hand. At six foot three, he towered over Southall, making her look smaller than she really was. He liked it that way.

'I'm Acting Superintendent Barry Evans,' he said. 'I shall be filling in for Superintendent Bain while he's away.'

Southall was unimpressed by Evans's attempt to intimidate her.

'Yes, I know. The CC told me. Do you know how long Superintendent Bain will be away, sir?' she asked.

'He's not as young as he used to be and these things can take time,' said Evans. 'Who knows, maybe he'll take this as a sign that it's time to retire.'

'Really?' said Southall. 'He's never given any indication he wants to leave.'

'Yes, well, he wouldn't discuss it with his subordinates, would he?' said Evans dismissively. 'And regarding the team, I can't say I'm impressed with what I've seen so far, although I have to admit that despite the apparent lack of discipline, you seem to have managed some impressive results. What should I put that down to, Southall, your brilliant detective skills, or just plain luck?'

'I think there's a bit more to it than luck, sir, and it's not just down to me,' said Southall. 'I'm lucky to have an experienced DS, a willing team of young detectives and a very supportive boss.'

'Yes, well, I'm sure Superintendent Bain does his best.'

'He's the best superintendent I've ever worked for, sir, and DS Norman agrees.'

'Hmm. DS Norman strikes me as rather insubordinate. Perhaps that's why the younger officers have no discipline.'

Impatient to get out to the crime scene, Southall decided that this was an argument that could wait until later.

'He didn't seem to know what he was doing earlier,' continued Evans. 'But then, at his age, he's probably getting a little long in the tooth for police work. Maybe it's time he retired too.'

'He was retired, sir. Superintendent Bain talked him into rejoining to help train the younger detectives.'

'Yes, but he's not getting any younger, is he? And you just said the younger detectives know what they're doing, although I remain to be convinced of that. As I said, they seem to lack discipline. Two of them haven't even turned up for work this morning.'

'DC Morgan tells me their car broke down, but they're up and running now and they're on their way out to the Dragon Forest,' said Southall. 'I can assure you we have a good team, and DS Norman is an important member of it. In fact, I would go so far as to say he's the glue that binds them together, and I'm a great believer in the old adage that if it ain't broke, why fix it.'

Evans could see that Southall was going to be no push-over, but if he wanted to take Bain's place, he was just going to have to find a way to persuade her it would be in her best interests to comply.

'I have to make a call, and then I'll be out to join you,' he told her. 'I just wanted to touch base. You'll find I'm a bit more hands-on than Superintendent Bain, but that means I'll be on hand if you need anything.'

'Right, thank you, sir. If that's all, I should go and catch up with my team.'

'Yes, of course,' said Evans.

'Smarmy bugger,' muttered Southall, as she made her way back down the stairs.

* * *

At about the same time as Southall was knocking on Acting Superintendent Evan's door, Norman was arriving at the main car park of the Dragon Forest. One of the two missing detectives, DC "Frosty" Winter, was already on site and as Norman pulled into the car park, walked over to meet him.

'How come you got here before me?' Norman asked.

'Catren rang and suggested we come straight here,' said Winter.

Norman glanced at his footwear. 'Do we really need wellies?'

'It's okay here in the car park, and the gravel paths aren't too bad,' said Winter, 'but the rain was torrential yesterday. If you go off piste the grass is sodden, and the crime scene is pretty muddy.'

'Right,' said Norman, heading for the boot of his car.

A cordon had been set up to stop visitors going into the forest. At the end of one of these paths, a harassed-looking uniformed officer was doing her best to appease some disgruntled dog walkers. She was pointing towards a large log-built building which served as visitor centre and cafe, presumably suggesting they make do with a coffee before heading off.

At a second path, another officer was talking to two fifty-something red-faced men dressed in jogging gear, who didn't appear particularly upset at having their activity curtailed.

Norman nodded towards the uniformed officer talking to the dog walkers.

'I feel sorry for the uniforms,' he said. 'She's having her ear chewed off by dog walkers while we just swan in and out as we like.'

'Yeah,' said Winter. 'I can still recall what it's like trying to explain that we can't tell them anything and that we're just doing our jobs. I could never understand why they take it so personally.'

'That's the great British public for you,' said Norman. 'They want us to solve crimes, but they don't want to be inconvenienced in the process. Are the uniforms taking names and addresses?'

'Yep. I've asked them to collect names, addresses, phone numbers and any relevant info.'

'Good,' said Norman. 'Where's the body?'

Winter pointed to one of the well-worn gravel paths leading into the trees, and they set off in that direction.

'In a clearing in the middle of the forest,' Winter said.

'Is it far?'

'About two hundred yards,' said Winter. 'Forensics and the pathologist were here just now, but there's a small car park on the other side that's nearer the clearing, so I told them to head that way. There's another Uniform keeping it clear for them.'

'You mean there's a car park that's closer and you didn't think to tell me?' asked Norman.

Winter smiled. 'I have your welfare at heart, Norm. I figured the exercise would do you good.'

'Don't you worry about that. My dog makes sure I get plenty of exercise. A few more weeks up and down that damned hill and I'll be ready to tackle Everest.'

Norman was pleased to find that the uniformed officer was doing her job. She wouldn't let them onto the path without entering their names on a clipboard, even though she knew very well who they were.

He smiled at the officer.

'Good work,' he said. 'And here's a friendly warning. We have a new guy acting as temporary superintendent at Llangwelli. He claims to be hands-on, and has suggested he might turn up here. I hope he won't, but he's trying make an impression so be on your toes just in case. Okay?'

'Thanks, Norm,' she said. 'I'll spread the word among the guys.'

'What's with the acting super?' asked Winter as they continued walking. 'Is Superintendent Bain leaving?'

'I hope not,' said Norman. 'As I understand it, he's just getting a new hip.'

'Have you met the new guy?'

'Oh yes,' said Norman. 'He was already there when I strolled in nearly two hours late. To make matters worse, Sarah was called up to see the CC so she wasn't there, and you two didn't do yourselves any favours by being late as well. The only one in the office was Catren.'

'He wasn't impressed then.'

'Oh, he was impressed all right. Unfortunately, the impression he got was the wrong one. It didn't help that I didn't jump to attention the minute I saw him either. He's got me down as insubordinate.'

Grinning, Winter raised an eyebrow.

'Insubordinate? You, Norm? Surely not.'

'A word of advice,' said Norman. 'Just be careful around this guy for a while. And don't let him find out about you and Judy.'

Winter blushed. 'I don't know what you mean, Norm.'

'Don't play the innocent, you know exactly what I mean,' said Norman. 'Talking of Judy, where is she?'

'She's gone back to the office to take over from Catren so she can come out here. Do you think she'll be okay with the new boss?'

Norman sighed. 'If she's lucky he'll be on his way here by the time she gets to the office. Of course, that won't be so lucky for us, but it is what it is. As for the other thing, I don't care what you two get up to in your own time if it doesn't interfere with your work, but I don't think Acting Superintendent Evans is the sort to turn a blind eye.'

'Does the boss know?' asked Winter.

'Does she know what? About Evans?'

'No. The other thing you mentioned.'

'You mean about you and Judy moving in together? Of course she does!'

'I suppose Catren's been blabbing—'

'Catren hasn't said a word,' said Norman. 'Trust me, your secret is safe with her.'

'Then how—'

'Jeez, come on, Frosty, wake up. We're detectives. We notice things. It's what we do.'

To Winter's relief, they were almost at the clearing.

'The body was buried in a shallow grave,' he said. 'The pathologist thinks the heavy rain we've had must have washed some of the soil away. He and his guys are excavating it as we speak, but they say it could be a slow job.'

Another cordon had been stretched around the perimeter of the clearing. A man in matching dull green trousers and jacket was talking to another uniformed officer at the entrance to the clearing.

'Who's the guy in green?' Norman asked Winter.

'Gareth James. He's the forest manager. He's got a small office and workshop behind the visitor centre.'

'Did he find the body?'

'A dog walker saw what he thought was some rubbish that had been fly-tipped and reported it to him.'

'Fly-tipping? Is that likely, all the way out here?'

'Yeah, that's what I thought,' said Winter. 'But at least he did report it, even if he didn't give much thought to how it got there. At least it meant he and his dog didn't go poking around the crime scene.'

'Yeah, that's a definite plus,' said Norman.

The man in green turned as they approached.

'Mr James?' said Norman. 'My name is DS Norman.' He nodded towards Winter. 'I understand you've met my colleague.'

James shook Norman's hand.

'Terrible business,' he said. 'We've never had anything like this happen before.'

'What exactly did you see?'

'At first, I thought it was some rubbish that had been buried and then exposed by the rain. There was some fabric showing, and when I took a hold of it, I realised there was a hand underneath.'

'Did you touch anything else?' asked Norman.

'Just that bit of fabric. I probably should have checked further, but I panicked.' James's face had taken on a haunted expression. 'I . . . I didn't know what to do so I called you guys. Should I have tried to get them out? Could I have saved them? I feel awful. There must have been something I could have done.'

'Not from what I've been told,' said Norman. 'Calling us was the right thing to do. We can handle it from here.'

'Is there anything I can do to help?'

'At the moment we'd like you to close the forest to visitors, and keep everyone away from this clearing.'

'How about if I send them the other way?' suggested James. 'Just so they don't come near the clearing.'

'In my experience, curiosity will drive at least one person to "accidentally" find an alternative way here,' said Norman. 'And even a loose dog can disrupt a crime scene. It won't be for long. Maybe a day or two.'

'We don't even stop people coming on Christmas day . . .'

'Look, Mr James, you've had a nasty shock,' said Norman. He nodded to Winter. 'DC Winter is going to take you back to your office. He'll help you get the site closed, and then when you feel a bit better you can give him a statement. How does that sound?'

'Yes, a statement. Of course.'

As James turned to head back down the path, Norman frowned at Winter. 'Keep an eye on him,' he whispered.

Winter gave Norman a thumbs up and fell in step with James.

Norman donned a white over-suit provided by the uniformed officer and looked across the clearing. It was roughly the size of four football pitches, and a white pop-up tent had been erected about twenty yards in from the far side. A small team in similar over-suits were working in and around the tent.

'Is it usual to have a clearing like this in the middle of a forest?' Norman asked the uniformed officer.

'Well, I know they have firebreaks, but they're nothing like as wide as this, and they run in straight lines,' said the officer. 'But then this whole forest seems a bit weird if you ask me.'

Norman had no intention of getting involved in a discussion about the weirdness of the forest.

'Oh well, I guess standing around talking won't get me any closer,' he said.

'It never works for me,' said the officer, and raised the cordon tape for Norman to duck under.

As Norman trudged across the clearing to the pop-up tent, he slowly scanned the clearing. Glancing back, he noticed that the uniformed PC who had issued his over-suit was now in conversation with a man in running gear. After a few seconds the runner headed reluctantly back towards the main car park.

'How the hell did he get this far?' muttered Norman as he watched the man leave. Then, satisfied the runner had gone, he opened a tent flap and peered inside.

'Morning, Bill. What have we got?'

Dr Bill Bridger, the pathologist, looked up. He was wearing the familiar white forensic suit and a face mask, but his eyes were crinkled in a smile.

'Morning, Norm. Female, mid to late teens or possibly early twenties.'

'I don't suppose there's any ID?' asked Norman without much hope.

'Your pessimism is thoroughly warranted,' said Bridger.

'How close can I come?'

'Keep to the plates and you'll be fine.'

Norman stepped carefully along the metal plates that had been placed on the ground to protect the scene from contamination, stopping just short of a shallow grave about two feet deep. The body of a young woman lay face up in the grave, partially wrapped in a muddy white sheet.

'So, not Caucasian,' said Norman.

'I'd suggest probably from the Middle East or perhaps Asian,' said Bridger.

'What's that, a shroud?' asked Norman.

'It's hard to tell,' said Bridger. 'She is naked underneath, so it could be.'

'I'm guessing you're going to tell me the rain has washed away any trace evidence,' said Norman.

'At this stage I'd say that's a pretty good guess,' said Bridger. 'Though from my point of view it could be worse. At least this soil will wash off easily. It would be a real bugger to clean her up back at the lab if it was clay.'

'Have you got anything at all?'

'There's a seriously powerful torch, and a spade found nearby.'

'Really?' said Norman. 'Was it close enough to be what was used to dig the grave?'

'I don't know for sure yet, but if I was a gambling man . . .'

'That's a bit careless, if it is,' said Norman. 'How close is nearby?'

'Too close to be a coincidence in my opinion. And I can't imagine many dog walkers carry a spade to clear up after their dog.'

'Take it from me, dog walkers carry poo bags, not spades,' said Norman. 'Any idea how long she's been here?'

'I can't say for sure, but the soil she was buried in isn't compacted, and there's no significant decay, so I'd say not long. A couple of days at most.'

'Time of death?' asked Norman.

'Come on, Norm. You know I can't tell you that.'

'Take a wild guess.'

Bridger grinned beneath his mask. 'I'm a scientist, Norm; I don't make wild guesses. But what I will say is she was probably dead before she was brought here.'

'Aha!' said Norman. 'How long before?'

'Now you're pushing your luck too far.'

'What else can you tell me?' asked Norman.

'Footprints,' said Bridger. 'Loads of them. But after the downpour we've had we'll be damned lucky to find any good enough to identify. And don't forget this forest is open to the public, so I wouldn't get your hopes up.'

'That's a great help,' said Norman.

'I aim to please,' said Bridger. 'There is one thing that might be of interest.'

'What's that?'

'I think whoever placed her here did it with respect, and she wasn't just thrown in.'

'Respect? Buried out here in the forest?' said Norman.

'I know it's hard to believe, and I could be totally wrong—'

'But you're more often right,' said Norman. 'So, come on, let's hear it.'

'Okay, well, it might not be significant, but it's the way she's been laid out — on her back, legs together, arms crossed over her chest, eyes closed.'

'Like it was a proper burial,' said Norman.

'Exactly,' said Bridger. 'And the sheet wasn't just tossed on top of her, she was wrapped in it like a shroud, and it covered her face as if to keep the soil off.'

'So, you think someone murdered her, stuck her in a shallow grave out here where no one was supposed to find her, but was concerned enough to take care of her body?'

'When you put it like that, it does sound unlikely, doesn't it?' said Bridger.

'Yeah, but unlikely doesn't mean it didn't happen,' said Norman. 'At this stage of the investigation I'm open to all possibilities. How long do you think you'll be here, Bill?'

'The SOCOs will be here for hours, but once I've got the body fully uncovered, I'd like to move her back to the lab as soon as I can. Say, half an hour?'

Norman's mobile phone began to ring. It was Southall.

'Yo, Sarah,' he said and listened.

'That was Sarah,' he said to Bridger after finishing the call. 'She's just arrived at the main car park. She says can you hang on, she wants to see the body in situ.'

'No problem,' said Bridger.

'I'll just go and meet her,' said Norman.

He made his way back across the clearing and reached the uniformed officer just as Southall came into view further down the path, heading their way.

'That jogger I saw you talking to, what did he want?' asked Norman.

'Just being nosey, wanted to know what we're doing,' said the PC.

'Did he say how he got here?' asked Norman. 'I thought we had the place closed down.'

'We've got the car parks locked, but they can't block off the footpaths, and there are plenty of those.'

'Any idea how many?' asked Norman.

The PC shrugged. 'Sorry, no idea.'

'What's up?' asked Southall as she reached them.

'Just some nosey jogger,' said Norman. 'You must have passed him on your way here.'

Southall shook her head. 'Not seen a soul.'

'There you go,' said the PC. 'There must be another path.'

'Is it important?' asked Southall.

'Probably not,' said Norman. 'But a map of the forest might be handy, just to see how many different ways in there are.'

Southall quickly got herself suited and booted, and she and Norman set off across the clearing.

'Have you met this new acting boss?' asked Norman.

'I met him briefly before I came out here.'

'What d'you think?' asked Norman.

Southall grimaced. 'I think he's after Nathan's job. He reckons he won't come back after his operation.'

'Jeez, he's gone in for a new hip, not a heart transplant,' said Norman. 'He's only having the month off because he's owed so much leave.'

'That's what I understood,' said Southall. 'Now I'm wondering if they're angling to kick him while he's down, and force him out.'

'I always got the impression that although almost every-one at Headquarters hates Nathan because he's a maverick, the chief constable appreciates him because he himself is sur-rounded by "yes men" and Nathan is a breath of fresh air.'

'Yes, but what if Evans dreams up a scenario that makes Nathan look bad?' Southall said.

'Ha! He can try,' said Norman. 'But I've known Nathan a long time and he's no fool. I bet if he thinks someone is going to try and force him out, he'll be ready for them.'

'I do hope so,' said Southall. 'It was a rushed meeting with Evans — he had to get to a meeting, and I was in a hurry to get out here — so maybe I just read him wrong.'

'If you read him as a first-rate arsehole, that's how I did,' said Norman. 'But I get your meaning. We should forget this conversation ever happened and give the guy a chance.'

'Yes, let's forget I said anything.'

'As if that's going to happen,' said Norman.

Southall followed Norman across the clearing, stepping carefully across the metal plates, and smiled at Bill Bridger. She looked down at the grave. 'So, what have we got here, Norm?'

'All we know at this stage is that the victim is a young woman with no ID. She's naked, was wrapped in the sheet, and then placed in the shallow grave and covered with soil.'

'Do we think the grave was prepared beforehand?' asked Southall.

'The SOCOs found a spade and a torch nearby, so it looks as if someone carried the body all the way out here, dug the shallow grave, wrapped the body in the sheet — or maybe that was done before she was brought here — placed her in the grave, then buried her,' he said.

Southall looked at Bridger. 'Does that scenario make sense to you?'

'It could have happened like that,' said Bridger.

'All we have to figure out is who she is, where she came from, and why anyone would want to do that to her,' said Norman.

'That's where the detective bit comes in,' said Bridger. 'As I've told you before, I'm here to do the scientific stuff that helps you guys work out who did it and why.'

'But if the grave was filled properly, she might never have been found, right?' said Norman.

'Maybe it was bad luck,' said Bridger. 'If it hadn't rained so much it's possible she wouldn't have been found, regardless of how well she was buried.'

'That means whoever did it either wasn't local or they were stupid,' said Norman. 'Anyone who lives here would have known it had to rain within a day or two. I mean, when doesn't it?'

'Unless, of course, she was supposed to be found,' said Southall.

'You mean you think this could be a warning to someone?' said Norman. 'But who? And look at her face. Does she look like a gangster?'

'I don't know, Norm,' said Southall. 'What does a gangster look like these days?'

'Can I take the body away now you've seen it?' asked Bridger.

'Yes, of course,' said Southall. 'We'll get out of the way while SOCOs do their work.'

* * *

'Have we anything to go on?' Southall asked Norman as they headed back.

'The only person who might be any help is Gareth James, the forest manager. He's the poor guy who went to investigate what he thought was going to be some rubbish only to find it was a body. He was pretty shaken up, so Frosty took him back to his office. That was a while ago, so hopefully he'll be okay to give us a statement.'

'Right then, Norm. I suggest we go and see if Mr James can help us.'

* * *

They found Winter and Gareth James in the cafeteria drinking coffee. Norman made the introductions.

'Forest manager. I didn't realise there was such a thing,' said Southall. 'Has anyone gone missing in the forest?'

'Not recently. The last one was a ten-year-old boy, but that was over a year ago and we found him. He'd just wandered off on his own.'

'Can I ask what your job entails?' Southall asked.

'It's more about maintaining the environment than anything. That includes trying to make sure people use the forest rather than abuse it.'

'Do many people use it?' asked Norman.

'Dog walkers and bird watchers mostly. We have the occasional party of students, and scouts sometimes camp here, that sort of thing. Organised groups must book, but we're open to the public, so if someone wants to come and walk they're free to do so.'

'What's the significance of the clearing through there?' asked Norman.

'Ah. That's where the dragons gather.'

Norman raised an eyebrow. 'Dragons?'

'Not now, of course,' said James. 'According to legend, the local people used to offer human sacrifices to appease the dragon, and it took place in the middle of the forest. The clearing is supposed to have been where the dragons landed.'

'Really?' said Norman, dubiously. 'And do you believe that?'

'I think it's bollocks,' said James, 'but if people want to believe it, what's the harm?'

'Quite a lot if someone is crazy enough to offer such a sacrifice hoping they can entice a dragon to land.'

James gasped. 'Jesus, that's not what happened, is it?'

'We're not sure exactly what's happened yet,' said Norman.

'We did try planting new trees there, but they wouldn't grow,' said James. 'Nothing grows well there, even grass struggles to survive. The Pagans say it proves that the dragons did actually come.'

'Pagans?' said Norman.

'Yes, you know, ancient hippie types. Nature worshippers.'

'You mean like the people who descend on Stonehenge to celebrate the solstices?'

'Those are mostly Druids, aren't they?' said James. 'But, yeah, that sort of thing.'

'And they come here?'

'They come to the clearing several times a year to celebrate whatever it is they celebrate. We tried to stop them in the past, but they just kept coming, some of them from miles away. In the end we reached an agreement that they could use the clearing for their ceremonies, but they had to book in advance, so we knew when they were coming.'

'Are there that many of them?'

James guffawed. 'There used to be hundreds, but from what I've seen there are barely a dozen nowadays.'

'And they use the clearing?' asked Southall.

James nodded.

'Why there, specifically?'

'There's a path runs due east, straight towards where the sun rises on the first day of spring. I think it's a coincidence, but they claim it's how the dragons navigated, and it proves the site has been significant for centuries.'

'When were they last here?' asked Norman.

'A few nights ago.'

'How many nights ago?'

'It would have been the thirty-first, Halloween, so that's, what, four nights ago? I can check. The booking will be in my diary.'

'That would be very helpful,' said Norman. 'And could you let us know where to find these Pagans?'

'Yes, no problem.'

'How many access points to the forest are there?' asked Norman.

'There's the main car park where you guys are all parked. Then there's a small car park on the opposite side of the forest, and another small one on the western side. But there are numerous footpaths leading in, and if someone wanted to walk across fields, they could reach the place from almost anywhere.'

'Well, thank you, Mr James, you've been very helpful,' said Southall. 'But I'm afraid that for the time being, we're going to have to cordon off the clearing and the three car parks. And anyone who tries to enter the forest will be turned away.'

'Have you any idea how long for?'

'The clearing could be closed for a few days, but the rest will probably be for no more than a day or two. Really, it depends how long it takes us to make sense of what happened.'

'Yes, I understand,' said James. 'If you can hang on for a minute, I'll go back to my office now and get that information for you.'

As he headed back to his office, Norman, Southall and Winter slowly made their way out to the car park.

'If you can access the forest from almost every direction, that's not going to help us find where the killer brought the body in, is it?' said Winter.

'You really think someone would have carried that body across miles of fields?' asked Norman.

'What if she was alive until they got to the clearing?' countered Winter.

'I'll grant you there's an outside possibility she was made to walk, but I'll put my money on one of the car parks,' said Norman.

'Do you have a theory?' asked Southall.

'At this stage? I wish,' said Norman. 'But my guess would be we can forget the main car park. Too much risk of someone else being there.'

'But what if it was late at night?' asked Winter.

Norman winked.

'Still too risky. I'm thinking it would be a nice quiet spot for a boy with a car to bring a willing girlfriend. At least it would have been in my day.'

They heard a door slam, and Gareth James came hurrying across. 'I was right. The Pagans were here on the night of Halloween.'

'That was last Thursday night,' said Southall. 'Do you know what time they left?'

'They're usually here until the early hours, even after dawn sometimes.'

'At this time of year?' asked Norman.

'I couldn't say for sure,' said James, 'but they were gone before I arrived for work at eight o'clock. Here's the address of the couple who make all the bookings.' He handed a sheet of paper to Southall.

'Elis and Sian Williams,' Southall read out loud. 'Are they married?'

'I guess so,' said James, 'but it is only a guess. I don't really know them.'

'Are they the leaders of the Pagans?' she asked.

'Again, I'm guessing,' said James. 'But they do make all the bookings.'

Southall studied the sheet of paper again. 'Leaders or not, it's somewhere to start. Thank you, Mr James.'

'If there's anything else I can do . . .'

'Just keep the forest closed for now. We'll let you know when we've finished.'

James turned and headed back to his office.

'Evans should have been here by now,' said Southall.

'Yeah, so should Catren,' said Winter. 'Judy went back so they could change places.'

'Judy was just driving in as I was leaving,' said Southall.

'That doesn't sound good,' said Norman.

'You're right,' said Southall. 'So, how about you and Frosty pay the Pagans a visit, and I'll head back to the ranch in case Evans is giving Catren and Judy a hard time.'

CHAPTER TWO

The house they were looking for turned out to be a small-holding set back from the main road. As they drove along the tree-lined driveway with neat paddocks either side, they could see that the old farmhouse had been remarkably well renovated.

'I know I'm supposed to keep an open mind,' said Winter, 'but this isn't exactly what I was expecting.'

'And what exactly were you expecting?' asked Norman.

'I have visions of a shabby old shack with chickens and filthy animals running loose,' said Winter.

'Well, I see chickens and animals aplenty,' said Norman, 'but they ain't filthy. And that house looks none too shabby either.'

They drove up to the house and parked alongside a large van and a nearly new Mercedes saloon.

'They keep their vehicles as clean as their animals,' observed Norman as they made their way up to the front door.

* * *

Norman estimated the man who answered the door to be in his fifties. He stood around six feet six inches tall, with shoulders wide enough to fill the doorway. He had a huge grey beard, a weathered face and his long hair, also grey, was tied back in a ponytail. He looked down at them in silence, studying their faces through dark, hostile eyes.

Winter took an involuntary step back, but Norman wasn't so easily intimidated.

'Elis Williams?'

The man folded two massive arms across his chest.

'Who wants to know?'

Norman produced his warrant card.

'My name is Detective Sergeant Norman, and this is my colleague, Detective Constable Winter. We'd like to ask you a few questions.'

'Oh yeah. What about?'

'I understand you're a Pagan, is that right?'

'Yes, I have Pagan beliefs. There's no law against that, is there?'

'Not that I'm aware of,' said Norman. 'Are you part of a group?'

'I play bass in a rock band, if that's what you mean,' said Williams.

Norman frowned but managed to suppress his irritation.

'I was thinking more in terms of a group of fellow Pagans.'

'Oh, that group. Yeah, there's a group of us with shared beliefs.'

'Do you meet up regularly?'

'We meet when we've got something to celebrate.'

'I understand you made a booking at the Dragon Forest on the night of thirty-first October,' said Norman.

'Is it a crime to visit the forest these days?' asked Elis.

'That would depend on what exactly you were doing in the forest,' said Norman. 'Was this gathering for one of your celebrations?'

'Well, it was Halloween, but we didn't go there searching for witches.'

'So, what *were* you doing?'

'Reflecting on the fragility of life.'

'That's a bit vague,' said Norman.

Somewhere behind Williams, the voice of a woman called, 'Who is it?'

'It's the police,' he said, taking a step back.

'That'll explain why you're being so unhelpful then.' A dark-haired woman with wide brown eyes peered around Elis Williams from about the level of his elbow. The lines on her face suggested she smiled often. She was smiling now. She appeared to be about the same age as the man, and Norman assumed she was his wife.

'Mrs Williams? I'm DS Norman and this—'

'Never mind the formality,' she said, squeezing past her husband. 'Call me Sian.'

Although she was half the size of her husband, it was immediately apparent who really wore the trousers in this house. Williams muttered something under his breath, turned and retreated into the house.

'Now then, what can we do for you?' asked Sian.

'We're investigating a crime that occurred in the Dragon Forest. We've been told your Pagan group were in the forest on the night of thirty-first October, and we'd just like to know why you were there, and what you were doing.'

She stepped aside. 'Sure I'll tell you, but you don't have to stand out there in the cold. Why don't you come on in?'

'Mr Williams didn't seem too keen to let us in,' said Norman.

'Oh, don't take any notice of Elis. He's a bit protective; sometimes behaves more like my bodyguard than my husband, but he's a pussy cat really.'

'Well, if you don't mind,' said Norman.

'We're always willing to help the police,' she said, leading them through to an enormous kitchen where Elis was sitting at a huge wooden table. 'Pull up a chair and sit down. Elis will make us a cup of tea, won't you, Elis.'

It was an instruction rather than a question, and Elis didn't demur. With a grunt, he got up to make the tea.

'Right,' said Sian. 'What do you want to know?'

'Is it okay if my colleague takes notes?' asked Norman.

'Go ahead,' she said. 'We've nothing to hide.'

'Why were your Pagan group in the Dragon Forest last Thursday night?' asked Norman.

She sighed. 'I'm assuming you don't want me to go into Paganism in any depth.'

'Please spare us the depth,' said Norman. 'Simple would be good, and quicker.'

'Okay. We were celebrating what's known as Samhain.'

'And what might that be when it's at home?' asked Norman.

'Our New Year.'

'Do you need to go into the forest to do that?'

'It's the tradition. Pagans have been celebrating Samhain in the Dragon Forest for centuries.'

'And how many of you were out there?'

She looked across at Elis.

'Twelve was it, or fourteen?' she asked.

'Fourteen,' Elis said.

'There we are,' she said. 'Fourteen. Elis can make a list if you like.' She flashed a smile at her husband, who sighed and reached for a pen and notepad.

'Fourteen? Is that it?' said Norman.

'How many were you expecting?' asked Sian.

'I don't know really,' said Norman. 'But it's hardly a match for the Druids at Stonehenge. Hundreds gather there to celebrate the solstice.'

Sian smiled patiently. 'Well, we're not trying to outdo the Druids, Mr Norman. We just do our own thing.'

'But fourteen though,' persisted Norman. 'Is it worth it?'

'If you want to get into numbers, have you seen the size of most church congregations these days? It's the strength of belief that matters, not the number of people.'

'You've got me there,' conceded a chastened Norman. 'That's a good point. And I apologise. I didn't mean to cause any offence.'

'I can assure you I take no offence,' said Sian. 'We're used to people not having the slightest idea of what we're about.'

The brief awkward silence that followed was relieved by Elis Williams placing a tray with four mugs of tea on the table. He pulled out a chair and sat down. In silence, he handed the list of Pagans to Winter. It seemed his wife was to be doing all the talking.

'How long were you out there in the forest?' asked Norman.

'I think we got there at about seven thirty, and we left around midnight.'

'Not an all-nighter, then?' asked Norman.

'Ha. I wish,' said Sian. 'When I was in my twenties maybe, but I can't stay awake that long these days.'

'How do you get out there?' asked Norman.

'We have permission to drive one vehicle to the clearing, and we have a key to open the gate from the car park. So, we meet in the car park, then drive up in our van. And no, we don't cheat and take all our cars.'

'Did you see anyone else out there?'

'There was no moon, so it was quite dark. We had to use lamps to see what we were doing.'

'And you didn't see any lights, or hear anything?'

'No, nothing,' said Sian.

'Forgive my curiosity, but isn't it a bit late to be starting your year when everyone else is preparing for the end of theirs?' asked Winter.

'Samhain marks the end of the harvest and the beginning of winter.'

'So, it's a bit like harvest festival in church?' asked Winter.

'Not exactly,' she said patiently. 'Where do you think the Church got the idea from? People have been celebrating the harvest for millennia, long before the Church even existed, simply because it's the end of the growing cycle and the crops are all in. And when you think about it, it makes perfect sense for the harvest to signify the end of the year.

'But there's more to it than that for us. Samhain is also the time when we honour our ancestors and our loved ones who have passed. It's an acknowledgement of the continuous circle of life and death, the interconnectedness of all life and the importance of living in harmony with the Earth's cycles.'

'It almost sounds as if you were reading from a book,' said Norman.

'That's a concise version. I could go on for hours. Of course, you could always Google it . . .'

'Yeah, perhaps we will,' said Norman.

'Although there's no guarantee of the accuracy of what you might find there.'

'Yeah, that's true enough,' said Norman. 'But getting back to the night in question, tell me, how exactly do you celebrate this event?'

'We go out to the forest where we have a bonfire, a feast, and perform rituals to remember the dead,' said Sian.

'Oh really?' said Norman, his radar twitching. 'And what do these rituals entail?'

'Poems mostly, and readings.'

'Poems?' said Norman.

'Yes, poems. And readings.'

'What sort of readings?'

Sian smiled.

'Ones that celebrate new beginnings, and—'

'Reflect on the fragility of life,' said Winter, looking up from his notes.

'There you go,' she said. 'Your young man's keeping up.'

'And that's all?' asked Norman.

'Look,' said Sian. 'We've been using the clearing in the Dragon Forest for years, and there's never been a problem before. Perhaps if you would tell us what we're supposed to have done, we might be able to help you.'

'And you don't sacrifice things?' asked Norman.

'Sacrifice things? Of course we don't sacrifice things. Our ancestors might have done thousands of years ago, but

34

these days our beliefs are strong enough. We don't need something like that to reinforce them.'

Norman didn't look convinced.

'Look, we're not devil worshippers. Our belief is based on respect for nature and for the Earth.'

'Like the green movement,' said Winter.

Williams sighed.

'Yes, if you like,' she said wearily. 'Though sadly, they've caught on a bit too late. Tell you what, why don't I give you some literature to read? Then you might have a better understanding of what we're about.'

'Literature?' asked Norman.

'Just a couple of leaflets, but it explains the Wheel of the Year. It'll tell you what we celebrate, and when, and why. That, in turn, will tell you when we go to the Dragon Forest.'

She reached into a drawer and produced two leaflets which she handed to Norman.

'You have to admit it's unusual though, isn't it?' he said.

'What is?' asked Sian.

'Being a Pagan.'

'A lot of people need something to believe in to help them make sense of the world. And if established religion doesn't provide it, they look elsewhere.'

Norman nodded. 'Yeah. I guess I can't argue with that.'

Sian smiled. 'Well, there we are then. Our little group just happen to share a belief in Paganism.'

'Is it a recent thing for you two?'

'Elis introduced me to it when we first met, which was forty years and three kids ago, wasn't it, love?'

Elis nodded and began to speak, for the first time since they'd entered the kitchen.

'The thing is, when I was a kid at school, they used to fill our heads with stories about a big guy up in the sky who created the world in seven days. The other kids all seemed to accept it without question, but I just didn't see how anyone could be expected to take it seriously, no more than I could accept the story about an old guy with a white beard and a red suit who flies around on a sleigh delivering presents on Christmas Eve.'

Norman nodded. He could relate to that.

'I was always fascinated by how things grew. Insects, animals, plants, all of the natural world,' continued Elis. 'So, when I came across the Pagans and their belief that nature is sacred, and that natural cycles carry deep meaning, it made perfect sense. I mean, you can see nature and you can touch it. It's all around us!'

Norman finished his tea and glanced at Winter.

'I think we'll get out of your hair and let you get on with your day now,' he said. 'Thank you for your help.'

'Is that it?' asked Sian.

'As I said before, we're investigating a crime that took place in the forest,' said Norman. 'At this stage we're trying to establish who was out there, when they were there and if they saw anything.' He pulled a business card from his pocket. 'If you think of anything that seemed out of the ordinary, my number is on the card. Give me a call, anytime.'

Sian took the card. 'I'm not sure we can tell you anything more.'

'You never know,' said Norman. 'Sometimes we speak to someone, and then a couple of days later they remember something that seemed too trivial to mention at the time, but which eventually proves to be important.'

* * *

'When we get back to the office, I'd like you to do a background check on those two and then start working through that list of names he gave us,' said Norman as Winter started the car and headed back to Llangwelli. 'Let's see if any of our Pagans have anything to hide.'

'He was one big guy, wasn't he?' said Winter. 'I'm not sure I can see him as a pussy cat like his wife said, but I suppose he wasn't so bad once she took over.'

Norman chuckled. 'Yeah, it wasn't hard to see who ruled the roost, was it? I might be wrong, but I'm guessing he's all mouth and no trousers. He might have been a hard man back in the day, but I suspect he changed once Sian arrived on the scene. He can still use his size to intimidate, of course, but I bet he doesn't dare take it any further unless she tells him to.'

'Do you reckon she does? I didn't think she seemed the type,' Winter said.

'You mean you bought all that "willing to help the police" crap?'

Winter shrugged. 'Keep an open mind, right?'

Norman smiled. 'As it happens, I think you're probably right, but you can never be too sure.'

'And that's why you need me to check them out, right?' asked Winter. 'Make sure there's no previous.'

'Exactly,' said Norman.

They drove on in silence for a few moments.

'You know, it's weird to be on the same page as a guy like that,' Norman said, 'but I felt much the same as him when I was a kid.'

Winter frowned. 'I'm not with you.'

'About God and all that,' said Norman. 'Even as a little kid I could never understand how anyone could accept that stuff without question. The "all-seeing big guy up in the sky" thing made no sense to me either. I mean, how could he possibly be everywhere and see everything? It didn't make sense.'

'Ah, right,' said Winter. 'I see what you mean. But, if you don't believe in God, what do you believe in?'

'If you had asked me that question before I moved down here, I would have said I don't know, or even that I don't really believe in anything. But that was before I discovered what it's like to live in a beautiful place like this, with the sea and the valleys and the fields all close by.'

'And now?' asked Winter.

'Now I see things differently, and I realise how lucky I am. And when I do stuff like restoring our garden and making it more nature friendly, or even when I'm just out on the hill with the dog breathing it all in, it makes me realise I'm just a tiny, insignificant part of something so huge I can't even begin to get my head around it. That something is nature, and no one can doubt that it really is everywhere. And, just like Elis said, I can see it, and I can touch it any time I want. You can't do that with God.'

'Wow,' said Winter. 'That's profound. I've never thought that way about living here.'

Norman looked at him. 'I expect that's probably because you've always lived here, and you don't realise how lucky you are. Like anything that's always there, we tend to take it for granted. Trust me, when you've been raised in the city and then you come and live somewhere like this, it changes your outlook. For me, it's like coming to live on another planet.'

'Some people who come here hate it,' said Winter. 'They go back as soon as they can.'

'I'm not saying it's for everyone,' said Norman. 'There again, maybe those people didn't give it a chance. If you come here thinking you're going to hate it, then for sure you will. I've never been able to understand why you youngsters who were raised here want to leave and go to the city.'

'Jobs and opportunities, Norm, jobs and opportunities. That's the reason.'

Norman sighed. 'Yeah. I can't dispute that, I suppose. The city's where the money is.'

'And we all have different tastes, right?' said Winter.

'For sure,' said Norman. 'And thank goodness we do, or life would be so dull it doesn't bear thinking about.'

Winter glanced across at Norman and smiled.

'D'you know, Norm, I can't decide if you're a closet hippie, or if this is a roundabout way of you saying you're going to become a Pagan.'

'Me? A hippie?' Norman laughed. 'Although looking back, I wouldn't have minded being part of the "summer of love", but that was big in the sixties and seventies so I missed out on it by a couple of decades. As for becoming a Pagan, ha, I don't think I'll be going that far. Though the more I think about it, the more I think Elis is right. Believing in nature makes more sense than anything else.'

* * *

At around the same time as Norman and Winter were speaking with Elis and Sian Williams, Southall was pushing through the doors into the main office at Llangwelli station. Judy Lane was sitting at her desk.

'Is he here?' Southall hissed.

'If you mean Superintendent Evans, I thought he was with you.'

'We haven't seen him,' said Southall.

'That's strange,' said Lane. 'I saw Catren give him directions to the forest.'

'When was this?'

'Not long after I got here,' said Lane. She looked at the clock. 'Over an hour ago now.'

'Have you got your car sorted out?'

'I dropped it off at the garage,' said Lane. 'That's why it took me a bit longer to get here.'

'Where's Catren?'

'Over the road getting coffee.'

'She should have been out at the crime scene,' said Southall.

'Superintendent Evans told her to stay here. He told her murder was a job for experienced officers, not juniors.'

'Oh, he did, did he?' said Southall. 'I think I'm going to have to point out to him how much experience this team actually has in dealing with murders. And how the hell does he think anyone's going to gain experience if they never go near a murder scene?'

Catren Morgan backed her way through the doors carrying a tray with three coffees.

'I saw you drive into the car park,' she explained to Southall. 'I guessed you'd like one.'

'I hear Acting Superintendent Evans thinks you're too inexperienced for a murder scene.'

'I think he's living in the past,' said Morgan, putting the tray down and handing out the drinks. 'Obviously us women are too fragile to handle the sight of a dead body.'

'Judy says he left for the crime scene over an hour ago.'

'That's right, he did,' said Morgan.

'So how come I didn't set eyes on him?' said Southall.

'Well, I gave him directions,' said Morgan innocently.

'Or to be more accurate, he snatched your directions from you,' said Lane.

'It's possible my directions may have been a little vague,' said Morgan.

'How vague?' demanded Southall.

'Well, I suppose they would have been quite vague for someone who doesn't know the area,' said Morgan. 'The thing is I wrote them for myself, but as I know that area fairly well, it was really just a reminder.'

'Oh, God. He's probably been driving around scratching his head,' said Southall.

'Surely if he's got anything about him, he should have been able to find it,' Morgan said.

'I hope for your sake he did,' said Southall. 'I want him to see we're a slick team, a well-oiled machine, not a bunch of idiots who can't find their own arses with both hands!'

'Right. Sorry,' said Morgan. 'But it was me who got it in the neck when he arrived and there was no one else here . . .'

Southall sighed. 'Oh well, at least I know what to expect when he gets back here. Now, I know we don't have much to go on yet, but at least we can get a murderboard started.'

They had barely started when a red-faced Evans poked his head through the doors.

'DI Southall. My office. Now!' he barked, withdrawing his head and heading for the stairs and his own office.

The three detectives exchanged looks.

'I wonder what that's about,' said Lane.

'He doesn't look all that happy, does he?' said Southall.

'That's a bit of an understatement,' said Morgan. 'If this is my fault, I'm sorry, boss. I'll make it up to you, I promise.'

'Let's not jump to conclusions,' said Southall. 'But if it is your fault, I'll definitely hold you to that promise.' She took a deep breath and headed for the door. 'You two carry on with that board. I'll go and face the music.'

Southall made her way up the stairs and stopped outside the door with the brass plate indicating that the office was that of *Det Supt Nathan Bain*. Wishing it was Bain on the other side of the door, she knocked.

'Come.'

Southall pushed the door open and walked in.

'Ah, Southall,' Evans said, looking up.

Southall began to pull out a chair.

'No need to sit,' said Evans. 'This won't take long.'

'Sir,' said Southall, standing in front of the desk.

'I suppose you know why I called you up here?'

'As we missed you at the crime scene, I assume you'd like me to bring you up to speed with the murder,' suggested Southall.

'You didn't miss me at the crime scene because I didn't find the bloody crime scene,' hissed Evans. 'That stupid girl gave me the vaguest directions I've ever seen. I've been driving round in circles for the last hour.'

Southall had thought about her response on her way up the stairs.

'With respect, sir, I understand you took directions from Morgan that she had written for herself, and not for you.'

'What's that got to do with anything? They were as good as useless.'

'I can understand how they would have been useless to someone who didn't know the area,' said Southall. 'But the thing is, the directions you took from DC Morgan was just a reminder for herself. She's lived in this area all her life, so she knew where the forest was. She just wasn't sure which road the car park was on.'

'Well, I think she did it on purpose,' said Evans. 'Why would she need directions for herself?'

Southall made a show of looking bemused.

'As I said, sir, DC Morgan knows the area and just needed a reminder—'

'What was she doing heading to a crime scene anyway?'

'We believe the younger detectives won't learn anything sitting in an office.'

'From what I understand, the junior detectives here can't be trusted with real police work.'

'Can I ask where you heard this information, sir?'

'Everyone knows this is the place they send the—'

'Ah, I see,' said Southall. 'I'm afraid you've been listening to old news, sir.'

'Old news? What do you mean *old* news?'

'It's true Llangwelli station was once known as the last chance saloon, but that has changed since Superintendent Bain took over. He recognised the latent talent here and realised they just needed mentoring and encouraging. That's why he recruited DS Norman from retirement.'

'Ah, yes, DS Norman. I can see his influence in the complete lack of discipline in this place, and this directions fiasco is just one more example. It's just what I would expect from a place that lacks discipline. And having been here for a few hours now, I'm beginning to wonder if your success rate is all it's made out to be.'

'The results speak for themselves,' said Southall. 'You even mentioned them earlier. That didn't happen by luck, or by accident. It was the result of a lot of hard graft from a small team of excellent detectives, mentored by DS Norman and me. I believe each one of them will go far.'

'That's your considered opinion, is it, Detective Inspector?'

'Yes, it is, sir,' said Southall.

'I should warn you there has been talk of closing this station.'

'I am aware of that.'

Evans's eyes narrowed. 'Oh, are you, indeed?'

'Superintendent Bain has kept me informed, at the chief constable's behest.'

This obviously came as a surprise to Evans, although he tried not to show it.

'Well, in that case, DI Southall, you should take this as a warning,' said Evans menacingly. 'Any more ill-discipline and I will be recommending to the CC that Llangwelli station be closed as soon as possible. Is that clear?'

'Yes, sir,' said Southall through gritted teeth.

'Good. Now, I have some calls to make, and you need to get your team working this investigation. I'll be down to review the case later.'

Just in case Southall hadn't understood that the meeting was over, he picked up the phone and began thumbing through a diary on his desk. 'Please close the door on the way out,' he said without looking up.

Furious, Southall made her way from his office, somehow resisting the urge to slam the door behind her.

Muttering, 'Wanker,' she stomped back down to the office.

* * *

It was late afternoon when Norman and Winter returned to the office. Morgan and Lane were hunched over their desks and Southall was in her office, but she came out to meet them as soon as they walked in.

Norman went across to the back wall of the office where they had mounted a huge whiteboard. A large map of the forest dominated the centre of the board. The three car parks were conspicuous, and now it was clear just how many footpaths led into the forest. They seemed to come from all directions.

Without an identity for the victim, she remained a nameless, post-mortem photograph pinned to the board alongside the map. The only name on the right of the board was that of Gareth James, the forest manager. The word "Pagans" had been added to the left of the map. And that was about it.

'It's going well then,' said Norman as Southall joined him.

'As you can see,' said Southall. 'Judy is trawling through missing person reports, and Catren is doing a background check on Gareth James, but apart from that we've nothing to go on until the post-mortem and forensic reports come in. I was rather hoping you might have something to report.'

'I've got these leaflets about Paganism.' Norman brandished the leaflets and put them down on the nearest desk. 'It gives us a taste of what they're about, but not much more.'

'Did you learn anything that helps us?' asked Southall.

'I can add the names of the couple who lead the Pagan group.' He wrote the names Sian and Elis Williams on the board. 'And Frosty has a list of all the Pagans for background checks.'

'Is that it?' asked Southall.

'They admit being in the clearing in the middle of the forest on the night of thirty-first October from seven thirty until midnight.' He added this information to the board. 'But they didn't see or hear anyone else out there.'

'What did you make of them?' asked Southall.

'They didn't make us feel we should be requesting a search warrant anytime soon,' said Norman. 'The guy, Elis, likes to think he's a big, scary, hard man, but it's his wife who wears the trousers. He might have a past, but I suspect that since she came along he's kept out of trouble and does what he's told. I reckon she can be pretty feisty if she feels threatened, but she didn't come across as someone we should be worried about. As I said, Frosty's going to do background checks on the whole group, but I'll be surprised if he finds anything.'

'Right, let's have a quick roundup,' said Southall. 'Judy, how are you doing with the missing persons?'

'Sorry, I've found nothing within fifty miles, so I've widened the search area to the whole of the UK. It's running now, but it's not looking hopeful. There are plenty of young women missing, but none that match our victim.'

Southall nodded. 'Catren, anything about our forest manager that should be cause for concern?'

'From what I can see, Gareth James is pretty much squeaky clean,' said Morgan.

'What, nothing?' asked Norman.

'He's got three points on his driving licence for speeding,' said Morgan. 'But that is the full extent of his criminal record.'

'I didn't think you were going to find much, if I'm honest,' said Southall.

'Yeah, I thought he seemed genuine,' said Norman.

'And he was clearly shocked at finding the body,' said Winter.

'Right. In view of what we know so far, I think there's not much point in staying late tonight,' said Southall. 'We've absolutely nothing to go on until we have the post-mortem and forensic reports, so I suggest we get off home, get a good night's rest and make an early start tomorrow. Norm and I will be at the post-mortem first thing, and you all have tasks to be getting on with.'

'That sounds like a plan,' said Norman. 'I'll just write up what happened with the Pagans, and then I'll be off.'

CHAPTER THREE

'I'm not going to be revisiting my breakfast, am I?' asked Norman.

The pathologist, Dr Bill Bridger, smiled.

'You're okay, Norm. I know how much you enjoy watching the gory bits, so I came in early and got them out of the way before you arrived.'

'What can you tell us?' asked Southall.

'The victim is a teenager, sixteen to eighteen years old. Four feet ten inches tall, weighs barely six stone. Black hair, brown eyes.'

'Jeez, she's just a kid,' said Norman.

'I don't think she died where she was buried,' said Bridger, carefully folding back the sheet covering the body far enough to show her neck and head. 'And I believe she may have been brought to the burial site in a car.'

'Carpet fibres on the body?' asked Norman.

'Not on the body, but there were on the sheet she was wrapped in.'

'That only proves the sheet was in a car,' said Southall.

'And that's why I said "may have been" brought in a car,' said Bridger.

'Is there any way you can be sure, one way or the other?' asked Southall.

Bridger pursed his lips. 'We found a small oil stain on the sheet, and a matching one on the body.'

'You think the oil came from the boot of a car?' asked Norman.

'If you can find a car with a matching oil stain and I can prove it's the same oil—'

Southall sighed. 'Good God, Bill. How are we supposed to find that car? The crime scene is pretty remote and there are no CCTV cameras for miles.'

Bridger spread his hands. 'You asked me what I can tell you. If it helps, we might be able to find a manufacturer match for the fibres. That might narrow it down a bit.'

'Okay, that's a fair point,' conceded Southall. 'What else? Cause of death?'

'It's an unusual one, that's for sure.'

'Unusual how?' asked Southall.

'Well, there are bruises on her arms suggesting she was being held down, and more bruising and a couple of cracked ribs point to someone kneeling on her chest.'

'Strangled?' suggested Norman.

'Something like that,' said Bridger. 'I believe someone was trying to smother her.'

'You mean she was suffocated,' said Norman.

'I think she probably would have been, but her heart stopped before that happened. I believe she was literally scared to death.'

'Is that a thing?' asked Norman. 'I know people say they were scared to death, but I thought that was just a turn of phrase.'

'It's rare, but it can happen,' said Bridger. 'If you're scared you get an adrenaline rush—'

'Which is the fight or flight thing,' said Southall.

'That's right,' said Bridger. 'Normally it won't do you any harm, but if your heart is damaged, or diseased, it may not cope, and the rush could trigger a cardiac arrest.'

'Was her heart diseased?' asked Southall. 'She seems very young for that.'

'Not exactly. Have you ever heard of broken heart syndrome?'

'That's something else I didn't know was a real thing,' said Norman.

'It's usually a temporary one-off event that's caused by overwhelming stress.'

'Leaving your family at a young age and being smuggled into a foreign country must be stressful,' said Southall.

'Exactly,' said Bridger. 'The condition is often associated with grief, which is why it's called broken heart syndrome.'

'And she could well have been grieving as a result of leaving her family behind,' said Norman.

'It's most common in women over fifty, but there are exceptions. The effects can last anything from a few days or longer, but treated correctly, most people recover and are none the worse for it.'

'But this girl didn't recover,' said Southall. 'How come?'

'After examining her heart, I believe she had the misfortune to have suffered recurring events. Untreated, each one would have weakened her heart further, until the inevitable cardiac arrest.'

'I thought you said it was a one-off thing,' said Norman.

'It nearly always is,' said Bridger. 'I'm going to seek expert opinion, but just imagine a scenario where someone already has a weakened heart, perhaps caused by these adrenaline rushes, and then she undergoes God knows how much stress leaving her family and travelling here, and then, after all that, she's attacked. Cumulatively, I can't think of anything more likely to scare her to death.'

'Jeez, what a way to go,' said Norman, gloomily. 'If she was naked, does that mean she was—'

'No, there's no sign of sexual assault,' said Bridger. 'In fact, she was still intact.'

'A virgin? I suppose that's something,' said Southall.

'Makes you wonder why they took her clothes,' said Norman.

'Perhaps her clothes would have made it easier to identify her,' said Southall. 'I take it you didn't find anything?'

'We didn't find anything on site,' said Bridger, 'and there are no distinguishing marks on her body. Her dark hair and skin tone suggests she could have Middle Eastern heritage but that's just an educated guess. I've taken samples for DNA analysis which will tell us more.' He pulled back the other end of the sheet to reveal her feet. 'But she does have the number thirty-seven tattooed on the sole of her foot.' He pointed to her left foot. Norman took a couple of steps forward, bent and peered at it.

'I don't like what that suggests,' he said.

'What about time of death?' asked Southall.

Bridger looked at his notes. 'Being out in the cold wet ground didn't make it easy, but I estimate she died sometime between early Thursday evening and Friday morning.'

'Hedging your bets there, Bill,' said Southall. 'Can't you be a little more specific?'

'You know very well how I feel about guessing. I'll be much more specific when the test results are in, but that could take two or three days.'

'Can't you make an exception for once,' said Southall irritably. 'You've given us a timeframe that covers more than twelve hours. Surely you can narrow it down a bit. It's not as if we're going to hold you responsible if you're a few hours out.'

Bridger sighed. 'Okay, since you ask so nicely, I'll say between eight p.m. on Thursday and two a.m. on Friday.'

'Any idea when she was buried?' asked Norman.

'I'd say some time on Friday night.'

'Why Friday?' asked Southall.

'We know it rained fairly heavily from late Saturday afternoon until after midnight on Sunday, yet the soil beneath the body was relatively dry.'

'You think it wasn't raining when she was buried,' said Norman.

'Right,' said Bridger. 'And if we assume the torch we found was taken there by whoever buried the body, that suggests it must have been dark. Hence, I'm thinking Friday night.'

'That will give us somewhere to start,' said Southall. 'I suppose it's too early to have anything from Forensics?'

'It's early days, but we have made a start,' said Bridger. 'I'm afraid the spade we found had no fingerprints on it, but the torch was much more obliging. We've got two different prints from it, but at this stage we haven't found a match on the database.'

'I guess that would have been too convenient, wouldn't it?' Norman said.

'Is that it?' asked Southall.

'Jeez, Sarah, give the guy a chance,' said Norman. 'There's enough there to get us started.'

Bridger smiled at him.

'Thank you for bringing the voice of reason to the proceedings, Norm,' he said, looking pointedly at Southall.

'All right, I apologise,' said Southall. 'It's been a bad day.'

'We've got a new boss keeping Nathan's seat warm while he's away,' explained Norman. 'And he says he's going to be very much hands-on.'

'Ah, I see,' said Bridger. 'Now I understand why one of you is so touchy this morning.'

Southall looked sheepish.

'I do get it, Sarah,' he said. 'You've got used to running things your own way, and now someone wants to take that control from you. I understand, honestly I do, but making my life hell isn't going to change the situation.'

'I've apologised once,' said Southall. 'I hope you're not expecting me to keep on apologising.'

Bridger winked at Norman.

'I think I know you well enough to understand how unlikely that would be,' he said. 'Anyway, getting back to work, I'm assuming you want to show this new boss that you can manage just fine without his interference, but so far I'm not helping you to do that.'

'Yeah, something like that,' said Norman. 'And we also think he sees this as an opportunity to take Nathan's place permanently.'

'Ah, I can see how that does complicate things,' said Bridger. 'So, basically, you're damned if you do a good job, and you're damned if you don't.'

'That's it in a nutshell,' said Southall. 'But it goes against the grain for us not to do our jobs properly, so we'll just go ahead, and deal with the fallout when, or if, it happens.'

'I'm sure I'll have more for you later, but you know what it's like. You can't hurry test results, it's a waiting game. Always is,' said Bridger. 'And, apart from the oil stain, which was so obvious we couldn't miss it, we've barely started testing the sheet she was wrapped in.'

'Do you think you'll get anything from it?' asked Norman. 'I thought any evidence would have been lost since it was covered in soil and then rained on.'

'Don't forget it was wrapped around the body, so not all of it was covered in mud, or soaked by the rain. Fingers crossed, we might get lucky. Also, as you know, there were numerous footprints and tracks found around the edges of the clearing. The rain has made it difficult to even be sure which way they're heading, but we think the vast majority head to and from the main car park. We're never going to be able to sort those out in a million years, so we're assuming they've been left by dog walkers and other visitors to the park.'

'My gut tells me that whoever did this wouldn't have risked using the main car park, even though it was late at night,' said Norman.

'I agree with Norm,' said Southall. 'And I think you're right not to waste time on those footprints.'

'Due to the weather, we haven't found any distinct enough to get a perfect cast anyway,' said Bridger. 'But we did find what we think are footprints that lead off in the opposite direction, heading towards the small car park that we used.'

Realising what this might imply, Southall jumped straight in.

'You mean your guys didn't consider they were driving all over the car park where—'

'Come on, Sarah, cut us some slack here,' said Bridger. 'They might be a small team of SOCOs, but they are professionals. Of course they realised the possibility. That's why they took casts of all the tyre tracks they found in that car park before we went in.'

'Oh, right. Of course. I'm sorry,' said Southall, looking crestfallen.

'You said you "think" they're footprints,' added Norman. 'Why think?'

'At first we couldn't make sense of them because they were so widely spaced, but then we realised—'

'Whoever left the footprints was running,' said Norman. 'But if they only lead away—'

'Because of the size of the prints, I think we're probably talking about a man,' said Bridger. 'The footprints were only left because he was running away. If he came in the same way but was walking, and careful where he stepped, he could have got there without leaving any prints at all.'

'Carrying a body?' asked Norman. 'In the dark?'

'She was so light a big, strong guy would hardly notice,' said Bridger. 'And we know he had a powerful torch.'

'So that's really it, is it?' asked Southall. 'I suppose it's better than nothing, but there's no definitive evidence, is there?'

Bridger beamed. 'Well, perhaps there is. You see I've saved the best until last.'

'What is it?' asked Southall.

'You're going to have to make dinner tonight,' said Bridger.

'I might, if I'm home in time,' said Southall. 'But I won't if you don't tell us what it is.'

'I found some dried blood beneath the victim's left breast.'

'She was cut? You didn't mention any wounds, and how does that help us if you didn't find a weapon of some sort?'

'That's the thing,' said Bridger. 'There was no knife, or any other weapon, because there are no wounds on her apart from the bruises.'

'So, how did the blood get there?' asked Norman.

'I think whoever buried her cut his hand.'

'So, you're saying it's not her blood?' asked Southall.

'Yes, that's exactly what I'm saying.'

'So, there's a good chance it's the killer's blood?'

'I would say there's a very good chance. I'll know more once it's been analysed.'

* * *

'Don't you and Bill talk work when you're at home?' asked Norman as he and Southall walked back to their car.

'Sorry?' said Southall.

'That seemed like it was all news to you,' said Norman.

'That's because it was all news to me,' said Southall. 'Bill didn't come home last night. He worked all night trying to hurry things along for us.'

'And you're still not satisfied?'

'It's not that,' said Southall, but didn't elaborate.

Norman started the car and pulled away.

'Oh, I get it. You don't approve of him working over-night, right?'

'Don't get me wrong, I appreciate what he's doing, and that he's doing it to help us,' said Southall. 'But I don't want him overdoing it. I keep telling him he's no use to any of us if he makes himself ill, but will he listen?'

'So that's why you were giving him such a hard time,' said Norman.

'That's just the half of it,' said Southall. 'He got so engrossed in his work he forgot to tell me he wasn't coming home. When I woke up at two a.m. and he wasn't there, I nearly had a heart attack.'

'He can't help it,' said Norman. 'He's always been a workaholic. We've all been there, haven't we?'

'Well, I think he needs to become a bit less of a workaholic,' said Southall. 'I've managed to do it, you've managed to do it. Now he needs to do it.'

* * *

Nine thirty a.m. and the whole team were now gathered before the freshly updated whiteboard.

'Before you start, can I just add something to the board?' asked Lane.

'Of course,' said Southall.

Lane went up to the board, taking the lid from a pen. 'I hope you don't mind, but I don't like to think of her as just "the victim". So, I looked up the Arabic for unknown.' Beneath the photograph of their victim she wrote the word *Majhul.* 'I don't know about anyone else, but to me it seems to lend her a bit more dignity.'

'I think that's an excellent idea,' said Southall.

'Yeah, I like it. Well done, Jude,' said Morgan.

'Right,' said Southall. 'Now we've got some information to work with let's—'

The doors banged, and all five detectives swivelled round. Acting Superintendent Evans was standing in the doorway, the doors swinging closed behind him.

'Oh, crap, just what we need,' muttered Norman under his breath.

'Good morning, everyone,' said Evans, taking in the scene.

There was a collective mumble of greetings.

Evans walked over and studied the board. 'You've a name for the victim?'

'Er, well, yes and no,' said Southall.

'What does that mean?'

'*Majhul* means "unknown" in Arabic. We feel it's more dignified than calling her "the victim" all the time.'

'I'd have thought it was a bit late to be worrying about her dignity,' Evans said sardonically.

'It's never too late to restore a bit of dignity,' said Norman. 'She was a human being, and she didn't ask for what was done to her.'

Evans seemed about to retort, but chose to swallow it. 'Don't mind me,' he said, 'I need to catch up with the investigation, and I'm keen to see my team at work.'

Norman bristled at the "my team", but before he could open his mouth Southall managed to dig a discreet elbow in his ribs. Meanwhile, she was wondering what had happened to the belligerent Evans of yesterday.

'Carry on, everyone,' said Evans. 'Don't let me cramp your style. Just pretend I'm not here.'

'Right,' said Southall, turning back to face the whiteboard. The others settled back in their seats.

'If we look at the timeline, we know that on the night of Thursday, thirty-first October, the Pagan group met in the main car park at seven thirty, then made their way to the clearing, where they remained until midnight.'

'They were there to celebrate Samhain,' Norman informed them. 'Basically, that's a sort of harvest festival. It's also the start of the Pagan new year.'

'How do they celebrate?' asked Morgan.

'According to Sian Williams, they have a fire, a feast, and what she called rituals, which seem to consist of poetry readings and reminiscing about the past,' said Winter.

'I don't recall seeing any charred bits of ground,' said Southall thoughtfully.

'We didn't cover the entire clearing,' said Norman, 'we left that to Forensics. But, come to think of it, I didn't see any mention of it in their report.'

'Maybe they didn't think it was relevant,' suggested Morgan.

'Frosty, when we've finished this update, get on to Forensics and ask them about it,' said Southall.

'Yes, boss.'

'Did they go to the clearing on foot?' asked Morgan.

'Elis and Sian have a van,' said Norman. 'They all pile into the van and leave their cars in the main car park.'

'Dr Bridger thinks Majhul died sometime between eight p.m. on Thursday and two a.m. on Friday, but she didn't die where she was buried,' Southall said. 'The evidence suggests she was buried on Friday night. That's somewhere in the region of twenty-four hours between death and burial. So, two questions: where was she murdered? And where was her body kept during those twenty-four hours?

'There was a small oil stain on the sheet and on the body which could mean she was in the boot of a car,' continued Southall. 'This is backed up by fibres found on the sheet the body was wrapped in which are probably a match for the sort of carpet found in the boot of a car.'

'All very well,' said Norman. 'The problem is we have no idea what car we're looking for. There's no CCTV at the small car park, and although Forensics have a couple of nice tyre treads, they don't lead us to a definitive make of car.'

'What about the spade, and the torch left at the scene?' asked Lane. 'Any fingerprints?'

'There were no prints on the spade,' said Norman.

'So he must have worn gloves,' said Lane. 'Whoever did this knew what they were doing.'

'You'd think so,' said Southall. 'But then we've got a torch with not one, but two different sets of fingerprints. Sadly, they don't match anyone on the database.'

From the back of the room, Evans coughed loudly. 'So, find the fingerprints that match those on the torch, and you have the killer.'

'I'm not so sure,' said Norman. 'The thing about the fingerprints bothers me.'

'You're overthinking, DS Norman,' said Evans. 'It seems straightforward enough to me.'

'You're saying he was savvy enough to wear gloves to handle the spade, but not to carry the torch?' said Norman. 'To me, that doesn't add up.'

'Maybe there were two of them,' said Evans.

'Don't you think the clever one carrying the spade would have made sure the other guy wore gloves, too?'

'All right. Perhaps he doesn't like getting his hands dirty,' said Evans.

'He's worried about that, but he doesn't mind handling a dead body?' said Norman.

'Perhaps he blisters easily,' said Evans.

'For the first time in my life, I've been doing a lot of gardening lately,' said Norman. 'My hands blistered at first, so I used gloves but, trust me, latex tears when you're digging. You need heavy-duty gardening gloves.'

'I think you're wrong,' said Evans. 'In fact, I think you've both got this all wrong. It seems obvious to me. These Pagan people need bringing in. They know the site, they were there on Thursday, and they've got a van for moving the body.'

'What about a motive?' asked Morgan.

Evans drew himself up to his full six foot three and looked down his nose at this junior detective. 'Are you questioning my judgement?'

'No, sir,' said Morgan. 'But—'

'How would I know what their motive is?' snapped Evans. 'Perhaps they wanted a human sacrifice.'

'Human sacrifice?' spluttered Norman. 'You must be joking. Where has that come from?'

Evans's face was beginning to grow dangerously red.

'DS Norman,' he said. 'Just remember who you're talking to. I'm in charge here, and if I tell you to question someone, you damn well get out there and do it.'

'With respect, sir,' said Southall. 'I think—'

'"With respect"? What crap,' said Evans. 'There isn't a single one of you people who has any idea what respect is. I am especially disappointed in you, DI Southall. I distinctly told you yesterday that I wanted to be kept up to date, yet when I came down to see you, there was no one here. You had all gone home, and there was hardly anything on the board.'

'There was very little on the board because we had very little to put on the board,' said Southall. 'I didn't see any point in keeping everyone here when we had nothing to go on since we were waiting for the post-mortem and forensic reports which I knew wouldn't be ready until this morning.'

'Well, you should have told Forensics to get a move on,' said Evans.

'You can't hurry tests,' said Southall. 'They take time. It's a fact of life.'

'And you could have told me you were leaving early,' Evans said.

'When I came up to your office to update you, you weren't there,' said Southall.

'Oh? What time was that?'

'Just after five p.m.,' said Southall.

'Yes, well, I had to nip out for a while.'

'I'm sorry, but Superintendent Bain always lets me know if he's not going to be around or he's going home early, because he knows I'm a detective, not a mind reader.'

'I'd watch your tone, if I were you, Southall,' hissed Evans, heading for the door. 'Just do as I say, get those bloody Pagans in here and do your jobs.'

'We can't just go barging in there without a search warrant,' said Southall. 'And that will take time to arrange.'

'You'd better get on with it then, hadn't you,' said Evans. 'And, Southall, rest assured I will be speaking to you later.'

* * *

They watched in stunned silence as Evans marched out.

'Well, isn't he the cheery one this morning?' said Norman.

Morgan turned to Southall. 'Can he speak to you like that in front of us?'

'He just did, Catren.'

58

'Yes, but that doesn't make it right,' said Morgan. 'I think you should make a complaint.'

'I'll tell you one thing,' said Norman. 'You wouldn't find Nathan Bain speaking to anyone like that. If he had a gripe with any of us, he'd tell us so in the privacy of his office.'

'Yes, well, Evans isn't Nathan Bain, is he?' said Southall. 'Anyway, you all heard what he said. We need to interview the Pagans. All fourteen of them.'

'Are you sure we should be doing this, Sarah?' asked Norman. 'Surely it's a complete waste of time.'

'I hate to say it, but I have to admit he does have a point,' said Southall. 'The Pagans know the forest, they were there on Thursday night, and they have a van. That's an avenue of enquiry we can't ignore.'

'Don't tell me you think they made a human sacrifice too?' asked Norman.

'I think it's highly unlikely, but I'm keeping an open mind,' said Southall.

'Seriously?' asked Norman. 'My gut is telling me this particular avenue of enquiry is going to end in a cul-de-sac.'

'Look, Norm, if you don't want to do it, I can always take Catren,' said Southall.

'I'll sort out the search warrant,' said Lane.

* * *

'Mrs Williams? I'm Detective Inspector Southall, and this is my colleague, DC Morgan.'

Sian Williams cast an eye over the two warrant cards.

'If it's about what happened in the forest, we've already spoken to DS Norman, and a young man called, um, Winter, I think it was,' she said.

'Yes, I know,' said Southall. 'But we're investigating a murder, and we have a few more questions.'

A look of horror crossed Sian's face.

'Murder? We don't know anything about any murder.'

'We'd also like to have a look around, if that's okay,' added Southall. 'And we'd like to look inside your van.'

Sian Williams planted her feet firmly in the doorway and folded her arms.

'Oh, no. You're not looking at anything without a search warrant.'

'Got something to hide?' asked Morgan.

'No, I haven't, girly,' said Sian. 'But I know my rights.'

'There's a search warrant on the way,' said Southall. 'Perhaps we can come in and have a chat while we wait.'

'And there again, perhaps you can't,' said Sian. 'We've already had a chat with DS Norman and I really don't feel like going over the whole thing again. A better idea would be for you to go and sit in your car and wait.' She stepped back and slammed the door.

Southall turned away from the door with a sigh. 'Well, that went well. I thought Norm said they were helpful.'

'Yeah, but then Norm and Frosty only came for a cosy chat,' said Morgan. 'They weren't here to search the place.'

'Yes, I suppose that's true.'

'What do you want to do now?' asked Morgan.

'Well, I'm not going to stand here in the cold, so I suppose we'll have to do as she said and wait in the car.'

* * *

It was another hour before Norman turned up with the search warrant, and a small forensic team. This time Sian did let them in, but not before telling Norman how disappointed she was.

'We told you what we knew,' she said. 'Elis even made you both a cup of tea.'

'I'm sorry, Sian,' he said. 'But look at it from our point of view. You were there in the forest the night the murder took place.'

'Ergo, we must have done it! How many people were in Oxford Street when that bomb went off? Did they all become suspects because they were in the area?'

'That's hardly the same thing, and you know it,' said Southall.

Still addressing Norman, Sian cocked her head in Southall's direction.

'Someone get out of bed on the wrong side this morning, did they?'

Ignoring the dig at Southall, Norman said patiently, 'Look, we're not accusing you of anything—'

'Seems to me you are from where I'm standing.'

'How about if there was another way you could look at it,' said Norman.

'What other way?'

'Helping us now could eliminate you from suspicion.'

Sian was obviously unconvinced.

'Believe me, we don't enjoy doing this kind of thing,' he said, 'but we have to, it's part of our job. Now, whether you like it or not, we have a warrant and we're going to search the premises, and it would be a lot easier for all of us if you co-operated.'

Reluctantly, Sian stepped aside for them to enter. Southall led the team upstairs, while Norman talked Sian into making him a cup of tea while he tried to calm her down.

Twenty minutes later, Southall joined them in the kitchen. Norman looked up as she came in. She shook her head.

'Didn't find anything, did you?' asked Sian. 'I told you you wouldn't.'

'You've had plenty of time to hide any evidence,' said Southall.

'So you say,' said Sian. 'If we had any evidence to hide.'

'Where's your husband?' asked Southall.

'He's gone out. Believe me, if he'd known you were coming, he would have stayed here to welcome you.'

'We need to talk,' said Southall. 'And before you start complaining again, we can either do it here, or we can take you down to Llangwelli station.'

Sian could be belligerent when she wanted to be, but she also knew when she was beaten.

'Okay,' she said. 'I'm not going to give you the satisfaction of dragging me off to a police station.'

While Sian was giving Southall and Norman a hard time in the kitchen, Morgan was outside with one of the forensic team searching the van. Morgan was going through the cab, and so far, had found nothing of any consequence. Mia, the forensic technician, was just starting in the back when Catren heard her call out.

'Come and take a look at this.'

Morgan made her way around.

'There's all sorts of crap in here, including a lot of soil,' said Mia from inside. 'Plenty to get samples from.'

'Is that a pile of cushions at the back?' asked Morgan.

'Looks like it,' said Mia. 'Perhaps they carry passengers, although I wouldn't fancy being in the back of this thing. You'd get flung all over the place.' She pointed to the floor just inside the doors. 'Anyway, never mind the cushions, look at this. The whole floor has been boarded up and fitted out with carpet, apart from this area just inside the doors. Even the sides are carpeted.'

'Why would they only carpet two thirds of the floor and leave that part out?' asked Morgan.

'Maybe they cut it off because there was an oil stain on it?' suggested Mia.

'That's just what I'm thinking,' said Morgan. 'You carry on here, Mia. I think I'd better get Norm.'

Morgan hurried back to the house and followed the sound of voices into the kitchen.

'Sorry to butt in,' she said, 'but there's something you need to see.'

Southall watched Sian, whose eyes widened briefly. It was the first time she had shown the slightest sign of alarm.

'What is it?' Sian asked.

'Nothing for you to worry about, Sian,' said Southall. 'You and I can stay here and carry on talking, DS Norman will take care of it.'

Norman followed Morgan out to the van.

'What have you found? Anything incriminating?' He followed her to the van, where the forensic technician was busy taking samples from the floor.

'Mia noticed it,' said Morgan, pointing to the floor. 'We're thinking this piece may have been cut off because it had a suitably incriminating oil stain on it.'

'Yeah, that's a possibility,' said Norman.

'You're not convinced?' asked Morgan.

'I didn't say that, but I can think of several reasons why someone might have cut that piece of carpet out. And oil only features in one of them.'

'Oh,' said Morgan, deflated.

'I'm not trying to piss on your parade,' said Norman. 'But unless you have that missing bit of carpet, you'd be hard pressed to make a case. You need something incontrovertible like those carpet fibres Mia's gathering. Now, if they match the fibres on the sheet the body was wrapped in, we could be in business.'

Norman watched while Mia finished taking samples of the fibre. 'Mia, I know you've probably taken dozens already but, before you finish, could you take a couple of close-up photos of the edge of the carpet, where it's been cut?'

'Sure, no problem.'

'Any particular reason?' asked Morgan.

'I just want to see how smooth it is,' said Norman. 'If it's a rough edge, it would indicate it was done in a hurry. If the edge was cut neatly, it might have been done like that for a reason.'

Mia was taking a closer look. 'It looks as though the edge has been bound.'

'They've had all weekend to make it neat and tidy,' said Morgan.

'Yeah, that's true,' said Norman. 'They've also had all weekend to re-carpet the entire back of the van if they had something to hide.' He stepped back and looked over the van. 'They've also had all weekend to wash any evidence away, but we can all see the inside of this van hasn't been cleaned in weeks.'

'I thought we were trying to find proof they had a body in here,' said Morgan.

'I'd like to think we've trained you better than that,' said Norman. 'Our job is not to assume we know what happened and then make evidence fit our narrative, but to find evidence that helps us prove what happened, even if that means proving it wasn't the way we would like it to have happened.'

'You don't think they're guilty, do you?' asked Morgan.

'The way I see it at the moment, the only thing they're guilty of is believing in Paganism, and as far as I'm aware, that's not a crime.'

'How come you're so sure they're not involved?'

Norman frowned. 'I didn't say I was sure they're not involved, I'm just saying I've yet to see any evidence that suggests they are.'

'What about the missing piece of carpet I've just shown you?'

'Okay, Catren, what does that actually prove?' asked Norman.

'That the carpet has been cut,' said Morgan.

'Exactly,' said Norman. 'But it doesn't prove when it was cut, or why. Yes, that missing piece of carpet might have oil on it that matches the sheet, and it might be the thing that cracks the case, but instead of assuming we already know the answer, we need to ask the owner to tell us why it was cut. And there's another thing we can do.' Norman turned to the forensic technician, who was regarding them with an amused expression. 'What's the floor under the carpet like, Mia?'

She lifted the edge of the carpet and peered underneath. 'It's clean, almost like new.'

'That suggests the carpet has probably been there for some time, right?' said Norman.

Morgan sighed. 'Okay. It looks as if you're right,' she said. 'I'm sorry. I should know better than to argue with you.'

'It's not about arguing with me,' said Norman. 'It's about not jumping to conclusions. Anyway, we can talk about it later. You and Mia finish up here—' he pointed to a barn nearby — 'and then take a look inside that barn. I'll go and ask Sian Williams about the carpet.'

'Right,' said Morgan.

She and Mia watched Norman head back to the house. 'What's up with Norm? It's not like him to be so crabby,' said Mia.

'Our temporary boss. He's a bit of a shit,' said Morgan. 'He's ruffled everyone's feathers, especially Norm's.'

'Ah. Sounds like a new broom and all that comes with it,' said Mia.

'God, I hope not,' said Morgan. 'He's only been here five minutes, and he's already pissed everyone off. I'd hate to think it was going to be like that all the time.'

* * *

Norman made his way back into the kitchen and rejoined Southall and Sian Williams.

'What's the problem?' asked Sian.

'Why has the carpet in the back of your van been cut back?' asked Norman.

'Cut back?' said Sian. 'I'm sorry, I don't know what you mean.'

'Let me rephrase the question,' said Norman. 'Is there any particular reason why the back of your van has carpet up the side walls, but on the floor, it only goes just over halfway to the back doors?'

'Oh, I see what you mean,' said Sian. 'We often carry animal feed, muddy dogs, and all sorts of other stuff that makes a mess. If the carpet goes all the way to the doors, it gets ruined.'

'So why have carpet at all?' asked Southall.

'If you're in the back of a big van like that it's like being in a drum,' said Sian. 'The carpet up the sides absorbs a lot of the vibrations and reduces the noise. Boarding and carpeting the floor does the same thing, and if you're sitting in the back, makes it more comfortable.'

'Are you supposed to carry passengers?' asked Southall.

'Not really,' said Sian. 'We only do it when we're ferry-ing everyone from the main car park to the clearing.'

'You mean when you have your gatherings?'

'Yes, that's right. Never on the roads, and only at about five miles an hour.'

'What sort of stuff do you carry that makes such a mess?' asked Southall.

'As I said, animal feed, dirty dogs, but it's the firepit that makes the most mess.'

'Firepit?'

'We have permission to have a bonfire when we're on the clearing, and out of respect for the wildlife that lives in the surrounding forest, we take an old metal firepit with us so we can contain the fire. It's a big metal thing my husband made. We agreed it with the forest manager, as it means we can light a fire without the risk of burning the entire forest down.'

'How big are we talking?' asked Norman.

'Big enough that it takes two strong men to lift it,' Sian said.

'And you're saying you take it to the clearing, keep a fire burning until midnight and then bring it home again?' asked Southall. 'Isn't having a hot firepit in the back of your van a bit risky?'

'It would be,' said Sian, 'if we brought it home with us. Elis and his mate go and collect it the following morning. It's burnt out and cold by then.'

Southall didn't look convinced.

'If you're searching the barn you'll see the firepit, and the old tarpaulin we stand it on and use to cover the top. It's supposed to stop the ash from going everywhere. It's not per-fect, but it does a reasonable job. We did have carpet all the way to the back doors originally, but Elis forgot the tarpaulin one morning and ruined it. That's why he cut it back.'

Southall drummed her fingers on the table.

'I tell you what,' said Sian. 'As you obviously don't believe me, why don't you go and see for yourself. Or ask Gareth James, the forest manager. He's even helped Elis load it onto the van a couple of times.'

'Exactly how many times a year do you have these gatherings and bonfires?' asked Southall.

'We celebrate the eight Sabbats,' said Sian, 'so, that'll be eight times.'

'Sabbats?' asked Southall.

Sian nodded towards Norman. 'I gave him a leaflet that tells you when they are and what they're all about. And Gareth James will have a record of our bookings.'

Southall looked at Norman.

'Yeah, that's right, it's one of those leaflets I brought to the station,' said Norman.

'Look, are you going to be much longer?' said Sian. 'I've got a life to live.'

'I'd like a statement about Thursday night,' said Southall. 'We can do it here, or we can do it at Llangwelli station.'

Sian sighed wearily. 'Well, obviously I don't want to go to a police station.'

'Good,' said Southall. 'It shouldn't take long.'

'I'll go and see how Catren's getting on,' said Norman.

When he got to the barn, Morgan and Mia were just coming out.

'Anything?' asked Norman.

'Bales of hay and straw, and the sort of paraphernalia you'd expect to find on a smallholding. Nothing out of the ordinary, apart from what looks like a humungous firepit.'

Norman nodded. 'Has it been used recently?'

'I'd say so,' said Morgan. 'It's got ash in the bottom.'

'Was there a tarpaulin with it?'

'Yeah,' said Morgan. 'How did you know?'

'It adds up with what Sian just told us.'

'What happens now?' asked Morgan.

'By the time we get back and write this up, I would imagine that will be it for today,' said Norman. 'And I'm guessing that tomorrow we're going to waste another whole day interviewing and taking the fingerprints of the other thirteen members of the Pagan group just so we can keep our temporary boss happy.'

CHAPTER FOUR

Wednesday, 6 November, 08.30

'Right then, DI Southall,' said Evans. 'I was led to believe you were a well-oiled team, but now I've been able to observe you for a couple of days, it seems to me you are lacking in both leadership and organisation, so I'm going to be a lot more hands-on. Starting from now.'

'Lacking leadership and organisation?' said Southall. 'Whatever gives you that idea?'

'Well, for a start, there was only one officer on the premises yesterday.'

'But the rest of us were running all over the place interviewing Pagans, as you asked.'

'But DC Lane is a junior officer!'

'With several years' experience, who is more than capable of running the office,' said Southall.

'If she has all these years of experience, why hasn't she gone on to qualify as an office manager?'

'Because, in the past, she was held back by senior officers who weren't prepared to give her a chance and foster her talent.'

'That's not the point,' spluttered Evans.

'I think it's entirely the point,' said Southall. 'Young officers will never reach their full potential if they're never given a chance to flourish. DC Judy Lane is developing into a fine office manager because we recognised her talent and allowed it to flourish.'

'That's all very well, but she is not qualified as an office manager. That's DS Norman's job.'

'As we're a small team, and short on numbers, Superintendent Bain likes to use horses for courses,' said Southall. 'Norm's experience is of much more use out in the field, and Judy has a penchant for case management. It's never been a problem before.'

'And talking of qualifications, what exactly is your situation regards being Senior Investigating Officer?'

Southall had been expecting this to come up.

'I have one more step to go,' she said.

'So, how does this work, then?'

'Superintendent Bain is mentoring me,' said Southall.

'And what exactly does that mean?'

'He oversees all the investigations.'

'Yes, but does he lead the investigations? Is he out there in the field with you?'

'In view of the staffing levels, that would be impractical. He allows me to lead, on the understanding that I keep him informed. He's always there to step in, offer feedback and advice should I need it.'

'This is all most irregular,' said Evans. 'A DC as office manager, a DS who doesn't seem to know the meaning of the word "respect", an untrained DI as SIO. It's an outrage!'

'And yet it works,' said Southall. 'Our success rate proves it. And it's because this station operates so successfully on a shoestring budget that the chief constable allows us to remain operational.'

'Are you sure the CC really knows what goes on here?' asked Evans, grimly. 'I suspect Bain has been hiding the truth, but you needn't think I'm going to. Do you understand what I'm saying, DI Southall?'

'Yes, I do, sir, but I think you'll find that Superintendent Bain isn't keeping anything from the CC.'

Evans stared at Southall in frosty silence. Southall returned the stare. She wasn't going to be cowed by his bullying.

Eventually, he cleared his throat. 'So, what have we got on the Pagans?'

'Nothing from their statements,' said Southall.

'Nothing at all? Surely there must be something?'

'Their statements are all consistent, without being so alike as to suggest they were rehearsed.'

'Of course,' said Evans. 'That's because they've had days to get their stories straight.'

'That's not what we think,' said Southall.

'"We"? Who's we?'

'The team,' said Southall. 'The five of us got together yesterday afternoon, compared the statements, and agreed that there was a very high probability that they are all true.'

Evans grunted. 'And you think three DCs are qualified to make such a judgement, do you? Isn't that your job as acting SIO?'

'The final decision is mine, but we're a team, and I like to involve everyone as much as I can,' said Southall. 'It's valuable experience for them, and as far as I'm concerned, the more input the better.'

'What about Forensics?'

'We're waiting on their report,' said Southall.

Evans sighed. 'Well, can't you hurry them along? Don't they know we're investigating a murder?'

'As they were the poor devils who had the horrible job of removing the body from a shallow grave, I think you can be assured that they are perfectly aware of that, and don't need any unnecessary reminders,' said Southall. 'In my experience, putting pressure on them is only likely to delay the results.'

'So, basically, you're no further forward,' said Evans.

Southall kept her own counsel as to whose fault that might be.

'We're still running background checks. I'm not optimistic, but you never know, they might throw something up.'

'It's got to be the Pagans,' insisted Evans. 'I'm telling you now, that girl was a sacrifice to whatever weird heathen gods they believe in. Now, Southall, I suggest you get your finger out and prove it. Or do I need to show you how to do your job?'

'No, sir, that won't be necessary,' said Southall through gritted teeth.

'Right then. Close the door on your way out,' said Evans dismissively, and bent over some paperwork on his desk.

Seething, Southall stared at the top of his head, willing all sorts of dastardly things to rain down on it, then she turned on her heel, marched out of the office and closed the door very firmly.

* * *

Down in the main office, Norman was answering a call from Bill Bridger.

'Where do you want to start?' asked Bridger.

'How about the carpet fibres?'

'The carpet they've used in the back of their van is a short pile household carpet. You won't be surprised to hear it isn't the sort usually used in cars.'

'And don't tell me, it doesn't match the fibres you found on the sheet,' said Norman.

'Correct,' said Bridger. 'You're on fire this morning, Norm.'

'I'm not sure about on fire,' said Norman. 'But I am flaming mad that we're wasting our time, and yours, testing stuff that we know isn't going to be a match. What about fingerprints?'

'The good news — if you are a member of the Pagan group,' said Bridger, 'is that none of their fingerprints match the prints found on the torch.'

'I can't say that surprises me either,' said Norman. 'I didn't for one minute think they would.'

'But it's not all bad news on the fingerprint front,' said Bridger. 'There was a partial print in the blood found on the body. It doesn't match anyone on the database, but it is a match for one of the prints on the torch.'

'Aha!' said Norman. 'That ties in with your theory about the guy cutting his hand. Pity it doesn't match anything else.'

'Talking of things that don't match, I've also got the results for the dried blood we found on the body,' said Bridger.

'At last, something that might actually be useful,' said Norman. 'Come on then, let's hear it.'

'Right, so, the victim's blood is group A positive, whereas the dried blood we found is group O positive.'

'So, they're different,' said Norman. 'That ties in with your theory about the guy cutting his hand.'

'That's right,' said Bridger.

'What does that mean in terms of percentage of the population?' asked Norman. 'Isn't it about half the population that's O positive?'

'A bit lower than that,' said Bridger. 'It's thirty-five per cent to be precise.'

'That's not much better, is it?' said Norman. 'It certainly doesn't narrow the field down a great deal for us.'

'Sorry,' said Bridger. 'But it was always unlikely to be much better. To narrow the field significantly, you would have needed a blood group with a B in it, or better still group AB.'

Norman sighed.

'Yeah, but we both know I'm rarely that lucky,' he said. 'There again, I suppose thirty-five percent is better than the one hundred percent we started with.'

'Now that is positive, Norm, if you'll excuse the pun.'

'Pun excused,' said Norman. 'Is there anything else you can tell us, like the real identity of the victim? Judy has called her Majhul. It's Arabic for unknown. I mean, it's highly appropriate, but I'd rather know who she really is. Even if we knew where she came from it would help.'

'I'm afraid I've got nothing, at this stage,' said Bridger. 'I'm still waiting on the DNA results. I'll let you know as soon as I hear from them. In the meantime, I'll email a report with what we've got so far.'

'Okay, thanks, Bill,' said Norman. 'I'll speak to you later.'

He'd just hung up when Southall appeared.

'From the look on your face, I'm guessing that didn't go too well,' he said.

'That man is really getting on my tits,' said Southall. 'He can't understand why we haven't arrested the Pagans and charged them all with murder. He thinks our victim was a sacrifice to a heathen god.'

'Doesn't he understand the need for evidence, and there isn't any?'

'I've told him that. He seems to think there's plenty of evidence, but we're incapable of finding it.'

'Well, he's welcome to get out there and find it himself if he thinks he can do better,' said Norman. 'And he's going to be even more disappointed now, because Forensics haven't got anything to suggest the Pagans are involved either.'

'Honestly, Norm, right now I could happily punch him in the face.'

'Give it another day or two, and I think we'll be forming a queue for that particular pleasure,' said Norman. 'By the way, Bill's emailing a report over.'

'Anything useful?'

'As I said, nothing that's helps us immediately, but you'll see when it arrives.'

* * *

'Here's something you might find interesting,' called Lane. 'As we believe Majhul is Middle Eastern or Asian, I thought it might be useful to locate the nearest places where refugees might be staying. It's a long shot, but you never know, some-one might have gone missing but not been reported.'

'There isn't anywhere like that around here, is there?' asked Southall. 'I would have thought the nearest place would be miles away.'

'I thought so too,' said Lane, 'but there's actually a place in Llangwelli that takes in Syrian refugees and helps them integrate into UK life.'

'I had no idea,' said Southall. 'I've never heard of it.'

'It's small, and it only started operating a few months ago,' said Lane.

'Well, it's a very well-kept secret,' said Southall.

'Maybe they've chosen to keep a low profile for a reason,' said Norman. 'Not everyone welcomes refugees.'

'Where is it?' asked Southall.

'The old manor house in the middle of town. The one where they put up that huge Christmas lights display last year.'

'You mean where an illuminated Santa's sleigh was being pulled by four reindeer across the roof, and there were electric snowmen, elves and who knows what else all over the place?' asked Southall.

'That's the one,' said Lane.

'Jeez, yeah, I know the place you mean,' said Norman. 'The display was humungous. It caused gridlock in the traffic with everyone stopping to take it all in. No one here had ever seen Christmas lights on that scale before.'

'Shall I give them a call and ask if anyone's gone missing?' asked Lane.

'If someone is missing and they haven't reported it, it's unlikely they're going to admit to it over the phone,' said Norman.

'If they're registered, they'd report someone missing, or risk losing their licence,' said Southall. 'I'm more inclined to think Majhul was an illegal immigrant. Even so, I think it would be useful for me and Norm to pay them a visit. If nothing else we might learn something about Syrian refugees.'

'It wouldn't hurt to show them her photograph,' said Norman. 'You never know, someone might recognise her.'

'Do we have a name for the owner of the house?' asked Southall.

'It's a Mr and Mrs Delaney,' said Lane.

'Right then, Norm, let's go and have a chat with Mr and Mrs Delaney,' said Southall.

* * *

Like many small towns, Llangwelli had once had a thriving town centre, filled with a range of family-run businesses. But the inevitable arrival of supermarkets and huge shopping centres within a few minutes' drive had eventually put paid to that. The sad fact was that Llangwelli would have perished years ago if it wasn't for the tourist trade.

Built soon after Llangwelli became a town, the Old Manor had seen it thrive and then decline. Close to the centre of town, it had originally been the manor house, then later the town hall, and more recently it had been restored to serve its original purpose as a residence.

A low wall and hedge marked the boundary with the road. A gravel drive ran along the side of a vast expanse of lawn up to the front of the house, and then swept back round to the gates at the entrance.

'Jeez, look at this front garden,' said Norman as Southall turned into the drive. 'It's almost as big as a tennis court!'

'Except a tennis court with a U-shaped drive would be a bit of a health hazard for the players,' said Southall. 'But you're right, it's a good size, especially for the centre of town.'

'I wonder how much a place like this would cost,' said Norman.

'More than we could afford on our salaries.'

'You're right there,' said Norman. 'But then I wouldn't really want to live in a place this big. I'd get lost.'

As they neared the house, they could see that the drive branched off, running along the side of the house, presumably round to the back.

'It looks as though there's plenty more at the back,' said Southall.

'I've visited a few old houses like this,' said Norman. 'The bigger ones usually have stables, coach houses, outbuildings, kitchen gardens and all sorts out the back.'

'Nice work if you can get it,' said Southall, nodding her head at a large black Mercedes SUV, and a blue Mercedes saloon parked at the side of the house.

'You like those big ugly things?' asked Norman. 'I think they're about as stylish as a box on wheels. And do they really need four-wheel drive?'

'They're a status symbol, Norm. I'm sure they never leave the tarmac.'

Before they had even stepped from the car, the front door of the house opened to reveal a tall, forty-something woman with suspiciously black hair, dressed in expensive designer clothes. She stood in the doorway, legs apart and arms crossed.

'I believe that's what you'd call a "resolutely immovable posture",' said Norman as they got out of the car.

'It doesn't actually say welcome, does it?' said Southall. 'And she doesn't even know who we are yet.'

'I think she may have guessed,' said Norman.

The woman studied them suspiciously as they approached. 'Can I help you?'

Not a local then, thought Norman. Definitely a London accent.

'Mrs Sheila Delaney?' asked Norman.

'Depends who's asking.'

Norman made the introductions, and they produced their warrant cards.

'I'm DS Norman and this is my colleague, DI Southall. We're from Llangwelli police station.'

The woman regarded them thoughtfully. 'Is this about the parking fine? I know I haven't paid it yet, but I've still got a few days before it's due.'

'That's a little below our pay grade,' said Norman. 'And it would be between you and the local council.'

'I thought sending two detectives for a parking fine seemed like overkill, but then I'm not aware of having done anything else wrong.'

Norman wondered if she was anywhere near as clever as she thought she was, or if this was just a show of bravado.

'We're not here because you've committed a crime,' said Norman. 'We're investigating a murder, and we thought you may be able to help us.'

Sheila Delaney looked suitably shocked.

'A murder? Oh my God, that's awful. But what makes you think I can help?'

'We believe our victim may be Syrian, or at least from somewhere in the Middle East,' said Southall. 'And we understand you run a charity supporting Syrian refugees.'

Mention of the charity caused an immediate change in Sheila Delaney's attitude, and for the first time she smiled.

'Oh, I see. Of course, I'll help if I can. Come on in,' she said, stepping aside. 'Let's go through to the kitchen, it's nice and warm in there.'

The kitchen on its own was bigger than Norman's entire cottage, but the huge conservatory that had been added to it created an impressive light-filled space. It looked out over a garden which seemed impossibly long for a property in the centre of town.

'Wow,' said Southall. 'This is some kitchen.'

A girl of sixteen or seventeen was having breakfast, watching something on her smartphone. As they came in, she started, and with a guilty look switched off the phone.

'This is my daughter, Emilia,' said Sheila. 'These two detectives want to speak to me about my charity work,' she told Emilia. 'Isn't that nice?'

The girl smiled uncertainly at them, said hello and hurried from the room.

'Who'd have a moody teenager?' said Sheila, conspiratorially. 'Can't get a civil word out of her in the mornings. It's like walking on eggshells.'

'I don't have any of my own, but I've heard they can be hard work at that age,' said Southall.

'You can say that again,' said Sheila. 'Still, she'll be off to college in a minute and then I can relax.'

A man suddenly appeared through a side door, followed by a panting springer spaniel. Telling the dog to go and lie on his bed, the man looked enquiringly at Sheila.

Sheila introduced the two detectives.

'Ronnie Delaney,' he said, and shook their hands, smiling. He nodded towards his wife. 'What's she done now? Not speeding again, is it? I keep telling her we're only allowed to do twenty miles an hour around town these days.'

'It's just too slow,' said Sheila. 'Everyone says so.' She turned to the detectives. 'I bet you two think so, don't you?'

'As an officer of the law I'm afraid I couldn't possibly say,' said Norman.

'Very diplomatic,' said Sheila. 'Of course you can't say as much, but we all know you really agree with me.'

'We're investigating a murder, Mr Delaney,' said Southall. 'We believe our victim may be from Syria or the Middle East, and we're hoping you may be able to help us out, as we believe you provide shelter for Syrian refugees.'

'The charity is Sheila's baby,' he said. 'I know both our names are on the paperwork and what have you, but I just provide the funds.'

Delaney evidently didn't miss Southall's raised eyebrow. 'I used to run a successful business in London,' he explained, 'then I got lucky with a patent which enabled me to sell up and make a tidy profit. We came out of it with a potful of money. Sheila wanted to retire somewhere quieter than London, and she's always fancied Wales, so we ended up here.'

'Retired early then,' said Norman. 'I envy you.'

'You'd think that, wouldn't you?' said Delaney. 'But I got bored within a year. All that free time, great, right? But there's only so much gardening and golf you can do. I needed a hobby, so I bought a little delivery company. It's not full-time, but it keeps me occupied.' He looked at his watch. 'Talking of which, I need to get going.'

'I think Emilia's waiting for a lift to college,' said Sheila.

'Oh, and I forgot to mention, I'm also my daughter's chauffeur,' said Delaney at the door.

'So, Sheila, is the charity your hobby?' asked Southall.

'I don't know that you'd call it a hobby. It's more of a passion really. I know how lucky I am to have all this money, and I wanted to give something back,' she said.

'Any reason why you work with Syrians specifically?'

'It wasn't deliberate. We're still very small. In fact, I've only got room for two at a time, so it seemed sensible to choose refugees with a common language so that they can keep each other company. It just so happens that I was asked to take in two young Syrian women, so that's what I did. My dream is to convert all the outbuildings so we can accommodate more.'

'What exactly do you do?' asked Southall.

'Give them somewhere nice to stay for a start. Then I teach them English and help them understand enough of our culture so that they'll be able to stand on their own two feet and make a life for themselves here. I don't just teach them the good things about the UK, I also warn them about the negative aspects of it, including the hostility they may encounter. I mean let's face it, not everyone thinks we should take in refugees.'

'Is that why your charity keeps a low profile?' asked Norman. 'Have you had any trouble?'

'No. Everyone around here has been great about it so far,' said Sheila. 'But there's nothing to be gained by inviting trouble.'

'Have you ever lost a refugee?' asked Norman.

'I'm sorry?'

'Has anyone run away?'

'Oh, sorry, I see what you mean. No, never,' said Sheila.

Southall produced the photograph. 'Have you ever come across this young woman?'

Sheila studied the photograph. 'Is she the victim?'

'Yes,' said Southall.

'No, I don't know her,' said Sheila, handing it back to Southall. 'I'm sorry I can't help you, but she's not one of mine. Like I said, I've only got two. They are both about the same

79

age as the woman in the photo, but they're definitely still here. Why don't I show you round and you can meet them.'

Sheila led them out through a side door and across a small courtyard to a row of neat-looking outbuildings.

'These used to be the old stables,' she said. 'We've had them converted into flats so everyone has their own bedroom, bathroom and kitchen. There's also a common room where I give my lessons, and where they can relax, read, watch TV or whatever.'

'Can we see inside?' asked Southall.

'Yes, of course.'

Sheila showed them the common room first, where she introduced the two young refugees. They were no more than twenty years old, with the same dark hair and brown eyes as Majhul. Both wore hijabs and had been chattering animatedly but fell silent on seeing the two detectives. One adjusted her hijab to cover more of her face.

'It's okay, girls,' said Sheila. 'These people are from the police, but they are our friends. You're not in any danger.'

Norman smiled brightly and nodded to the two young women. 'Good morning.'

Shyly, they bowed their heads and gave a mumbled hello.

'They've not been here long and don't have much English yet, but they're learning fast,' explained Sheila.

'Can I show them the photograph?' asked Southall.

'It might be better if I do it,' said Sheila.

She took the photograph from Southall and showed it to the two girls. They both looked at the photo, then up at Sheila, shaking their heads.

'Sorry,' said Sheila, handing it back.

'They seem anxious,' said Southall. 'Is that normal?'

'Before they got here someone filled their heads with horror stories about what might happen to them,' explained Sheila. 'They pay people smugglers to take them across the Channel and then the smugglers try to scare them into working for them. These two were lucky. They managed to escape and have been allowed to stay. I'm doing my best to reassure them, but it takes time for them to know who to trust.'

'I take it you keep records,' said Norman.

'I've got all the relevant paperwork and permits in the house if you want to see them.'

'If you don't mind, before we go,' said Norman.

'Yes, of course,' said Sheila.

'If we're making the girls uncomfortable, maybe we shouldn't worry them any further,' said Southall.

Sheila reassured the two young women again, gave the detectives a brief look at the two small flats and took them back outside.

Norman pointed to a couple of large buildings further down the drive. 'What are those?'

'That's the old coach house and cowsheds,' said Sheila. 'That's our next project. We're hoping to make four more flats down there.'

'Well, thank you for showing us around, and good luck with it all,' said Southall.

'My pleasure,' said Sheila. 'I'm only sorry I can't help you identify your murder victim.'

* * *

Once Norman had checked the paperwork for the two girls, he joined Southall at her car.

'I take it everything is in order?' asked Southall.

'As far as I can tell,' said Norman. 'But, to be honest, I'm not very *au fait* with that stuff, so I took photographs. I'll get Judy to check it out when we get back.'

They drove away.

'What did you make of that set up?' asked Norman.

'It's a new one on me,' said Southall. 'It seems rather informal, but that's not necessarily a bad thing, is it?'

'What about the girls? I thought they seemed scared.'

'Well, wouldn't you be if you had arrived in a new coun- try and didn't know anyone. And if someone had filled their heads with crap about this and that before they got here, it's going to make it even worse.'

'Yeah, I suppose,' said Norman.

'Even so, I think we should ask Judy to do a background check and make sure this charity is real.'

CHAPTER FIVE

Thursday, 7 November, 09.00

The door to the incident room suddenly burst open, and Evans stood there, his face purple with anger.

'DS Norman!'

'That's me,' said Norman.

'I've just had an irate woman called Imogen Cooper on the phone.'

Norman frowned. Did he know that name?

'Imogen Cooper,' roared Evans. 'The woman I sent you out to interview on Monday.'

'Oh, yeah, that's right, I remember now,' said Norman. 'You did send me out there to interview her.'

'Well, now she's on the phone wanting to know why you didn't get there. You'd better have a good reason, because I had to come up with a plausible excuse off the top of my head. And I hate lying to the public.'

'I know what you mean,' said Norman. 'Lying is never a good thing, but why didn't you just tell her the truth?'

'The truth? What do you mean?'

'Yeah, don't you recall?'

'Recall what?'

'You sent me out there, and then, just as I got to her house, you called and diverted me to the Dragon Forest, because someone had found a body,' said Norman. 'If I recall correctly, your exact words were, "Forget that. It's too trivial to worry about now". So, I did as you said and headed for the Dragon Forest.'

'Yes, but—'

'Did I do something wrong by following your orders?' asked Norman innocently. 'I mean I suppose I could have gone back there later, but I assumed you'd want us to focus on the murder investigation rather than something so trivial, and it got so busy . . .'

'Ah, yes. That's right, I believe I did divert you,' said Evans, now red with embarrassment rather than rage. 'Of course, the murder is more important, but do you think you might be a good chap and head out there now?'

'Sure,' said Norman. 'It'll be better than wasting my time trying to find evidence against the Pagans.'

'What? What did you say?'

'I said it'll make a change from chasing the Pagans,' said Norman.

'Just make sure you don't take all day with Mrs Cooper,' said Evans, heading for the doors. 'I haven't given up on those Pagans yet.'

'No, of course you haven't,' said Norman as the doors closed behind Evans. He turned to Southall and winked. 'Did he just call me a "good chap"?'

'Yes, he did,' said Southall. 'But rather than basking in the moment, I think you'd better go and see Mrs Cooper, or you won't be a good chap for long.'

'I'm thinking I should probably take a member of the fairer sex with me,' he said. 'This is about an unsolicited photograph, so it might be a bit sensitive.'

'Take Catren,' said Southall.

* * *

It was just after ten a.m. by the time Norman and Morgan got to Imogen Cooper's house.

'I think it would be better if you take the lead on this,' said Norman as he switched off the engine.

'Woman to woman, right?' asked Morgan. 'Are you coming in?'

'Oh, yeah, but I think she'll probably feel more comfortable speaking to you.'

They made their way to the front door and rang the bell. Almost immediately a slim, youthful-looking woman with short brown hair and a cupid's bow mouth opened the door. She peered at them shortsightedly through the thick lenses of a pair of spectacles that made her brown eyes look huge, and frowned at them in displeasure.

'Mrs Cooper?' said Morgan. 'I'm DC Catren Morgan and this is my colleague, DS Norman. I understand you'd like to report a crime.'

'Yes, that's right, but I was expecting you on Monday.'

'I'm sorry about that, Mrs Cooper,' said Norman. 'That was me, but unfortunately we had an emergency come up and I had to attend.'

'You mean the body found in Dragon Forest?' she asked.

Surprised, Norman said, 'Erm, yes, it was.'

The frown was at once replaced by a sympathetic smile.

'Then I completely understand,' she said. 'Now I feel guilty for wasting your time when you have something so terrible to deal with.'

'I'm sure you won't be wasting our time,' said Morgan. 'We wouldn't be here otherwise.'

'Well, if you're sure . . . you'd better come in.'

She led them through to a sumptuously furnished sitting room and invited them to sit down.

'What exactly is the problem, Mrs Cooper?' asked Morgan.

'Please call me Imogen. I feel a bit of a fraud because it's not really my problem. The thing is, my daughter's class at sixth-form college have a WhatsApp group, and she has been sent an inappropriate photograph.'

'Did your daughter show you the photo?' Morgan asked.

'No. Well, not exactly. I could see she was a bit surprised by a message she'd received, so I asked her what it was. She didn't want to show it to me, but she left the phone on the table. I know I shouldn't have, but she had seemed so upset I couldn't resist looking.

'When I told her what I had done and what I thought of the photo, she didn't seem particularly interested in doing anything about it, and especially in going to the police. But eventually I convinced her it wasn't the sort of thing she should just accept. She didn't want to go to the police herself, because she didn't want her friends to think she's a sneak, so I said I would on her behalf.'

'Can I ask how old your daughter is?' asked Morgan.

'She's seventeen.'

'Is she here?'

'No, she's at college,' Imogen said.

'Can you describe the photo?' asked Morgan.

'I can do better than that. I persuaded her to forward the photograph to me so I could show it to you. That way she could tell her friends it was me who told the police, and it had nothing to do with her.'

'Can I see it?' asked Morgan.

Imogen found the photo on her phone.

'It's not the sort of thing that should be allowed, especially among teenagers who haven't even left school,' said Imogen, handing over the phone. 'It's not just Lizzie. There are other girls in that group, and they will have been sent the same photograph. If one of the boys in that group has sent it he needs to be stopped right now. I mean, who knows where it might end?'

'I don't suppose your daughter knows who the young woman in the photograph is?' said Morgan, studying the photo and trying to hide her dismay.

'Her friends are all nice girls,' Imogen was saying. 'I'm sure none of them would make an exhibition of themselves like this!'

Morgan passed the phone to Norman. The photo showed a pale, but not white, naked torso with small, grubby breasts. The face wasn't in the picture, but even so, a small detail caught Norman's eye, and he knew immediately that this photo had nothing to do with exhibitionism.

They had seen a similar smear of blood beneath a left breast very recently. He exchanged a significant glance with Morgan.

'And you're absolutely sure she didn't know the girl in the photograph?' asked Morgan.

'She swore she didn't know who it was, and I'm certain she was telling the truth.'

'Okay, Imogen,' said Morgan evenly. 'I agree that this needs looking into. Do you think you could send us the photo?'

'Yes, of course,' Imogen said. 'Give me your number and I'll do it right now.'

Norman produced his mobile phone and a second or two later, the photo appeared.

'And we'll need to know which sixth-form college this is, and the names of Lizzie's friends,' added Morgan.

'It's the Richard Llewellyn Sixth-Form College,' said Imogen. 'I don't know all of Lizzie's friends, but I can give you the names of half a dozen of those closest to her.'

'That would be great,' said Morgan. 'And we're going to need to talk to Lizzie. We can do it here, or she could come to Llangwelli station.'

'I think she'd prefer it if you could come here,' Imogen said.

'What time does she get home?'

'If you come after six we'll have eaten, which will give us more time.'

'We can do that,' said Norman.

* * *

A few minutes later they were in their car, speeding back to Llangwelli.

'It's definitely her, isn't it?' asked Morgan.

'It's one hell of a coincidence if it isn't,' said Norman grimly, staring at the photograph on his phone. 'I mean naked, lying on what looks like a grubby white sheet, streaks of mud on the body, and what looks like blood under the left breast . . .'

'It's got to be her,' said Morgan.

'I'll have to buy a hat if it isn't her,' said Norman.

Morgan frowned. 'Buy a hat?'

'Yeah, a hat,' said Norman. 'To eat.'

* * *

Norman ran to the incident room. Evans was there, and he turned on Norman as soon as he came through the door.

'Ha! About time,' he said. 'I was just on the point of conferring with the team about the Pagans.'

'Well, forget your conferring, that can wait,' said Norman.

'I beg your pardon,' Evans said angrily. 'How dare you barge in here and speak to me like that? And why did it need two of you to go?'

'We can talk about that in a minute,' said Norman, fishing his phone from his pocket.

'Listen here—'

'For God's sake, will you pipe down for a minute?' snapped Norman.

'I've never been spoken to like th—'

'Yeah? Well, I'm sorry, but you have now,' said Norman. 'You want to confer about the Pagans? Fine, go ahead and confer. If you want to bollock me, that's fine too, but before you do any of that you need to see this photograph Imogen Cooper just gave us.'

'This is no time for sharing photos,' said Evans.

'Trust me, you'll want to see this one,' retorted Norman. 'It could mean a big break in the case.'

Morgan, who had been parking the car, caught the last few words of their exchange. 'He's right,' she said.

Norman found the photo and showed it to Evans, who looked at it and then stepped back, appalled.

'What the hell are you up to, Sergeant?' Evans bellowed. 'We've got a dead woman to identify and her killer to find, and you're showing me this filth? What kind of game are you playing?'

'Take another look,' said Norman.

'A closer look,' added Morgan.

Evans glared at them. He was about to utter a dire warning, but something made him hesitate. It was the way they stood in front of him, almost quivering with excitement.

Norman held out the phone again.

'Who is she?' Evans asked.

'Can I see?' asked Southall. Norman took the phone from him and handed it to Southall.

'It's our victim,' said Morgan. 'The girl we're trying to identify.'

Evans shook his head. 'Just because she's naked, doesn't mean—'

'Oh, come on, open your eyes,' said Norman. 'It's obvious it's her! Look at the background. She's lying on a white sheet, and there's what looks like soil beneath it.'

Southall was comparing the photograph with those on their murderboard.

'There's no doubt it's her,' said Southall. 'The mud smears are the same and the patch of blood under the left breast is identical. Well done, Norm.'

'It was Catren who led the interview, not me,' said Norman.

'In that case, well done, Catren,' said Southall.

Evans looked at the photograph again. 'I don't know. The light is poor, and—'

'Take it from me, this is the same girl,' said Norman. 'The light isn't brilliant because this photo was taken in the middle of the night, probably using a phone. And it was taken before she was covered and buried.'

'So the photo was taken by the person who killed her,' said Evans. 'We've got him!'

'That only works if we assume that the person who buried her was also the killer,' said Norman.

'I think it's highly unlikely that more than one person was involved,' said Evans.

'Unlikely, but not impossible,' said Southall.

Evans obviously disagreed. 'Well, I hope you brought her in, the woman who gave you this photograph. What was her name again?'

'Imogen Cooper,' said Norman, 'and there's no way we're going to bring her in. The photograph was sent to her daughter. Mrs Cooper was just complaining about the content.'

'Then bring the bloody daughter in, for God's sake,' said Evans. 'These people need interrogating, not pampering.'

'Norm's right,' said Southall. 'As things stand, neither Mrs Cooper nor her daughter have any idea that this is a photo of our victim. The last thing we want to do right now is alert them.'

'Once we saw what we were dealing with, we just wanted to get out of there as quick as we could without arousing her suspicions,' said Norman.

'So, who is she?' said Evans, pointing to the photograph.

'We don't know,' said Norman. 'But if we can identify who the hell sent it to a sixth-form WhatsApp group, we might be able to find out who killed her, as well as who she is.'

Looking somewhat chastened, Evans turned to make his exit.

'Yes, well done, DS Norman and DC Morgan. Good work,' he said. 'Find out who sent it and who she is, but don't forget the Pagans. You mark my words, it'll all lead back to them.'

He stopped at the doors and beckoned to Norman, who rolled his eyes and made his way over to him.

'Now, Detective Sergeant, you've got away with it this time because you seem to have done rather well. But next time you speak to me, a little more respect will be in order, particularly if you want to keep your job.'

Norman bristled. 'Me? You didn't give me a chance. The moment I came through the doors, you jumped down my throat.'

Evans smiled down at him condescendingly. 'Yes, I did, but that's my privilege as the senior officer. The problem with you is that you seem to have difficulty comprehending that fact.'

'Oh, I *comprehend* it all right,' said Norman. 'But in my book, respect is earned.'

'That may be so in your book, Norman, but it's my book now, and don't you forget it.'

'I've also been around long enough to know that it's not always ability that gets people up that greasy pole. Sir.'

Evans gave him an evil smile, and pushed the doors open.

'Then you'd better hope I don't come sliding back down that greasy pole, Detective Sergeant, because if I do, I'll be using you to break my fall.'

'I'd expect nothing less of you,' said Norman, but Evans had already gone.

Norman joined Southall at the board, to which she was just pinning a copy of the photo.

'What was that about?' she asked.

'He says I don't show him enough respect, and that I should be nice to him if I want to keep my job.'

'He threatened to fire you?'

Norman gave her a rueful smile. 'To be fair, I did disparage him in front of the whole team. He can't just ignore that, can he? So I suppose I should be grateful it was only a threat.'

'Be careful, Norm. He seems intent on making his mark on this place, so please, don't make an easy target of yourself. I don't want to lose you.'

'I'll try and keep out of trouble, but I can't promise it,' said Norman. 'He gets my back up every time I clap eyes on him.'

Southall shook her head. 'Anyway, getting back to the job in hand, I take it you've arranged to interview the daughter?'

'Any time after six tonight,' said Norman. 'Her mum says she was worried her friends might think she's a grass, so I've a feeling she's not going to be best pleased to find she has been volunteered to speak with us.'

'Do you want me to take it?' asked Southall.

'I think it might be better if I sit this one out, don't you?' said Norman. 'Lizzie Cooper is a seventeen-year-old who's never been questioned by the police before. She may not relate very well to an old fart like me. I think a softly-softly approach is probably better.'

Southall grinned. 'I find you perfectly relatable.'

Norman smiled back. 'That's nice to know, Sarah, but that's because you're nearer my age, and you've been stuck with me long enough to get to know me.'

'I'm not "stuck with you", I'll have you know,' said Southall. 'And if I am, it's because I choose to be. And don't worry, I'm happy to interview Lizzie Cooper.'

'What about the rest of this WhatsApp group? I think we should speak to them all.'

'Why don't we arrange to speak to them tomorrow at the college?' said Southall.

'Good idea,' said Norman. 'It will be a lot easier than visiting them one by one at home.'

'And just in case Lizzie Cooper can't "relate" to me this evening, I'll take Catren with me.'

'Now that's a plan,' said Norman. 'If she can't relate to Catren, we're in seriously big trouble.'

* * *

Norman had phoned ahead to let Imogen Cooper know that Southall and Morgan would be interviewing Lizzie, and not him. So, shortly after seven p.m., Imogen Cooper ushered them into her sitting room, where Lizzie was waiting for them looking nervous.

Lizzie Cooper was a younger version of her mother, with the same cupid's bow mouth and intense brown eyes, but without the glasses, and with hair that reached halfway down her back. Both were slim, and Southall thought they could easily have been mistaken for sisters.

'I take it your mum explained why we're here, Lizzie,' said Southall once the introductions had been made and they were all seated.

'About the photo, right?'

'Yes, that's right.'

Lizzie tucked a strand of hair behind her ear and looked resentfully at her mother.

'I wish I'd never let her see it now. I had no idea it was going to cause so much fuss.'

'Catren and I have seen the photo,' said Southall. 'We both agree that we would find it inappropriate and unacceptable if it had been sent to us.'

'There, you see, Lizzie. I told you it was out of order,' said Imogen.

'Do you usually share photographs like this among your WhatsApp group?' asked Southall.

'No, of course not.'

'So, what's the group for?'

'We set it up in our class a couple of years ago so we could ask each other for help with homework and stuff. We still use it for that, but now we also use it to arrange nights out and things like that.'

'So, it's just people in your class who're in the group?'

'That's right,' said Lizzie.

'And you don't usually send photos?'

'Well, yes, of course we do, we are friends! But we never send each other anything like that.'

'Is the girl in the photo one of your friends?' asked Morgan.

'Eww. No,' said Lizzie, horrified. 'None of my friends would display themselves like that.'

'So, it's definitely not one of the girls in the group showing off?' asked Southall.

Lizzie rolled her eyes. 'I just said so, didn't I? I have no idea who she is.'

'If you don't know who the girl is, do you know who sent the photo?' asked Morgan.

Lizzie shifted uncomfortably, her eyes darting between Southall, Morgan and her mother. 'I don't. And even if I did, I wouldn't . . . I mean I don't want to fall out with anyone in the group.'

'It's good to be loyal to your friends, as long as that loyalty isn't misplaced,' said Morgan. 'The way I see it, whoever sent this doesn't deserve to be your friend.'

Lizzie licked her lips nervously.

'I think you do know who sent it, Lizzie,' said Southall. 'The thing is, if you don't tell us, we're going to have to question everyone in the group.'

'Please don't do that,' said Lizzie. 'The thing is, no one else has mentioned it, so I don't know if it was sent to the whole group, or it was only sent to me.'

'But, if it's a WhatsApp group, wouldn't it have been sent to everyone?' asked Morgan.

'It wasn't sent through the group. It was sent to me personally.'

'Then you must know who sent it,' said Morgan.

Lizzie shook her head. 'I didn't recognise the number it came from.'

'Okay,' said Morgan, 'but do you have an idea who would have sent something like that to you, personally?'

Lizzie kept her lips firmly closed. After giving her a moment or two, Morgan decided it was time to apply a little pressure.

'I have no idea why you feel you should be protecting this person, Lizzie, but this can work one of two ways,' she said. 'You can tell us now, or we can get a warrant to impound your phone.'

'And, if that happens,' added Southall, 'we'll have the right to access everything that's on it. That means we can read every message you've ever sent or received on that phone. So that's texts, WhatsApp messages—'

'All right, you've made your point,' said Lizzie hastily.

'So. The name?'

'His name is Jack Foster.'

'And just so we're clear, you're saying you think Jack sent the photo, even though you didn't recognise the number it was sent from?'

Lizzie nodded. 'He's the most likely.'

'Is he a friend of yours?' asked Morgan.

Lizzie pulled a face. 'No way. He's only in the group because he's in our class. When he joined the class at the end of last year, we added him to the group, but it was a big mistake. We didn't know him back then, but now we know what he's like everyone hates him. He's a total creep.'

'Has he sent you photographs before?'

'He's sent messages, but never anything like this.'

'From the same phone number?' asked Southall.

'No, he's never used this number before. But I know he likes to mess around with phones and computers, and he's used different numbers to message me before.'

'Have you any idea why he sent it?' Southall asked.

'He's always trying to impress me because he keeps saying he wants to go out with me. I've told him he hasn't got a chance, but he won't take no for an answer.'

'He sounds like a right charmer,' said Morgan. 'But why would he think this photograph would change your mind?'

Lizzie glanced at her mother. 'He's been telling me for ages what a good time he could give me if I'd only get naked with him.'

Imogen gasped.

'It's alright, Mum, don't worry. I told him I thought he's probably never even seen a real naked woman, and if he ever got his hands on one, he wouldn't know what to do with her. I think this photo is supposed to prove me wrong, but all it proves is that he's an even bigger creep than I thought.'

'Have you any idea where he got the photo, Lizzie?' asked Southall.

Lizzie shook her head. 'No idea. I mean, he's never going to get a girl the way he behaves, but his dad's got money. Maybe he paid her.'

'What makes you think that?' asked Southall.

'Just look at the state of her. I mean, she looks so dirty.'

'Do you know where Jack lives?' asked Southall.

'I know it's somewhere near Llangwelli, but I'm not sure of the exact address.'

Time to go. Southall gave Morgan a glance

'Well, if you could just let us have that mobile number, I think we've taken enough of your time for now,' said Southall.

Lizzie passed her phone to Morgan, who made a note of the number.

'Obviously we'd rather you didn't mention this to anyone else in the group, Lizzie, especially Jack Foster,' said Southall.

Lizzie rolled her eyes. 'Don't you worry, he's the last person I want to speak to.'

Southall and Morgan gathered their things and got ready to leave.

'Just one more thing, Lizzie,' said Southall. 'Can you tell us where you were on Friday night.'

'What, last Friday?'

'That's right, Friday the first.'

'We were down the pub. The Foresters Arms.'

'Who's we?' asked Southall.

'There was me, Ianto Harris, Emilia Delaney, Harri Willis, Leah Graham and her boyfriend, Afan Mason.'

'Aren't you a bit young to be drinking in a pub?' asked Southall.

'We don't touch alcohol,' said Lizzie. 'Horrible stuff. Do you know what it does to your body?'

Southall looked at Imogen, who rolled her eyes. 'Lizzie and her friends are quite evangelical when it comes to healthy living. She's a nightmare to feed.'

Southall smiled sympathetically. 'We'll be in touch.'

* * *

'What's the plan then, boss?' asked Morgan as Southall started the car.

'First, we check out that phone number,' said Southall. 'Unless the boy's a complete idiot, it'll be a burner, but we need to make sure.'

'Then find an address for Jack Foster and arrest him?'

'I think not,' said Southall. 'We don't know for sure that it was Jack who sent the photograph. And if he did send it, as things stand he has no idea we know about it. Also, Lizzie is unaware that it's a photo of a murder victim. I think a better approach might be to gather all the members of the WhatsApp group together at college tomorrow, and—'

'And when we've spoken to them all, we can take Jack Foster to one side,' said Morgan.

'Exactly,' said Southall.

CHAPTER SIX

Friday, 8 November

It had taken Southall a personal visit and a large amount of cajoling to persuade the principal of Richard Llewellyn Sixth-Form College to allow the police into the college to interview the students belonging to the WhatsApp group. He was only persuaded when Southall mentioned they may have been potential witnesses in connection with a murder but, even then, he would only allow it if all the parents of the students in question were contacted first.

It was lunchtime when Southall asked for an update.

'The mobile phone turns out to be an unregistered burner,' said Morgan.

Southall nodded. 'I would have been surprised if it wasn't,' she said. 'So where are we with the parents? We've got a dozen kids to interview, and if we leave it much longer we're going to have to wait until tomorrow.'

Judy Lane looked up from the list on her desk.

'Between us we've managed to get hold of all the parents, and they've given us permission to speak to their sons and daughters,' said Lane. 'One or two were a bit anti, but once we pointed out that they weren't suspects but potential witnesses, and that there would be a member of staff sitting in on the interviews, they couldn't really raise any objections.'

'I think we should get over to the college and go ahead, then,' said Southall.

'This might save you a little time,' said Lane. 'Four of the students were away on a field trip last week. I checked with the tutor who was on the trip with them, and she assures me they didn't get back until very late on Friday night. Their parents were waiting for them to get back so they could take them home, and they confirmed that the minibus they were travelling in didn't get back to the college much before midnight. Another one was, and still is, off sick with glandular fever. And then there's Jack Foster, who's been off sick all this week.'

'Oh, great,' said Norman. 'He's the one we really need to speak with.'

'How many does that leave?' asked Southall.

'There are six we have permission to speak to,' said Lane. 'That's Lizzie Cooper, Ianto Harris, Emilia Delaney, Harri Willis, Leah Graham and Afan Mason.'

'Aren't they the same six Lizzie said were in the pub on Friday night?' Southall said to Morgan.

'Sounds like it, boss.'

'What are you thinking?' Norman asked Southall.

'It's probably nothing,' she said. 'From the way Lizzie spoke about them, I'm just wondering if this is a clique within the bigger group and, if so, just how close they all are.'

'You think Jack Foster is trying to join the gang, and they won't let him in?' asked Norman. 'It might explain why he sent the photo.'

'How does that work?' asked Morgan.

'He could have sent it out of spite because they won't let him in, or it could be as Lizzie Cooper said, and he's got weird ideas about what would appeal to a girl.'

'I'd like to think spite was the more likely motive,' said Morgan. 'If not . . .'

'Yeah, you're right,' said Norman. 'He must have a seriously warped mind if he thinks something like that would appeal to anyone.'

'I think the issue of how he comes to have the photo in the first place is just as worrying to me,' said Southall.

'It's probably a bit left field as ideas go,' said Morgan, 'but what if the gang came up with the idea of sending the photo so they can point the finger at Jack Foster?'

'Of course I haven't met these kids,' said Winter, 'but do you think they really are that devious?'

'I've long stopped being surprised by how underhanded people can be,' said Norman. 'And age has never been a barrier to that.'

'Right, we need a strategy,' said Southall. 'I think we should interview them individually. They must be aware of the murder by now, so let's ask them where they were on Friday night, and if they know about the photo. At this stage we don't mention when we think it was taken, or that it's a photo of the murder victim. Is everyone clear on that?'

There was a chorus of "yes, boss".

'Right, then. Let's go,' said Southall.

* * *

They had divided themselves into two teams, each accompanied by a tutor, as the appropriate adult. Southall and Morgan spoke to the three girls, and Norman and Winter interviewed the three boys. By three thirty, they had finished and were comparing notes, and something soon became glaringly obvious.

'Their stories are identical,' said Norman.

'Almost word for word, by the sound of it,' said Southall.

'Well, what an amazing coincidence,' said Norman sardonically.

'And none of the three we spoke to had to think for a second,' said Winter. 'If you asked me what I did last Friday, I'd have to think about it before I could tell you.

Nevertheless, having said that, I can't believe any of them are involved in the murder.'

'I won't argue with you about that, Frosty,' said Southall, 'but they're definitely hiding something.'

'It worries me that Jack Foster has been off sick all week,' said Norman. 'What if he's involved in the murder and they're all covering for him?'

'But they said there were only the six of them in the pub, and anyway, didn't Lizzie Cooper say they all hated him?' said Winter. 'If that's true, why would they protect him?'

'I'm probably being over-suspicious,' said Norman. 'But what if this thing of hating him is just part of the story they've dreamt up?'

'Maybe Norm's right and me and you have got it wrong, Frosty,' said Southall. 'Maybe they are all involved in the murder, and if that's the case, perhaps Catren's theory about the group sending the photograph and blaming Jack Foster isn't so left field after all.'

While they discussed the possibilities, Morgan had been on the other side of the room, speaking to someone on her mobile phone. Now she came back to join them.

'The landlord of the Foresters Arms has just told me that a group of six or seven students were in the pub until closing time. He knows Afan Mason's family, and he says Afan was one of them. His girlfriend, Leah, was there too.'

'Right, fair enough,' said Southall. 'That confirms where they were, but do we believe they all went straight home afterwards?'

'Did you say "six or seven students"?' Norman asked Morgan.

'That's what the landlord said. He says they'll be on the CCTV. Do you want me to go over there and have a look at the footage? It's only five minutes away.'

'Yes. Good idea, Catren,' said Southall. 'Let us know what you find.'

'We're thinking Jack Foster was student number seven, right?' Winter asked. 'So why didn't his name come up in any of the statements?'

'And if he was there with them, you have to wonder why they didn't say so,' said Norman.

'It was obviously a collective decision not to mention it,' said Southall.

'It looks that way,' said Norman. 'But again, we come back to why they would protect someone they are supposed to hate. Unless, as I said, all that hate stuff is bullshit.'

'They definitely know something they're not telling us,' said Southall.

'Maybe they'd be a bit more talkative if we put a bit of pressure on them,' said Norman. 'Tell them why we're really asking.'

'Yes, I think you're right, Norm,' said Southall, 'we should, and I think we should get them all together when we tell them.'

* * *

Ten minutes later, six not quite so confident students were gathered in the room with one of the tutors, with Southall, Norman and Winter standing in front of them.

'I'm sorry we had to drag you back in here like this,' said Southall. 'But I'm afraid we have a problem with your statements.'

'What problem?' asked Afan Mason. 'We told you where we were and what we were doing.'

'Yeah, you did,' said Norman. 'Every one of you said the same thing, and every statement was more or less word for word.'

'Well, there you are then,' said Afan. 'That proves we were where we said.'

Norman smiled. 'Yeah, but does it, though? You see, when you've been doing this as long as we have, you can tell when people have rehearsed their stories. And d'you know how we can tell? Because rehearsed stories are always identical, whereas real stories always vary a little. They amount to the same thing, but they're never the same word for word.'

Their expressions were beginning to look even less confident now, and Southall wasn't about to make them feel any easier.

'As we speak,' she said, 'one of our colleagues is at the Foresters Arms looking through the CCTV footage for Friday night. Now, the landlord tells us there were seven students in the pub that night. Would anyone like to tell us who the seventh student was? Or shall we sit here and wait until the officer calls us from the pub?'

'This is getting scary,' whispered Leah to Afan. 'I think we should tell them.'

'Tell us what?' asked Norman.

'Nothing,' said Afan. 'It's just that me and Leah didn't go straight home after the pub. If her dad finds out, he'll go ballistic.'

'Let me stop you right there,' said Southall. 'Before you feed us any more lies—'

'I'm not lying,' protested Afan.

'From Leah's expression, it seems she's not as comfortable telling lies as you are, Afan.'

Afan turned to Leah, who kept her gaze averted.

'As I was saying, I think you need to know the reason why we're here speaking to you,' said Southall.

'Well, go on then, why *are* we here?' asked Afan, obviously trying to put a brave face on it. 'My dad's not going to be impressed when he finds out I've been interrogated by the police without his knowledge.'

'Actually, all of your parents have given us permission to speak to you,' said Southall.

'My dad knows? Well then, he must have said we're entitled to a solicitor as we're under eighteen.'

'Yes, Afan, he knows we're here, and we told him you are entitled to have an appropriate adult present, which is why Mr Tomlinson is here.'

She turned to the tutor, who nodded, and said to the students, 'All your parents are happy with it.'

'If they weren't happy, we wouldn't be here and you would all have to come to Llangwelli station,' said Southall. 'We thought you'd prefer it this way. And trust me, Afan, you have no idea what an interrogation is, whatever you might think.'

'What about a solicitor? I'm entitled—'

'This is an informal witness interview,' said Norman. 'But as DI Southall said, if you want to pay for a solicitor, we can always upgrade it to a more formal, recorded interview, back at Llangwelli station.'

Afan was silent. Southall waited a moment before she continued.

'Right,' she said. 'Why are we here? Well, at first, we were investigating the sending of an inappropriate photograph, sent to Lizzie by someone we believe to be a member of your WhatsApp group.'

There was a chorus of vociferous denials. When the hub-bub died down, Afan said, 'You said "at first". That "at first" you were investigating a photograph.'

Norman smiled. 'I can see you don't miss much, Afan. Now that's a good thing, because we're also investigating a murder, and it just so happens that the photograph that was sent to Lizzie is that of the victim.'

The students all gasped. Lizzie Cooper put her hand to her mouth. 'Oh. My. God.'

'I know it's horrible, Lizzie, but I'm afraid the photograph has been sent, and we can't un-send it,' said Norman. 'So, we were already trying to figure out how this murder happened and who the killer is, but now we've also got to figure out how that photograph found its way to Lizzie's phone. We think at least one person here knows more than they're letting on.'

There was a shocked silence.

'So, what you're saying is that you think whoever took the photo is the killer, and that it's one of us,' said Afan. 'Is that right?'

'I didn't actually say that,' said Norman. 'But I can't rule it out as a possibility.'

'You have to be joking.'

'There's nothing funny about murder, Afan,' said Norman. 'It's our job to consider all possible scenarios, whether you like it or not. And we must also consider why you guys aren't telling us everything.'

There was an uncomfortable silence and a lot of fidgeting. Southall gave it a few seconds before she spoke.

'I should warn all of you that if you change your stories now, we won't charge you with wasting police time, or obstruction, but if you persist with your stories and we later find you are lying, we won't be so lenient.'

The shared look of alarm told Southall all she needed to know.

Norman's phone started ringing. He moved to the back of the room to take the call, and then returned.

'Okay, that was our colleague at the Foresters,' he announced. 'The CCTV footage shows all six of you in the pub on Friday night. But there's also a seventh student with you, on the edge of your group. We think we know who he is, and we can find out easily enough, but would anyone care to tell us, and save us all a bit of time?'

'Yes,' said Lizzie Cooper. 'It's Jack Foster.'

'So, Jack was there with you,' said Norman. 'But when we asked you, you all said there were just six of you. Would anyone care to tell us why not one of you mentioned him?'

'He's not part of our group,' said Afan.

'And yet there he is on CCTV,' said Norman. 'My colleague says the CCTV suggests he's sitting with you guys. It seems to me that he thinks he's one of your group, even if you don't see it that way.'

'He's a hanger-on who won't take a hint,' said Lizzie.

'Does anyone know why he's not here today?' asked Southall.

'Does anyone care?' asked Afan.

'That's not a very nice attitude, is it, Afan?' asked Norman.

'You don't know Jack Foster,' said Afan.

'You really don't like him, do you?' asked Norman. 'Why is that?'

'Us six have gone through school together since we were kids, so we've been friends for years. He only started at college a year ago, so he's just not one of us.'

'He's a year older than the rest of us and he thinks that makes him special,' added Lizzie.

'A year older?'

'I think he was kept back a year before he came to college. I don't know why.'

'I hate him,' said Afan. 'He's always pestering Lizzie and the other girls.'

'Sounds as if you'd like to see the back of him, right?' asked Norman.

'For sure,' said Afan.

Norman and Southall shared a look. Maybe Catren Morgan's theory about who had sent the photograph could be right on the money.

'We'll talk about this later, Afan,' said Southall. 'For now, let's go back to what Leah was trying to tell us about Friday night.'

All eyes turned to Leah, who seemed to shrink under their gaze. Then Lizzie spoke up.

'Seeing as it was me, or at least it was my mum, that started all this. I'll tell you what happened on Friday night.'

'Okay, Lizzie,' said Southall. 'Go ahead.'

'There have always been rumours about Pagans taking part in human sacrifices in the clearing at the centre of the Dragon Forest, and because of that there are ghosts and dead bodies out there. I know one of their festival things happens on Halloween, so I had this stupid idea that we could get Jack to come with us to the Dragon Forest on the Friday.

'I guessed that, knowing him, he'd want to prove how brave he is. I thought if we could get him into the forest and leave him there, he might finally get the hint that we don't want him hanging around.

'So, we arranged to go to the pub, making sure Jack overheard us talking about it, and sure enough he turned up uninvited. So, after the pub closed, we all went to the forest.'

'And you took Jack with you?' asked Southall.

'He was in his dad's car. He followed us.'

'And then what happened?'

And Lizzie began to tell the story of what had happened that night in the forest . . .

CHAPTER SEVEN

Friday, 1 November, 23.30
The Dragon Forest

The group of six friends made their way along the path from the Dragon Forest car park to the clearing. Barely enough moonlight filtered through the trees, and when passing clouds hid even that, a blanket of darkness enveloped them. They had prepared for this eventuality, however, and the three boys each carried a decent torch.

About fifty feet ahead, they could see the powerful beam of the torch of a seventh person. Although Jack Foster was a year older than the others, he was in the same sixth-form class, which didn't mean he was necessarily part of their group. They saw him as a needy hanger-on, disliked by them all, but he was the reason why they were here in the middle of the night. They had been walking slowly to allow Jack to go on ahead, just as they had planned.

Leah Graham shivered and pulled her woolly hat further down over her ears. 'I'm not sure this was a good idea. I don't like it. I think we should go back.'

Afan Mason, her boyfriend, squeezed her hand.

'Don't worry, Leah. I'll make sure the dragon doesn't get you.'

'That's not funny,' said Leah. 'Anyway, it's not the dragon I'm worried about. We all know Foster's a weirdo. How do we know he isn't leading us into some sort of trap?'

'How can he be leading us into a trap?' said Afan. 'He didn't know we were coming until we invited him half an hour ago.'

'I think Leah's right,' said Emilia Delaney. 'This place is creepy, and I can't believe we all agreed to come out here to see if there are any ghosts.'

'We can't go back yet,' said Harri Willis. 'And we didn't agree to look for ghosts. If you recall, that was just an excuse to entice Foster out here. You know what we planned; we know he'll want to be the big brave hero out front, so we let him get miles ahead and then we run back to the car park, let one of his tyres down, jump into our car and go home, leaving him out here.'

'Whatever,' said Leah. 'Right now, I don't care if we leave him or not. I just want to go home.'

'I'm still not sure if leaving him out here is the right thing to do,' said Emilia. 'It seems a bit extreme.'

'It's a bit late to start raising objections now,' said Afan. 'You were keen enough before. Anyway, he's got a spare wheel. It's not as if he'll have to walk home.'

'Of course it's right,' said Lizzie Cooper, the third girl among the group. 'He gives everyone the creeps, and even when we ignore him, he still won't go away. Maybe after this he'll get the message, and he'll stay away.'

'Keep your voices down,' hissed Ianto Harris. 'He might be weird, but he's not deaf.'

'Ianto's right,' said Afan. 'We've come too far to turn back now.'

'Okay, so how much further do we have to go?' asked Leah.

'He's not far enough ahead yet,' said Ianto. 'If we turn back too soon, he might catch up before we get away.'

'We should let all his tyres down,' said Lizzie.

'That would be too cruel,' said Emilia.

'What's cruel is having a perv like him leering at us all the time,' said Lizzie. 'I'll tell him why we left him out here if no one else wants to. I'll tell him why we hate him, too.'

'Lizzie's right,' said Leah. 'He's just a creep. He wouldn't know what to do with a girl. I don't think he'd even know where to start.'

'Well, he's not starting with me,' said Lizzie.

'Ooh, yuck! No way,' said Emilia.

'And that's exactly why we're out here tonight doing this,' said Afan.

Up ahead, the powerful beam swung around and pointed their way causing them all to stop. Then, apparently satisfied they were all present and correct, Jack Foster swung his torch back the other way again and began sweeping the area ahead of him.

'What's he doing?' asked Lizzie.

'Your voices were so loud he probably heard you talking about leaving him out here, and he's checking to see if we're still here,' said Ianto.

'I meant what's he doing now?'

'It looks like he's looking at something up ahead,' said Afan.

'He couldn't really have heard us,' said Lizzie. 'Could he?'

'Let's hope not,' said Ianto.

'What's he seen?' asked Emilia, alarmed.

'Don't panic, Emmy,' said Afan. 'There won't be anyone out here at this time of night.'

'We're here,' Leah pointed out.

'Well there won't be anyone else, then,' said Afan.

'Yeah, what are the chances, right?' said Harri.

'So, what do we do?' asked Lizzie.

'We can't turn and run now,' said Afan, 'he's not far enough ahead. You guys stay here. I'll go and ask him what he's waiting for.'

When Afan reached Foster, he realised they were at the end of the path and had reached the clearing.

'What's up, Foster?' asked Afan when he caught up. 'The girls are freaking out back there.'

Foster was still sweeping his torch beam ahead.

'I heard something.'

'Well, if there was anything out there, you'll have scared it away with that searchlight. You nearly fried our eyes when you turned round just now.'

Foster pointed the torch down at the ground.

'My dad likes to be able to see where he's going,' he said.

A loud rustling sound echoed across the clearing, making them both start. Foster stared at Afan.

'There! Don't tell me you didn't hear that.'

'It was probably a deer,' said Afan.

'Or a ghost,' said Foster. 'You said they're supposed to haunt the clearing. Well, here's the clearing, and ther—'

'Don't be a dick, Foster. Ghosts are silent. That's why they're so scary. They don't go crashing through bushes like that.'

'Come on, let's check it out,' said Foster.

'You go,' said Afan. 'I'll go back and tell the others. We'll catch up.'

'Chicken!' said Foster.

'If you say so,' said Afan. 'But I've got Leah to look after. Of course, you wouldn't know anything about that, would you? We've all noticed how your right arm is much bigger than your left one.'

Afan couldn't see it in the dark, but Foster was blushing furiously.

'I've got a girlfriend,' he said.

'Only in your wet dreams,' said Afan. 'You'd like to get your hands on Lizzie, but she won't even speak to you. I bet she is your wet dream. She is, isn't she?'

'I'll prove I've got a girlfriend,' said Foster.

Afan put his hand to his mouth and faked a yawn.

'Yawn, yawn, yawn,' he said. 'We've heard it all before, but we never get to see this girlfriend, do we?'

'I'll send you photos.'

'Yeah, right,' said Afan, turning to head back. 'If you had any photos of this mysterious girlfriend, you'd have sent them by now just to show off.'

Back along the path he could see the beams from the other torches coming to meet him.

Foster set off across the clearing, swearing to himself and moving his torch beam across the open area of the clearing.

'Where's he going?' asked Leah when Afan got back to them.

'We heard something up ahead. I think it was a deer crashing through the scrub, but he insists it was a ghost, so he's gone to find it.'

'A ghost?' shrieked Emilia.

Harri put an arm around her shoulders. 'Calm down, Emmy. There are no ghosts, all right?'

'We haven't got to go after him, have we?' asked Emmy.

They had reached the entrance to the clearing. They could see the powerful beam of the torch way ahead, moving forward.

'Is that enough of a start?' asked Leah. 'Is he far enough ahead yet?'

As she spoke, the torch seemed to drop to the ground.

'What's happened?' asked Leah.

'It looks as if he's fallen over,' said Afan, taking Leah's hand. 'Now might be a good time to head back.'

'But what if he's hurt?' asked Emmy.

'What if he is? Who cares?' asked Lizzie. 'Coz I don't. Come on, everyone, let's run!'

* * *

'So, you're telling us he fell over, and you just ran back to the car park and left him there?' asked Southall when Lizzie had finished her story. 'Didn't it occur to any of you that he might have been injured?' She stared at the six guilty faces. None dared return her gaze.

Norman was appalled. 'I can't believe it. You really don't care, do you? And they say you're the caring generation. Haven't any of you thought that maybe that's the reason why Jack's been absent all week?'

'He must be okay, or he couldn't have sent that photograph,' said Lizzie.

'That's if he did send it,' said Norman.

Lizzie stared at him.

'We don't know yet, do we?' said Norman. 'The phone it was sent from is unregistered, so it could have been sent by anyone. Heck, it could even be one of you guys.'

'That's absurd,' said Afan. 'Why would one of us send it?'

'Maybe you sent it so you could put the blame on Jack,' said Norman. 'You've already said you hate him.'

'That's ridiculous,' said Afan.

'Is it?' said Norman. 'You've already demonstrated a rare talent for lying.'

'That's not the same thing,' said Afan sullenly.

'No?' asked Norman. 'Well, it's certainly a step in the right direction, isn't it?'

Southall could see this wasn't getting them anywhere.

'Okay,' she said to the students, 'you can go now, but we'll no doubt be speaking to you again.'

'What about Jack?' demanded Afan. 'Aren't you going to arrest him for sending the photo?'

'You didn't give a damn what happened to him on Friday night,' said Norman, 'so why would you care what happens to him now?'

'I don't care!'

'Then you don't need to know, do you?' said Norman.

The students trooped disconsolately from the room, and Southall thanked Mr Tomlinson, the tutor who had been asked to sit in as the appropriate adult.

* * *

'I'm guessing we're heading to Jack Foster's now,' said Norman. 'D'you think he's going to be as evasive as this lot were?'

'I don't know,' said Southall. 'He might have been savvy enough to use a burner phone, but he's obviously not that clever because if he hadn't sent that photo to Lizzie in the first place, we'd never have known about any of this.'

'We still don't know for sure that he did send it,' said Norman.

'Well, we've just heard that he told the others he was going to prove he had a girlfriend, and we do know he was in the vicinity of the body, so he's my number one suspect, and I'd be very surprised if he wasn't yours too.'

'Yeah, you're right about that. And what with six witnesses saying they saw him fall into a hole, I can't wait to hear his explanation.'

'He's also eighteen,' said Southall.

'Which makes him an adult, and we won't need a babysitter when we speak to him,' said Norman. 'Do you want me to bring him in now, or leave him until the morning?'

'Frosty, do you think you can get hold of his GPS data? If we can prove his phone was out there, he hasn't got a leg to stand on.'

'I can try,' said Frosty, 'but this late on a Friday I can't guarantee I'll find anyone willing to help.'

Southall turned to Norman. 'Can you handle an early start on a Saturday morning?'

'How early?' asked Norman dubiously.

'Pick him up at eight.'

'Isn't he considered a flight risk?' asked Morgan.

'He's had a week to make a run for it. I'd have thought he'd have done it by now if he was going to,' said Norman. 'So I don't see him disappearing tonight.'

'What if he really is sick?' asked Morgan.

'I think he's more likely to be holed up at home wondering what he's got himself into, don't you?' said Southall.

'We'll risk it and find out in the morning,' said Norman.

'That's what I was thinking,' said Southall. 'Frosty, can you get up early tomorrow?'

'You think Norm needs me there in case Jack does a runner?'

Southall laughed. 'Yes, something like that.'

'No worries,' said Winter. 'I'll wear my running shoes just in case.'

'If he's going to make a dash for it, shall I come too?' asked Morgan.

CHAPTER EIGHT

Saturday, 9 November, 08.00

Saturday morning was grey and misty. Winter drew up outside the Fosters' house, where a black Mercedes SUV, a green hatchback and a small white van were parked on the drive.

'Jeez, look at that big ugly thing,' said Norman.

'What's that?' asked Winter.

'That damned great Mercedes boxmobile,' said Norman. 'Where do these people think they live, the Himalayas?'

'I agree they're not exactly the best thing for the environment,' said Winter, 'but I wouldn't say no if someone offered me one.'

'Yeah, well, luckily for you I don't think that's going to happen anytime soon,' said Norman. 'Getting back to business, it would have been handy if you could have got that phone data.'

'I did say we'd be pushing our luck asking late on a Friday,' said Winter. 'When the guy said he'd call back I had a feeling he wasn't going to.'

'Oh well, Jack Foster doesn't know we don't have proof, does he?'

'Bet you a tenner the Merc is the father's car,' said Winter, nodding at the cars. 'And the hatchback is his mum's.'

'You really think he lets his eighteen-year-old son drive a Merc that must have cost him well in excess of a hundred grand?' said Norman. 'Apart from the obvious risk of damage, it would cost a fortune to add a kid that age to his insurance.'

'Looking at the house, I don't think cost would be that much of an issue,' said Winter.

'What about the van?' asked Norman.

'Family workhorse vehicle?' suggested Winter.

'If it was me, that's what I'd let my kid drive,' said Norman. He glanced at the house. 'The lights are on so someone must be at home. I'll let you ask them about the cars if it's worrying you so much.'

'How are we going to play this?' asked Winter.

'We're just going to calmly tell Jack Foster we're taking him to Llangwelli so we can interview him. Then we'll see how he reacts.'

'Do you think he'll be a problem?'

'Your guess is as good as mine,' said Norman. 'Just remember, if he legs it, I don't do running.'

Winter rolled his eyes. 'Like I'm going to forget.'

'And I'm getting a bit old for fighting, too,' said Norman. 'But we've got no reason to think he's violent, so I don't think it'll come to that.'

'Unless he actually is a murderer,' said Winter. 'People like that tend to be capable of a bit of violence.'

'Would you murder someone and then take a bunch of friends to see your handiwork?' Norman said.

'The boss did say she thought he wasn't very bright.'

'D'you know, that's a fair point,' said Norman. 'I hadn't thought of it like that.'

He sat for a moment as if in thought, then abruptly opened his door.

'Come on, then,' he said. 'Let's find out if you're going to have to fight him.'

Winter followed rather reluctantly, unsure if Norman thought there really was going to be a fight, or if he was being wound up.

Norman knocked loudly. A minute later, the door was opened by a short woman with a round face and a shock of hair dyed a colour that Norman could only describe as "red ink". She frowned at them, raising an eyebrow streaked with grey.

'Mrs Maria Foster?'

The woman nodded. 'Yes?'

Warrant cards ready for inspection, Norman introduced himself and Frosty.

'Police? What on earth are you doing here?'

'We'd like a word with your son, Jack.'

'Jack?'

'Yes. You do have a son called Jack who attends Richard Llewellyn Sixth-Form College?'

'Why do you want to speak to him? What's he supposed to have done?'

'We'll discuss that with Jack if you don't mind,' said Norman.

'Well, I'm his mother and I do mind,' she snapped. 'He's had a hard week at college, and he needs a rest.'

'At college? You're sure of that, are you?' said Norman. 'Only we were there yesterday, and they told us they hadn't seen Jack all week.'

This was obviously news to Maria Foster. 'That can't be right.'

'I can't think of any reason why the college would tell us something that wasn't true,' said Norman. 'Can you, Mrs Foster?'

'Whatever,' she blustered. 'You're not speaking to him—'

'Jack's eighteen, right?' asked Norman.

'Yes, but I don't see what difference that makes—'

'The difference it makes is that being eighteen makes him an adult in the eyes of the law,' said Norman. 'If he was under eighteen, he would be entitled to have a parent or appropriate adult accompany him, but as he's no longer under eighteen . . .'

'Accompany him? Are you going to arrest him?'

'I was hoping it wouldn't come to that,' said Norman. 'But I'm running out of options.'

'Why?'

'As I said, Jack's an adult now—'

'Just tell me what he's done, would you.'

'All I can tell you is that we're investigating an allegation that's been made against him,' said Norman, patiently. 'If you'll just call him, we can take him to Llangwelli station, and I'm sure we'll get it sorted out in no time. We're also investigating a separate incident that happened on Friday night. We know Jack was in the vicinity, and we think he may have witnessed something. We need him to make a statement about that too.'

'Is there anything you're *not* accusing him of?'

Norman sighed wearily. 'Mrs Foster, if you could just call your son.'

Maria Foster made no attempt to move.

'Is Jack here or not?' demanded Norman.

'I don't know where he is,' she said.

While Norman was speaking, Winter had been looking up at the house. A curtain twitched at one of the windows.

'I don't like to disagree with you, Mrs Foster,' said Winter, pointing at the window. 'But I think you know exactly where Jack is. He has just been peeking at us through that window.'

Maria Foster glared at Winter.

'So Jack is inside, right?' asked Norman.

She said nothing. She didn't have to, her face told him all he wanted to know.

'Look, Mrs Foster, I get that Jack's your son and you want to protect him, but you're actually not helping him one bit. If anything, you're making it look as though he has something to hide, and that you know what it is.'

'I don't know anything. I didn't even know he hadn't been to college until you just told me.'

'Whether he's been to college or not isn't really my concern,' said Norman. 'The sooner you let us take him to Llangwelli to answer our questions, the sooner he'll be back home.'

'Why can't you ask your questions here?'

'It's just procedure,' said Norman. 'We don't write the rules, but I'm afraid we do have to follow them.'

'You're not going to arrest him, though?'

'Well, that wasn't my intention when we came here, but at this rate I'll be left with no choice. So, either he comes with us now, or I can arrange for uniformed officers to arrive in patrol cars with blue lights and sirens. If it was me, I wouldn't want that, but it's up to you.'

The sound of a scuffle was heard, coming from around the side of the house, and Catren Morgan appeared with a teenager in a tracksuit, hands cuffed behind his back. Morgan was holding a bloodstained tissue to her nose.

Winter immediately rushed to take the prisoner from Morgan, while Maria Foster gasped, her hand to her mouth. 'Oh, my God, what's happened?'

'Little bugger tried to kick me in the face,' said Morgan. 'I didn't duck quick enough. But it's just a nosebleed, nothing serious.' She looked at Norman. 'You were right to drop me off up the road. I caught him climbing over the back fence.'

'Take your hands off my son!' snapped Maria Foster.

'Doing a runner from the police is never a good idea,' said Norman. 'Nor is assaulting a police officer.'

'What do you expect?' she retorted.

'I expect you to advise your son to come with us rather than keep us standing on your doorstep while he makes a getaway,' said Norman.

'I did no such thing!'

'Maybe you didn't intend to,' said Norman, 'but it had the same effect. You can't deny that delaying us enabled him to attempt an escape.'

'I suppose you're going to arrest me as well.'

'I have a feeling you'd enjoy that, Mrs Foster,' said Norman. 'However, I wasn't born yesterday.'

'This is outrageous,' she said. 'Jack's done nothing wrong.'

'So why did he try to run away?' asked Norman.

Maria Foster ignored the question.

'You come here, try to force your way in, then you beat him up and arrest him!'

'If we forced our way in, how come we're still outside on the front doorstep?' asked Norman. 'And you seem to have overlooked the fact it's my officer with the bloody nose. Your son looks fine to me, but just to make you happy I'll have him checked over by a doctor when we get to Llangwelli.' He turned to Winter. 'Put him in the car and let's go.'

'I'll get you a solicitor, Jack!' shouted Maria after their retreating figures. 'You say nothing until he gets there.'

'Oh, by the way, Mrs Foster,' said Norman. 'Something I forgot to mention. I have a warrant to seize any computer, laptop, tablet, or mobile phone belonging to Jack.'

'You can't be serious.'

'It's because of the nature of the alleged offence,' said Norman.

'And what if I won't let you into my house?'

Norman shrugged and gave her a sad little smile.

'If you're hoping I'll try to force my way in, you're going to be disappointed, I'm afraid. I'll just make a call and then wait outside for a team of uniformed officers to arrive. But then, because you'll have had time to hide the evidence, I'll have to make sure they turn the entire house upside down. Do you really want that?'

'You're enjoying this, aren't you?'

'Actually, no, I'm not. I didn't intend it to turn out this way. You need to remember you could easily have avoided all this fuss by persuading Jack to come with us voluntarily. It was your choice to allow him to try and escape.'

A look of sullen resignation came over her face.

'Now,' said Norman, 'if you could just show me where to find this equipment, I'll be out of your hair.'

* * *

In the event, Maria Foster had been bluffing. There was no family solicitor to sit in on the interview with Jack. His father, Tom, had been out walking the dog when the drama unfolded, and had since arrived at Llangwelli station demanding to see his son. When his request was denied, he had suggested he should sit with Jack in lieu of a solicitor, but Southall wasn't having any of that either. It took a while, but eventually he backed down and allowed them to call a duty solicitor to be present during Jack's interview.

It was gone eleven o'clock by the time Southall and Norman sat down opposite Jack Foster and his appointed duty solicitor. Norman set the tape going and requested those present to give their names for the recording, and, finally, Southall began.

'So, where have you been all week, Jack?' she asked.

'I'm sorry?'

'The college tells us you've been absent this week.'

'I've been at home. I've not been feeling well.'

'Now that's odd, because your mother thought you'd been at college.'

'Yeah, well, she nags me if I don't go, so I go out in the morning, wait till she's gone to work and then go back home. It's what I always do when I feel like having a day off.'

'Which means no one can prove you were at home,' said Norman. 'How convenient.'

'Why do I have to prove it?' asked Foster. 'Is all this just about me missing college? It seems like a humungous fuss if it is.'

'Do you really think we care whether or not you go to college?' asked Norman.

Foster shrugged. 'I know you like to harass people, and right now, you're harassing me.'

'So, you're saying you don't know why we might want to question you. Is that right, Jack?' asked Southall.

'No idea,' said Foster.

Southall slid a copy of the photograph across the table.

Foster looked down at it and then back up at Southall. It was difficult to tell whether it was the image itself that surprised him, or the fact that the police had a copy of it.

'Have you seen this photo before?' Southall asked.

'I've seen it, yeah.'

'How come?'

'Someone sent it to me, and no, I don't know who.'

'It's been alleged you sent this photo to someone who hadn't asked for it and would have preferred not to receive it. Was it something you received and then forwarded?'

'No. Why would I do something like that?'

'Perhaps you were trying to impress someone,' said Norman.

'How would that impress anyone?' asked Foster.

Norman shrugged. 'I don't know. Maybe you were trying to prove that you've been with a girl.'

'I haven't done anything wrong, and I don't need to prove anything to anyone,' said Foster.

'How many phones do you have, Jack?' asked Southall.

'One, of course.'

'No unregistered phones?'

'Why would I have an unregistered phone?'

'If you only have one phone, is the photograph still on it?'

'No, it isn't,' said Foster, indignantly. 'I'm not a perv. I deleted it.'

'I'm glad to hear it,' said Norman. 'Do you have a girl-friend, Jack?'

'Not at the moment.'

'But you've had them, right? I mean, why not? You're a good-looking enough young guy, aren't you?'

Foster shifted in his seat. 'Yeah, I've had girlfriends, but I haven't got one right now. Okay?'

Southall tapped the photograph on the table.

'The thing is, Jack, this photograph you are accused of sending is a photo of a murder victim. Now that makes us wonder how you got hold of it. Can you tell us where you got it?'

'I already told you I was sent it, but I know nothing about where it came from.'

'Why do you have a plaster on your hand, Jack?' asked Norman.

Foster hastily withdrew his hand. 'I cut it. Not that it's any of your business.'

'Do you know what blood group you are?' Norman asked.

Foster looked puzzled. 'What blood group I am?'

'Yeah. You know what a blood group is, right?'

'Of course I know what a blood group is, but I don't know mine. Does it matter?'

'It could matter quite a lot,' said Norman.

'Whatever. I don't know, and I'm not sure I care either.'

'Oh, you definitely should care,' said Southall. 'You see, the young woman in the photo, the murder victim, is group A positive. Now, we found a smear of blood on her body that's O positive. Do you know what that means?'

Foster rolled his eyes. 'No, but I'm sure you're going to tell me.'

'What it means, Jack, is that the blood on her body isn't hers,' said Southall. 'And it's quite possible that it belongs to her killer. Now, if your blood group is O positive, what are we supposed to think?'

'You can think what you like. It's got nothing to do with me.'

'We took your fingerprints and a DNA sample when you came in. Why do you think we did that?' Southall said.

Foster shook his head.

'We did it so we can compare it with DNA and fingerprints taken from the scene where the murder victim was found,' said Southall.

'So what? Like I already said, it's nothing to do with me, so you're wasting your time.'

'That's right, Jack, we will be wasting our time if it's got nothing to do with you,' said Southall, 'but I'm pretty sure we'll find it has.'

'Can you tell us where you were on the night of Friday, first November?' asked Norman.

'I went to the pub with some mates from college.'

'Which pub was that?' Norman asked.

'The Foresters Arms.'

'That's a few miles from here. How did you get there?'

'I borrowed my mum's hatchback.'

'What time did you leave the pub?'

'We were there up to closing time, and then we all went home.'

Southall raised her eyebrows. 'You drove straight home? After you had been drinking?'

'I don't touch alcohol, and yeah, I went straight home.'

Southall slid a sheet of paper across the table.

'Are these the mates you were with?'

Foster licked his lips as he studied the list of names.

'Um, yeah, that's right,' he said, sounding rather less confident.

'Well, that's funny,' said Southall. 'You see we've taken statements from each one of them, and they all say the same thing, which is that far from going straight home, you all headed for the Dragon Forest. What do you say to that?'

Foster gulped, his eyes darting between the two detectives.

'Oh yeah, that's right,' he said. 'I remember now. I must have been thinking of another Friday.'

'Why did you go to the forest, Jack?' asked Southall.

Forest obviously thought he was on firmer ground. 'There's always been this rumour that some weirdo Pagan group goes to the clearing in the forest to have these ceremonies. They're supposed to make human sacrifices. I think it's a load of crap, but a couple of guys were saying there are ghosts out there. We thought it would be a bit of a thrill to go and find out.'

'Do you always carry a spade when you go to the woods?' asked Norman.

'A spade? I didn't have a spade. Ask any of the others, they'll tell you.'

'The others said you went on ahead of them.'

'Yeah, they're a bunch of chickens. Someone had to take the lead.'

'And was it "a thrill", as you put it?' asked Southall.

'Course not,' said Foster.

'What happened when you got to the clearing?' asked Southall.

'Nothing. There were no ghosts, so we went back home.'

Southall pursed her lips. 'Are you sure about that? Only the others say you went charging ahead when you got to the clearing, and then you appeared to fall over.'

'Then they ran off and left you,' said Norman. 'We're guessing that's when you lost your torch. Is that right?'

'Yeah, I dropped the . . .' Foster's voice trailed off. Realising he was walking into a trap, he turned to the solic-itor, who leaned towards him and whispered into his ear.

Foster listened, but seemed unsure what to do.

'I think now might be a good time to consider telling us the truth,' suggested Norman.

Foster looked back at the solicitor, who nodded.

'All right,' he said. 'I did go to the forest with the others. And, yeah, I fell over, and the others ran off and left me.'

'If they're your friends, why did they do that?' asked Southall.

'Because they're a bunch of losers,' said Foster. 'I expect it was Lizzie Cooper's idea. She's like their leader and she's always had it in for me. Was it her complained about me sending the photograph?'

'Who said anything about Lizzie making a complaint?' asked Norman.

'No one. I just assumed . . .'

'Now, why would Lizzie Cooper complain about you sending a photo if you didn't send it?' asked Norman.

'Because it's just the sort of thing she would do to get me in trouble.'

'Why would Lizzie want to get you in trouble?' asked Norman.

'I dunno, you'll have to ask her. I've never done anything to hurt her, and I didn't send her that photo.'

'Let's go back to Friday night,' said Southall. 'You said you fell over in the clearing. What exactly did you fall over?'

'I think it was a branch that had fallen off a tree.'

'It's called the clearing because there are no trees there,' said Norman. 'That's what a clearing is.'

'All right, I don't know what it was,' said Foster. 'One minute I'm walking along in the dark, and the next I trip over something, and I'm face down on the ground. It never came into my head to worry about what I had fallen over.'

'That's face down in a hole, right?' asked Norman. 'And this is where you came across the body?'

'No, I didn't see a body.'

'So, you managed to trip and fall onto a body, and yet you didn't see it?'

'I think I would have known if I'd fallen onto a body, don't you? I just said I didn't see a body.'

'And it was when you tripped and fell onto the body that you lost the torch, right?' asked Norman.

Jack was clearly rattled but stuck to his guns.

'How many times do I have to tell you? I didn't see a body and I didn't have a torch. I was using my phone as a light.'

'Your friends seem to think you were carrying a torch, and one with a pretty impressive beam,' said Norman. 'One of them even said it was like a searchlight. That doesn't sound like any sort of mobile phone I've ever come across.'

'And you're up to date with these things, are you?' Foster sneered.

Norman chuckled. 'Ha, you've got me there, Jack. I guess it's obvious I'm not the tech guy around here.'

'And you're quite sure you didn't lose a torch out in the forest?' asked Southall.

'Yes, I keep telling you that, but you don't seem to be listening to me.'

'So, your fingerprints won't match the prints on the torch we found in the clearing?'

'Well, of course they won't, because I wasn't carrying a torch,' said Foster. By this stage it wasn't clear if he was trying to convince the detectives, or himself.

Southall and Norman exchanged a look.

'We need to suspend the interview for a minute,' Southall said, addressing the solicitor. 'Is that okay?'

'Yes, I suppose so,' he said.

Norman made the necessary announcement for the tape and followed Southall outside.

'What do you think?' she asked. 'He's obviously lying about the body and the torch, but can we really picture him as a killer?'

'Well, there's clearly something odd about him if he's unaffected by finding a dead body,' said Norman. 'I'm sure he took, and sent, that photo, but I don't think he knew the body was there until he fell over it. As for murder? No way. He hasn't got it in him.'

'I think we can agree on that,' said Southall. 'What about burying the body?'

'Even though he's got access to his mother's car, I can't see him carrying a body around in it, can you? I mean, what if his mum wanted to use her car? As I said, I don't think he knew anything about it until he fell onto it. Besides, he doesn't look strong enough to carry a body more than about five yards.'

'I'm with you on that, too,' said Southall. 'Do you think he's a flight risk?'

'You want to let him go?'

'I think we're wasting our time asking him questions right now. He's just going to keep on denying everything. I think we release him now, and when we have the blood and fingerprint results, we can get him back in and start again. What do you think?'

'I think you're right. He should be a lot more talkative when he knows we've got the forensics to back us up, but I'm not so confident he won't do a runner. Don't forget he tried to escape this morning.'

'Hmm, yes, that's a good point,' said Southall. 'Do you think his mother knew he was going to try and get away?

'She was stalling us, but I'm pretty sure she was just being protective. I don't think it occurred to her that Jack would use the delay to make a break for it. She seemed to be as surprised as we were when Catren walked him round the corner in handcuffs.'

'Is his father still here?'

'I can't imagine he's gone,' said Norman. 'Not after all the fuss he made earlier. I reckon he thinks if he makes enough of a row we'll just back off and let him take Jack home.'

'Right. So, why don't we have a chat with him before we let Jack go?' said Southall. 'We can tell him we're releasing Jack into his custody as a responsible father and, hopefully, he'll keep his boy under control.'

'It won't do any harm to talk to the guy,' said Norman. 'But he's going to want to know why Jack's here. Are you really going to tell him?'

'If we let Jack go, I would imagine he'll have to explain at least some of it to his parents anyway.'

'I can't argue with that,' said Norman.

'So, I'm thinking it won't hurt to share a smidgen of what we know.'

'Okay. How formal do you want this to be?'

'Let's keep it informal for now,' said Southall. 'Just a friendly chat.'

* * *

Tom Foster had been sitting in the reception area, and jumped to his feet when he saw Southall and Norman walk in through the doors. He looked past them expectantly.

'Where's Jack?' he asked. 'You can't keep him here if he hasn't done anything. You're not keeping him here, are you?'

'We understand your concern, Mr Foster,' said Southall. 'We could release him pending further investigations, but after Jack's attempt to escape this morning, we're undecided. If we could guarantee he won't—'

'If you let him come home, I guarantee he won't run away, but what's this about further investigations? I don't understand what he's doing here in the first place. What's he supposed to have done?'

'If you're prepared to calm down and listen, we'll answer some of your questions,' said Southall. 'However, I need you to understand that if we do, we'll be bending the rules a little.'

Tom Foster looked confused.

'What do you mean "bending the rules"?'

'The thing is, normally we wouldn't discuss an open investigation with you. However, Jack is your son, and I'm sure that when he gets home he'll be telling you about it himself anyway, so, given that you've guaranteed to ensure he stays at home, I can't see the harm in cutting you some slack. You are going to make sure he doesn't run, aren't you?'

Tom Foster nodded. 'Yes, of course. I said I would, didn't I?'

'In that case we have a deal,' said Southall. 'If you'd like to follow us, we'll find somewhere quiet where we can talk.'

Foster followed Southall to an interview room, Norman bringing up the rear. Once they were inside, Foster looked around nervously.

'Is this an interview room?' he asked.

'Yes, it is, but don't worry, Mr Foster,' said Southall. 'This isn't an interview. It's just somewhere for us to chat without being disturbed. We're not recording anything.'

Foster didn't look completely convinced, but he sat down.

'Right,' he said. 'Why's Jack here?'

'It's been alleged that Jack sent a rather unpleasant photograph to someone.'

'What sort of photograph?'

'He sent a photograph of the almost naked body of a young woman.'

'Is that it? He's a teenage boy. I expect he sent it to one of his mates. They send photos to each other all the time. There's no need for all this fuss. I'll have a word with him and make sure he doesn't do it again.'

'I wish this was just about the sending of a photograph, Mr Foster, but I'm afraid it's not that simple,' said Southall. 'The young woman in question was the victim of a murder we are investigating.'

Southall waited quietly while Foster struggled to make sense of this. He opened and closed his mouth two or three times before finally saying, 'A murder victim? Well then, someone must have sent him the photograph.'

'That's what Jack says,' said Norman.

'Well, there we are then.' A light seemed to go on in Foster's head. 'It must have been one of your lot that sent it to him.'

'Jack knows a lot of people in the police, does he?' asked Norman.

Foster didn't answer.

'If you mean someone from within our investigation sent the photograph to Jack, we know that's not the case,' said Southall.

Foster's face was a picture of scorn. 'Well, of course you're going to say that, aren't you?'

'We're saying that because when we found the body she was buried in a shallow grave,' said Norman. 'The photo Jack sent was taken before she was buried. That's how we know it can't have come from us, and it's also why we're concerned to know where Jack got the photo.'

Foster began to bluster. 'Wait a minute. Are you suggesting . . . no way. Jack's a good boy . . . he couldn't possibly—'

'We're not accusing Jack of anything at this stage,' said Southall, 'but there are still some questions that need answering.'

'Like what?'

Southall slid two photographs across the table. 'We found this torch, and this spade close to where the body was buried. Witnesses say Jack took the torch from the boot of his car at the Dragon Forest on the night of Friday, first November and was carrying it when he fell over and lost it. Jack says it's not his.'

'We've got one like that,' said Foster, 'but I keep it in the back of my car.'

'Which is your car?' asked Norman. 'The Mercedes?'

'Yes, that's right, but I've got the hatchback this morning.'

'It's kept in your car? We were told Jack took it from the back of the hatchback.'

'The rule is if Jack goes out at night he takes the torch with him, just in case.'

'So, he would have had it with him that night?' asked Southall.

'He should have had it, that's the rule, but I don't think his mum would have checked to make sure. I know I didn't.'

'So, where is the torch now?' asked Norman.

'Knowing Jack, it's still in the back of the hatchback. He's not very good at putting things back where they belong.'

'So, it's in the back of the car that's outside?' asked Norman.

'Probably.'

'Can we go and have a look?'

'What, right now?'

'Is that a problem?' asked Norman.

'Not at all, it's an excellent idea,' said Foster. 'Especially if it proves that Jack's in the clear.'

Norman thought it was unlikely to do any such thing, but he didn't say so. He followed Tom Foster out to the car park and stood beside him as he opened the boot.

'Right,' said Foster, pointing to a box containing assorted tools and other paraphernalia. 'It'll be in there.' He stepped aside to allow Norman to look through it.

'There's no torch in here,' said Norman.

Foster elbowed him aside. 'Of course there is. Here, let me have a look.' He rummaged in the box before turning it over, spilling the contents onto the floor of the car. There was a wheel brace, a small jack, an anorak, a small tool roll, a towel and a few bits of rag, but no torch.

Foster stood up and scratched his head. 'That's funny. It should be in there . . .' He appeared to think for a moment or two, and then slapped his forehead. 'What an idiot I am. Of course it's not there. I lent it to a friend the other day and he hasn't given it back.'

'Right,' said Norman. 'So, your friend won't mind if I go and get it from him.'

'No can do,' said Foster. 'He's away. Flying out this morning, actually.'

'Perhaps you can give me his phone number so I can call him and confirm he has the torch.'

'He doesn't have a mobile phone,' said Foster. 'He's one of those weird people who thinks mobiles fry your brain.'

'My, how convenient,' said Norman.

Foster ignored the sarcasm. 'Can I take Jack home now?'

'Just one more thing,' said Norman. 'If you would just let us take your fingerprints—'

'Mine? Why do you want mine?'

'We have this torch we found in the forest,' said Norman. 'Now, hypothetically, if it was yours, it would have your fingerprints on it, right?'

'I suppose so, yes.'

'So, if your prints aren't on the torch we have, it will prove it's not yours.'

'Ah. I see what you mean,' said Foster. 'If my fingerprints aren't on it, it proves Jack couldn't have lost it in the forest.'

'That's exactly what I'm thinking,' said Norman. 'Will you do it?'

'Can I take Jack home after?'

'I'll have to check with DI Southall, but I don't see why not.'

'In that case, let's do it,' said Foster.

* * *

Two hours later, everyone had gone home apart from Winter and Lane, who were just tidying up and about to call it a day when Lane's phone rang. Putting her hand over the phone, she whispered to Winter, 'It's Tom Foster. He says his mate has returned the missing torch and can he bring it in now, so as to prove Jack can't have lost it in the forest.'

Winter rolled his eyes. 'Well, well, isn't that convenient?'

'What shall I tell him?' asked Lane.

'I was looking forward to getting home,' said Winter. 'But we don't want to be giving him grounds for complaint, so I suppose we'll just have to wait for him.'

Lane told Foster he could bring in the torch and ended the call.

'We might as well drop it in at the forensic lab on the way home. At least then we might get the fingerprint results back on Monday.'

Less than fifteen minutes after the call, Tom Foster was at the station. Winter met him in reception and held open an evidence bag for him to drop the torch into.

'We'll get this straight off to the lab,' Winter said with a smile. 'The sooner we get this sorted, the sooner you can relax.'

'Right, yes, that's fine. Thank you,' said Foster.

CHAPTER NINE

Monday, 11 November, 09.30

Bill Bridger had taken the rare step of coming to Llangwelli station to update the detectives on the latest forensic findings.

'Let's start with the tech stuff,' he said. 'Young Jack Foster might think he knows a bit about computers and phones, but our tech guys know a wee bit more. There's no evidence that he sent the photograph from his own mobile phone, but there is evidence to prove it was on there.'

'Yes, but he told us that,' said Southall.

'Ah yes, but he told you it was sent to him. We can prove he actually took the photograph.'

'That blows a huge hole in his story about not seeing the body,' said Norman. 'But it doesn't prove he sent the photo to Lizzie Cooper.'

'We can't prove he sent it from his own phone,' said Bridger. 'But our guys can prove he sent it to the burner phone, and they also found enough mobile phone location data from that burner phone to prove it was probably at his house.'

'Is it enough to convict him?' asked Winter. 'Just in case he tries to change his story.'

'They believe it is, and given a bit more time, they reckon they can prove it beyond doubt. Also, you won't be surprised to know the boy spends a lot of his time watching porn. There's a folder full of links to various websites on his laptop.'

'I suppose that's the flip side of him being an adult,' said Southall. 'We get to interview him without his parents, but he gets to watch porn.'

'It's not a recent thing,' said Bridger. 'We think he's been doing it for years.'

'I'm disappointed, but as you said, not even slightly surprised,' said Norman. 'Does he have a preference?'

'If you mean what kind of porn he likes, I'd say he's what you might call an all-rounder,' said Bridger. 'On the plus side, there's no actual kiddie stuff, but there is a "Young Asian Girls" site he visits a lot.'

'Is he paying to watch?' asked Southall.

'It's mostly free sites, but there are three that require a monthly subscription to watch.'

'And I'm betting they're not cheap,' said Norman. 'He's at sixth-form college and doesn't have a part-time job, so how can he afford it?'

'He doesn't have to. His father pays the subscription.'

There was a general sharp intake of breath at this.

'Did I hear that right?' asked Norman. 'He pays for his son to watch pornography?'

'What sort of parenting is that?' asked Southall.

'I'd call it the careless sort,' said Bridger. 'He uses his father's username and password, but I have a sneaking suspicion his father has no idea. And because it's a "no limit" subscription, he could watch it twenty-four seven if he wanted.'

'I guess as long as they're not both trying to log in at the same time, the father probably has no idea his son is watching it as well,' suggested Catren Morgan.

'Yes,' said Bridger. 'Although there is still the possibility that he willingly shares the subscription with his son.'

'I really hope not,' said Southall.

'Yeah, it doesn't bear thinking about, does it?' said Norman.

'I've thought of an equally unsavoury possibility,' said Morgan. 'What if he's blackmailing his father into paying? A sort of "let me watch or I tell Mum about it" scenario.'

'I'm not sure which is worse,' said Southall.

'I'll let you guys speculate about the hows and whys,' said Bridger. 'Anyway, that's the tech stuff for now, so, moving on, I can confirm Jack Foster's fingerprints are a match for one set of prints on the torch found at the burial site.'

'Well, that figures,' said Morgan. 'Didn't he say he lost the torch when he fell into the grave?'

'Yeah, but hang on,' said Winter. 'His father said their torch was the one he brought in on Saturday afternoon.'

'Talking about that,' said Norman. 'Does anyone else think it highly unlikely that his friend would have taken a five-mile detour on his way to the airport just to return a torch? Or am I just being a little cynical here?'

'I think we're all on the same page, Norm,' said Southall.

'And I suggest your cynicism is well justified, Norm,' said Bridger. 'The torch Tom Foster brought in to you on Saturday afternoon only has his fingerprints on it. It also looks suspiciously new. In fact, it's so new the batteries are just about fully charged.'

'You mean it's never been used?' asked Norman.

'I wouldn't say never used, but hardly.'

Norman scratched his head. 'I'm sure you're telling us something significant here, Bill, but my brain's working real slow this morning.'

Bridger smiled.

'It's my belief that the torch found at the burial site belongs to the Fosters. And the torch Tom Foster brought in to you on Saturday also belongs to the Fosters. But it's a new one.'

'So, you think he went out and bought a torch just like the first one so he could bring it to us?'

'Yes, that's precisely what I believe. You can only get that particular type of torch at the local DIY centre, and it wouldn't have needed much of a diversion to call in there and purchase one,' said Bridger.

'I knew there was something funny about it on Saturday,' said Winter, 'but I was in such a hurry to get home I missed it.'

'What?' asked Norman.

'It took us about half an hour to get to the Fosters' place, didn't it?'

'Yeah, thereabouts,' said Norman.

'Yet it was only about fifteen minutes from Judy putting the phone down to him arriving in reception,' said Winter. 'He must have been at the DIY centre when he called. I should have realised and questioned him about it.'

'So should I,' said Lane.

'But why would you?' asked Norman. 'You had no reason to think he'd be giving us a brand-new torch, and even if you had questioned him, it wouldn't have made any difference. If he's given us a new torch, he's obviously willing to lie about where it came from.'

'He could have said he called because he got halfway here and then realised we might not be here,' added Southall. 'You couldn't have proved any different.'

'Yeah, I suppose,' said Winter, still convinced he'd messed up big time.

'It's not you who messed up, Frosty,' said Southall. 'I think you'll find it's Tom Foster who has done that.' She turned to Bridger. 'If you're right about this being a new torch, and Frosty's right about him buying it on Saturday, there's a good chance Tom Foster would have been caught on the DIY centre's CCTV buying the torch.'

Bridger nodded. 'I should think that's a distinct possibility.'

'That works for me,' said Norman. 'I've used that store a lot over the last few months and I know they have CCTV all over the place. Best of all, if Bill's idea is on the money, we even know what time he was there.'

Southall turned to Morgan.

'I'm on my way,' said Morgan, reaching for her keys, phone and coat.

'Do you really think an eighteen-year-old could have murdered the girl and buried her in the forest?' asked Judy Lane.

'If you'd asked me that a couple of days ago, I'd have said no way,' said Southall. 'But so far the evidence isn't doing him any favours, is it?'

'And I wouldn't put it past his father to try and cover up for him,' said Norman.

'Is he a big lad?' asked Bridger. 'I know the victim didn't weigh much, but even so, it's a long way to carry a body from the car park to the clearing.'

'It is possible there was more than one person involved,' said Norman.

'And if daddy pays for his son to watch porn, it's possible they watch it together,' suggested Winter. 'And it's also possible they were acting out something from a video they watched.'

'Like Norm said, the father is probably covering for his son,' suggested Southall. 'Or, perhaps we've got it the wrong way round, and it's the father who's guilty and his son is covering for him!'

'Yeah, that's yet another possibility to add to all the others that are mounting up,' said Norman. He turned to Bridger. 'If you could find conclusive evidence that points to one definite suspect, it would help us enormously.'

Bridger gave him a rueful smile. 'I am doing my best, Norm, but I'm afraid I can only tell you about the evidence that's there.'

'Yeah, I know, Bill,' said Norman wearily. 'I'm sorry. I didn't mean to have a go at you.'

'Cheer up, Norm. It's not like you to be so pessimistic,' said Southall.

Norman sighed. 'I don't know what it is, but there's something just not right about this case. I feel we're missing something important, and that's why we can't tell the wood from the trees, if you'll excuse the pun.'

'In that case, let me conclude by telling you something that might help,' said Bridger. 'I wasn't going to mention it yet, but you sound as if you need something to raise your spirits.'

'I wouldn't say no,' said Norman.

'I'm making no promises, because it really is a long shot and it might well come to nothing.'

'Right now we'll take anything,' said Norman.

'As you know, I've been conducting tests on the sheet the body was wrapped in. Now I don't want to get your hopes up unnecessarily, but there's an outside chance we might be able to produce a DNA sample from it.'

'Yeah, but her DNA is bound to be all over it,' said Norman. 'Anyway, we already have photographic evidence from when she was found, so I don't really think we need further proof that she was wrapped in it.'

'Yes, of course, I agree completely,' said Bridger. 'But what if it's not *her* DNA?'

'You mean it could be the killer's?' asked Southall.

'Or perhaps the person that buried her, if they aren't the same person,' said Bridger.

'But we already have a blood sample from the body. Isn't that good enough?' asked Winter.

'Yes, but this was found on the sheet,' said Bridger.

'Oh no,' said Norman. 'Please don't tell me the guy got turned on burying her and decided to—'

'No, no, no, it's not that,' said Bridger. 'What I found was evidence that at some stage someone who handled the sheet may have shed a few tears.'

'You mean they cried over her?' said Winter.

'That, or maybe they got something in their eye and it started to water. Either way, it's the same stuff.'

'But if these tears are on the sheet, aren't they more likely to have come from the victim?' asked Winter.

'I don't think so,' said Bridger. 'Don't forget we think she had been dead for hours before she was wrapped in the sheet and buried.'

'Wouldn't the rain have washed the tears away?' asked Southall.

'The part with the tears was on the inside, so the rain didn't reach it. I'm guessing the person cried before they pulled it over her.'

'Seriously?' said Norman. 'Why would they do that?'

'Who knows?' said Bridger. 'Your guess is as good as mine.'

'But can you really get DNA from tears that have dried?' said Norman. 'I've never come across that before.'

'As I said, it's a long shot,' said Bridger. 'It depends on whether I can gather enough material to make a viable sample. But, even if we fail to get a full DNA sample, we might get something that will help. If nothing else, it might give you a bit of insight into the mind of the person who buried her.' He looked at his watch. 'Sorry. I'm giving evidence in court shortly, so I have to head off now.'

Bridger gathered his things and headed for the door.

'What did he mean about giving us insight into the mind of the person who buried her?' asked Winter.

'You have to ask why he was crying,' said Norman. 'If he was upset, why? Did he know her? Was he in love with her? Did he kill her, and then regret it? Jeez, maybe she was his daughter, and it was one of those "family honour" killings.'

'I'm not saying we should discount Bill's state-of-mind suggestion,' said Southall. 'But there are so many reasons why he might have been crying we could end up wasting a lot of time on something that turns out to be irrelevant. And, of course, he might just have poked himself in the eye.'

'Do you think it actually was an honour killing?' asked Winter.

'Anything's possible,' said Norman gloomily. 'Unless we can identify her, and where she came from, I doubt we're ever going to know what really happened.'

'So, if the DNA from the tears is different from Jack Foster's, it will prove there must be another person involved, won't it?' asked Winter.

'Yes, that's right,' said Southall.

'If it proves to be his father's, we're going to look pretty stupid,' said Norman. 'And wouldn't Evans love that.'

'D'you think that will happen?' asked Winter.

'If there are two people involved, the obvious suspects are Tom and Jack Foster,' said Southall.

'Armed with all this new forensic evidence, we can bring those two back in, and interview them again,' said Norman.

'Yes,' said Southall. 'I'll ask Uniform to head out there now, so that by the time Catren reports back about the CCTV, we're ready to start.'

* * *

Having made an unexpected appearance just as Judy Lane was answering a call, Evans stood in the doorway, listening.

'That was Uniform,' she called to Southall. 'Tom and Jack Foster aren't at home. According to Mrs Foster they were there an hour ago, but she has no idea where they are now.'

'What's that?' Evans asked.

'I sent two patrol cars to pick up Jack Foster and his father, but they're not at home,' said Southall.

'At home did you say? Good God, woman, I've just read your report and the way I see it he should have been charged and locked up straight after the interview.'

'Actually, we let his father take him home after the interview,' said Southall.

Evans stared at her in disbelief. 'You did what?'

'He was released into his father's custody on Saturday afternoon pending further investigations.'

'And now both he and his father are missing?' said Evans. 'Well, that's just bloody brilliant, isn't it? Why on earth did you let him go?'

'He says he didn't murder anyone, and he's even denying sending the photograph of the victim.'

'Well, he's bound to say that, isn't he?' said Evans.

'The thing is we now have forensic proof that he's lying about finding the body and sending the photograph, but we believe he's telling the truth when it comes to the murder,' said Southall.

'If he's lying about the photo, why on earth would you believe he's telling the truth about the murder?' Evans's voice went up an octave. 'Good grief, have you all gone soft?'

'We believe him because we have six witnesses who corroborate his story about tripping and falling into the shallow grave,' said Southall. 'We know he didn't take the body with him, and he couldn't have gone there to dig the grave if it was already there for him to fall into. Or are you suggesting he took his friends to the grave so he could show them what he'd done?'

'No, Southall. I'm suggesting they are probably all in it together!'

'I'm afraid I can't agree with that, sir,' said Southall. 'They're just a bunch of kids who went for a walk in the forest because they thought it would be a bit spooky and they wanted to see who would freak out first. They had no idea they were going to find a shallow grave, and apart from Jack Foster, none of them even saw the grave, or the body. They just saw Foster fall over, and then they all ran off and left him.'

Evans stood in front of her, studying her face for what seemed like an age.

'You'd better be right about this,' he growled. 'If you've released a murderer and his father has helped him abscond, heads will roll.'

He turned on his heel and stalked from the room. The doors closed behind him with a crash.

'I'm sorry,' said Lane. 'I didn't realise he was in the room when I called out to you.'

'Don't worry, Judy. At least now he can't complain he doesn't know what's going on.'

Norman, who had been out buying coffee for everyone, backed through the door. Seeing their glum expressions, he stopped short and raised his eyebrows.

'What's up? Don't tell me the lottery numbers didn't come up again.'

'Uniforms have just been to pick up the Fosters,' said Southall. 'Only they couldn't, because they've both gone .'

'Oh great,' said Norman. 'God's gift to arse-licking isn't going to like that when he finds out.'

'He already knows,' said Lane. 'I told him.'

'You what?' said Norman.

'It wasn't quite like that,' said Southall. 'Judy was just telling me about it when Evans walked in. It was just bad timing, that's all.'

'So what did he say?' asked Norman.

'He's going to fire me if we can't get hold of them.'

'We'll find them,' said Norman. 'If they've only been missing for an hour they can't have gone far.'

'They've only been missing for an hour if Maria Foster is telling the truth,' said Southall. 'Of course, if she's not, they could have been on the run since Saturday evening.'

'I thought it was supposed to be me who's not being positive about this case,' said Norman.

Lane's phone was ringing again.

'I know where Jack Foster is,' she said a minute later. 'That was Imogen Cooper. She says he's outside her front door, hammering on it like a mad thing.'

'He must be after Lizzie,' said Southall.

'There you go,' said Norman. 'I said they couldn't have got far.'

'Come on, Norm, let's go,' said Southall.

* * *

As they approached the Coopers' house, they could see a small white van parked haphazardly in the street outside.

'The Fosters own a van just like that,' said Norman, squinting at the registration number. 'I can't be sure, but I think it's theirs.'

'We know how Jack got here then,' said Southall pulling up behind it. They jumped from the car and were immediately assailed by the sound of loud banging, accompanied by shouted obscenities.

'Come on, Lizzie, I know you're in there,' Foster was yelling. 'You've got me into a whole load of trouble, and I want to know why!'

'All right, Jack, that's enough,' said Norman, coming up behind him. He seized the boy's arms and brought them up behind his back. 'The only one who got you into trouble was you, not Lizzie.'

'Take your hands off me,' cried Foster. 'You can't do this. Lizzie, tell them why you did this to me.'

Norman wrestled Foster away from the front door, turned him around and handcuffed him. 'That was a stupid thing to do, Jack.' He marched him towards their car, leaving Southall at the house to speak to the Coopers. 'You're in enough trouble already.'

'But I haven't done anything,' Jack yelled.

Norman swung Foster around and pushed him against the car.

'Ah, you bastard. These handcuffs are hurting me.'

'Well, whose fault is that? You wouldn't be in handcuffs if you hadn't been disturbing the peace,' said Norman. 'And, by the way, I would appreciate it if you didn't take my mother's name in vain.'

'Huh? I didn't mention your mother.'

'Oh, never mind,' said Norman. 'Now listen to me. I suggest you calm down and stop swearing at the top of your voice, especially as you obviously have no idea what those words even mean. Trust me, you really don't want to be charged with disturbing the peace on top of the other things you're being accused of, but I will do that if you don't get a grip.'

Foster began to protest again, although slightly less vociferously.

'Jack, just shut up and listen,' Norman said. 'In a few minutes we'll be taking you back to Llangwelli, and interviewing you all over again—'

'But why? I already told you what happened.'

'You told us a nice fairy story,' said Norman. 'Now, do you know anything about forensics, and what it's used for?'

Jack shrugged. 'A bit.'

'That's good. And knowing a bit about forensics, you might want to think about what it can tell us. And when you've thought about that for a while, you might consider how much better it would be for you if you told us the truth this time.'

'But—'

'Uh-uh,' said Norman, unlocking the car. 'I don't want to hear another word out of you until we're in the interview room, okay?' He opened the back door of the car. 'Now, sit in there and wait.'

'What, with these handcuffs sticking in my back?'

'Well, lean forward then,' said Norman. 'When we're ready to leave I'll undo them.'

'Yeah, but—'

'That's the deal, Jack. Or would you rather I left you like that all the way to the station?' Foster gave him a dirty look but said nothing. 'Good boy,' Norman said. 'You know it makes sense.'

Norman closed the car door and headed back to the house, meeting Southall on her way out.

'Are they all right?' he asked.

'Shaken but not stirred,' said Southall.

'Are they going to press charges?'

'Lizzie's all for it, but her mother's not so sure. She's going to think about it.'

'Had Jack been there long?' asked Norman.

'About half an hour.'

'Jeez, and he was hammering on the door all that time?'

'Apparently. He said he just wanted to talk to Lizzie. She says she might have spoken to him if he hadn't been so abusive.'

'He claims Lizzie's got it in for him,' said Norman. 'D'you think there's anything in that?'

'She certainly doesn't think much of him, but would she go out of her way to make trouble for him? I don't know, Norm.'

They were back at the car now and, as promised, Norman removed Foster's handcuffs. Just as he was about to climb into the front, a car pulled up behind them and Tom Foster jumped out.

'Have you seen Jack?' he asked.

Norman aimed a thumb at the back seat. 'He's in there.'

'I can take him home if you like. There's no need for you t—'

'Oh, no. Jack's not going home,' said Norman. 'He's coming with us. We have a few more questions for him.'

'Can I talk to him?'

Norman grimaced.

'No. I don't think that would be a good idea.'

'Why not? You've already questioned him, why do you need to do it again?'

'Yes, we have already questioned him,' said Norman. 'But, in the light of new evidence that's come up, we need to question him some more.'

'What new evidence?'

'I'm not at liberty to say. As a matter of fact, we'd like to ask you a few questions too.'

'Me?'

'That's right.'

'What do you want to ask me about?'

'If you follow us down to Llangwelli station, you'll be able to find out.'

Tom Foster hesitated.

'Look, Mr Foster, like it or not, we need you to answer a few questions. So, you can come with us now, voluntarily, or we can do it the hard way. It's entirely up to you, but I will point out that it doesn't look particularly good having a fleet of squad cars pull up at your house. Those boys enjoy putting on a show, so they tend to arrive with sirens going and blue lights flashing.'

This seemed to help Foster make up his mind.

'Okay. I think I'll come now.'

Norman smiled. 'Good move, Mr Foster.'

CHAPTER TEN

It didn't take long to get Jack Foster booked in, and in less than an hour they were settled in an interview room with the same duty solicitor in attendance.

'Right, Jack,' said Southall. 'We'd like to go over the night of Friday, first November with you again. And, just to put you in the picture, I'm warning you from the start that we know it was you who took the photograph of the murder victim found in the Dragon Forest and sent it to Lizzie Cooper.'

'I didn't—'

'Remember that little chat we had earlier about forensics?' said Norman. 'Well, you might have thought you had deleted it from your phone, but we have what you might call forensic technical experts, and they have found more than enough evidence on it to prove you took that photo. And enough tracking data to show that the phone from which the photo was sent to Lizzie was at your house.'

Jack looked at his solicitor, who shrugged and gave him a nod.

'You could start by telling us why you sent it,' said Norman.

'Lizzie is a bitch,' said Jack. 'We went out this one time, and apparently I wasn't man enough for her. She told everyone I couldn't do it.'

'By "it", do you mean have sex?' asked Southall.

Foster rolled his eyes. 'Duh, of course that's what I mean. But it wasn't that I couldn't perform. She was gagging for it. She said she always did it, even on first dates. That put me off, to be honest. I mean, if she's, like, that free and easy with it—'

'So why take the photograph and send it to her?' asked Norman.

'She said I'd never been with a naked girl and wouldn't know what to do with one, so I suppose I just wanted to prove she was wrong.'

'With a dead body?' asked Norman. 'D'you make a habit of interfering with dead bodies?'

'Of course not. And I didn't interfere with her.'

'Yet you did,' said Norman. 'You see, there was blood beneath her left breast, and a faint fingerprint in blood on it. It didn't take our pathologist long to work out that whoever that blood belonged to had put his hand on her breast.'

Jack, who'd been sitting with his hands on the table, immediately put his right hand on his lap, out of sight.

'You don't need to hide it,' said Norman. 'We know from the other day that you've a cut on your right hand.'

'Yeah, but I never—'

'Oh, but you did,' said Norman. 'Forensics again. Our forensic tests show that it was your blood on her body. Now, do you want to tell us how it got there?'

'But I wasn't there!'

'Look, Jack, you might think you're a criminal mastermind but, trust me, you're way out of your depth here,' said Norman. 'You already told us, on Saturday, that you were there in the forest with your friends. Remember?'

'Oh, yeah . . .'

'Not only that, but we also have proof you took a photo of the body. We also have your fingerprints, and your dad's, on the torch we found at the scene. Which proves it came from the boot of the car you were driving.'

'But that wasn't our torch. My dad brought ours to you on Saturday.'

'Is that what he told you?' asked Norman.

'He didn't have to tell me. It was our torch.'

Southall sighed heavily. 'It is pointless continuing to lie to us, Jack. As DS Norman just said, we already know you were at the scene. Now, apart from sending an indecent image, we're also talking about photographing and interfering with a dead body and failing to report that you had found a body. And, as if that isn't bad enough, we have more than enough evidence to charge you with murder—'

'Whoa! Now wait a minute. I didn't kill anyone. I wouldn't do that. I wouldn't know how.'

'You know we have your laptop, right?' asked Norman.

'Yeah, about that,' said Jack. 'When am I going to get it back?'

'I wouldn't hold your breath,' said Norman. 'Anyway, as I was saying, our tech guys had a good look at the laptop, and guess what they found?'

Deflated, Jack fell silent.

'You like watching porn, do you?' asked Norman.

'You're the one who said I was an adult,' said Foster. 'And as far as I know, there's no law against adults watching porn.'

Norman nodded. 'Well, that depends, especially if you were watching it before you turned eighteen. Or was access to your dad's porn subscriptions an eighteenth birthday gift? You do use your dad's subscriptions to access those sites, right?'

Foster looked puzzled, clearly not quite sure where Norman was going with this.

'Does your father know you use his login details?'

Foster licked his lips.

'Don't want to say? Okay, no worries,' said Norman. 'We can ask your dad when we interview him.'

Foster's eyes widened, but still he said nothing.

'As I said, we can check with him later. The thing is you seem to have access to a lot of sites. And I'm told one of them is a necrophilia site.'

'I don't know what that is.'

'Oh, but I think you do know, Jack, but I'll tell you anyway,' said Norman. 'The dictionary definition is: "being sexually attracted to dead bodies, or sexual activity with dead bodies". Now isn't that a coincidence?'

'What do you mean, a coincidence?' Foster's eyes suddenly widened in panic. 'I swear I didn't have sex with that dead woman. She was so cold—'

'Prefer them still warm, do you?' asked Norman.

The solicitor opened his mouth to object, but Norman beat him to it.

'You're right,' he said, holding his hands up. 'That was uncalled for. I apologise.'

'Can I have a minute or two with my client?' asked the solicitor.

'That sounds like a good idea,' said Southall. 'Let's take a break for fifteen minutes.'

* * *

Twenty minutes later, Southall and Norman were back, sitting across the table from Jack Foster and his solicitor.

'My client would like to clarify one or two things he said earlier today and on Saturday.'

Southall and Norman exchanged a glance. 'Fine,' said Southall. 'Please, go ahead, Jack.'

'First, about the porn subscriptions. They are my dad's, but he doesn't know I use his login details to watch stuff on my laptop.'

'Okay,' said Southall. 'Thank you for that. Anything else?'

Foster nodded. 'About that Friday night. We did go to the forest, me and the other six. I thought they had only invited me so they could prove what a coward I am. I went because I wanted to prove I'm not. But I needn't have bothered; it turns out I'm the least cowardly of the lot.

'I did go on ahead, and by the time I reached the clearing the rest of them were way behind. I thought I heard something up ahead, so I waited for them to catch up, but in the

151

end the only one who did was Afan Mason. I told him I'd heard a noise, but he said it was probably an animal — like a deer or something. Anyway, he said I should go on ahead while he went back to gee up the others. So I did. And that's when I tripped and fell into the hole.'

'That "hole" was a shallow grave, and I imagine there would have been a mound of soil alongside it that had been dug out,' said Norman. 'How come you didn't see it?'

'I wasn't looking down at the ground. I was trying to see what was making the noise up ahead.'

'With the light from a smartphone?' asked Norman doubtfully. 'Or are you now going to admit you were carrying the torch? Before you answer that, remember we have your fingerprints on it.'

Foster sighed. 'Okay, I admit I was carrying the torch.'

'And what happened then?' asked Southall.

'So, I'm lying face down in this hole with the breath knocked out of me. It was really dark because the torch had gone flying out of my hand when I fell. At first, I wasn't even sure what had happened, I thought whatever had made the noise had pushed me into the hole, but when nothing else happened, I realised I'd just tripped.

'Anyway, I didn't know where the torch had gone, so I started feeling around for it, and landed on a piece of cloth. I wondered what it was doing out in the forest, so I felt around a bit more and that's when I touched what seemed like skin, only it was really cold. I felt around a bit more and that's when I accidentally put my hand on her, um, boob.' He blushed and looked down.

'It must have been quite a shock finding a dead body out there in the middle of nowhere,' said Southall.

Jack nodded, keeping his eyes fixed on the table.

'What happened to the others?' she asked. 'Didn't they come to see if you were all right?'

'When I'd calmed down a bit, I looked back and they'd all gone,' said Foster. 'They ran off and left me. It turns out that was the plan all along.'

'And you say these people are your friends,' said Norman. 'If it was me, I think I might have started having a few doubts by then.'

'Yeah, well, I can see that now,' said Foster. 'When I joined their class I just wanted to be one of the gang, but now I'm glad I'm not. They think they're so cool, but they're really just a bunch of shits. And Lizzie Cooper is the biggest shit of them all.'

'Is that why you took the photograph and sent it to her?' asked Southall.

Foster nodded. 'Stupid, right? I can see that now. But I wanted to get my own back, do something to upset her and piss her off. I never thought she'd show it to her mum!'

'Whatever you might think of Lizzie, she didn't show the photo to anyone, including her mum,' said Southall. 'Her mother saw it by accident. It was her mother that made the complaint, not Lizzie.'

'Going back to the body,' said Norman. 'You say you touched her by accident as you were feeling around in the dark.'

'Yeah, that's right. At the time I didn't know I'd cut my hand. But that's how the blood got there.'

'Okay, but why didn't you report the body?' asked Norman.

'Because I thought I'd be held responsible.' He looked pointedly at the two detectives. 'And it looks as if I was right.'

'The reason we've got to this stage is because you've lied so much,' said Norman. 'If you had come forward as soon as you found the body, things would have been a lot different. Is that why you buried the body? So no one would know it was there?'

Foster's voice rose in alarm.

'Bury it? What are you talking about? I didn't bury the body! Once the reality of the mess I was in had sunk in, I couldn't wait to get out of there. I left the body exactly where it was and ran back to my car.'

'And this deer you thought you had heard earlier? Did you see it?' Norman asked.

'No.'

'So, how do you know it was a deer?'

'I didn't say it was a deer, I don't know what it was. It was Afan who said it was probably a deer.'

'What do you think it was?'

'How should I know? Deer, badger, fox, what difference does it make?'

'Tell us again what happened after you fell into the grave,' said Norman.

'I just told you. I was a bit winded from the fall, so I lay there until I got my breath back, and then I started to feel around.'

Norman frowned. 'That's the bit I don't get. You see, it would be perfectly understandable for any normal person to have panicked at this point, but you didn't. Instead, you reach out a hand to feel around. And then, when you feel cold skin, you still don't panic. You cop a feel, reach for your phone and take a photograph.'

'I didn't "cop a feel",' said Foster angrily. 'I touched her by accident.'

'And that's all you did? Are you sure you didn't take the cloth off her?'

Foster turned to the solicitor. 'You see, this is exactly why I didn't report finding the body.'

'We're just trying to find out what really happened,' said Norman.

'I think Mr Foster is making a valid point,' said the solicitor. 'He's volunteered to tell you what happened, but it would appear that because he's not telling you what you want to hear, you're putting words into his mouth in order to fit your narrative.'

'I'm sorry you feel that way,' said Norman. 'But if your client hadn't been so economical with the truth in our previous interview with him, we wouldn't now be wondering if this isn't another pack of lies.'

'Why don't we call a halt for now,' said Southall. 'I'm sure Jack would appreciate the chance to take a break and maybe have something to eat.'

'Is that it?' asked Jack. 'I can go home now?'

'I didn't say that,' said Southall. 'I don't think we can let you walk out of here just yet. You can wait in one of the cells for now, and we'll make sure you get something to eat.'

'Can I have a word in private, please, Inspector?' asked the solicitor.

'I'll take Jack downstairs and leave you to it,' said Norman.

'Does this mean you're going to charge Mr Foster?' asked the solicitor after they had gone.

'You've heard what he said,' said Southall. 'Do you really think we can just pat him on the head and tell him to go home like a good boy?'

'No, I suppose not. But what are the charges likely to be?'

'The same ones as before: interfering with a corpse, failing to report finding a body, sending an indecent image . . . We might even think about adding wasting police time to that. Oh, and we haven't yet ruled out murder.'

* * *

'So, what do you think of Jack Foster's revised story?' Southall asked Norman as they snatched a quick sandwich.

'I still don't think he's capable of murder,' said Norman.

'What about interfering with the body?'

'It's very convenient he happens to land in just the right position to reach out and touch her breasts, but we can't prove any different, can we?'

'Not reporting the body?'

'Can't argue with that one.'

'What about burying the body? Did he, or didn't he?'

'We need to speak to Afan Mason again and see if he confirms the bit about hearing a noise.'

'You think they disturbed whoever was digging the grave?'

'It makes sense,' said Norman. 'Say I'm out there in the middle of the clearing, thinking I've got all night to bury the body and then, before I've finished, I hear voices and see torches heading my way. What am I going to do? I haven't got time to finish what I'm doing, I can't risk staying where I am or I'll be seen, and it looks like there are too many of them to fight.'

'So, you run.'

'What else can I do?'

'And when Jack hears the noise of you running away, Afan assumes it must have been a deer,' said Southall.

'A perfectly reasonable assumption out there in the forest,' said Norman.

'So, who buries the body?'

'I do,' said Norman. 'I run and hide somewhere nearby, wait until the coast is clear, then come back and finish burying the body.'

'But if you assume these people have discovered the body, how do you know it hasn't been reported?'

'I don't,' said Norman. 'But it's a risk I have to take, because if I don't bury it now, it's sure to be found in the morning.'

'That could explain why it wasn't very well buried,' said Southall.

'It was a rushed job,' said Norman.

'But why leave the spade behind?'

'I got careless,' said Norman. 'Like I said, it was a rushed job. I realised later, but I couldn't risk going back again, and at least I knew it was clean because I was wearing gloves.'

Southall chewed thoughtfully on her sandwich.

'So, what do you think?' asked Norman.

'I think it ticks a lot of boxes regarding the burial, but does it get us any further when it comes to the murder?'

Norman sighed. 'Only if we can find out who was doing the digging, and even then, only if the digger is also the killer . . .'

'Come on,' said Southall. 'Let's go and have a chat with Tom Foster.'

* * *

By the time they sat down with Tom Foster, he was livid.

'Do you know how long I've been kept waiting?'

'Sorry about that,' said Southall. 'That's one of the problems with police work. We have finite resources, and we haven't yet found a way to be in two places at once.'

'It's a disgrace, that's what it is. And harassing innocent people like me and my son — it's outrageous. We have rights, you know.'

Southall smiled a humourless smile. 'Your son isn't complaining. He's being very helpful.'

'Yes, well, that's because he's still young and he doesn't know how these things should work. I expect you're baffling him with legal speak and taking advantage of his naivety. It's harassment, plain and simple.'

Southall smiled sweetly. 'I try to avoid legal speak as much as possible. And there's a solicitor present, should Jack become baffled.'

Foster managed an ungracious harrumph.

'And how exactly have we been harassing you, Mr Foster?'

'Well, this torch business for a start. It's ridiculous. I tell you it's not my torch, and do you believe me? You do not.'

'The reason we don't believe you is because both your fingerprints and Jack's are on the torch we found at the crime scene,' said Southall.

'And, in view of that, we'd like to ask you where you were on the night of Friday, first November,' said Norman.

Foster's mouth dropped open. 'You can't think I had anything to do with this.'

'Why not?' asked Norman. 'You keep telling us Jack's innocent, and your prints are on the torch we found. That being so, it's logical to conclude that we might have been looking at the wrong Foster.'

'But, of course, if you have an alibi . . .' said Southall.

'You're asking me to implicate my own son?'

'Not at all,' said Southall. 'We're simply asking you to tell us where you were, so that we can prove you couldn't have been involved.'

Foster thought about this for a minute.

'I was at a business association dinner. I got home well after midnight.'

'And we can verify this?'

'Just ask the association secretary, or any of the members. There were enough of them there.'

'Okay,' said Norman. 'I'll call when we finish up here.'

'I don't see how our fingerprints can possibly be on the torch you found,' insisted Foster. 'There must be some mistake. I brought my torch in on Saturday afternoon. I gave it to a young detective. He must have switched them.'

'You really think so?' said Norman.

'I can't see any other possibility.'

'Maybe you think we have a time machine here,' said Norman.

'Sorry?'

'That's the only way we could have switched the torches,' said Norman. 'The torch we found in the forest was tested several days before the one you brought in on Saturday.'

'While we're on the subject of torches,' said Southall. 'How do you explain the fact that the torch you brought in on Saturday, that you claim is yours, and that you and Jack both use, only has your fingerprints on it?'

'I don't understand . . .'

'Don't you think it's time you stopped playing this stupid game?' said Southall. 'Frankly, I'm insulted that you think we're so gullible.' She opened her laptop, swung it round and showed it to Foster. 'This,' she said, 'is CCTV footage from the local DIY store. It was taken on Saturday afternoon.'

Foster stared open-mouthed at the screen.

'The guy buying the torch look familiar to you?' asked Norman.

'Er, yes, it's, ah . . .'

'It's you, right?' said Norman.

'I needed to replace the one I was bringing in to you.'

'Twenty minutes before you came here and presented it to DC Winter?' asked Norman. 'You couldn't have done that on the way back home?'

Foster squirmed in his seat.

'This is no joke, Mr Foster,' said Southall. 'We could charge you with perverting the course of justice.'

'Look, he's my son,' pleaded Foster. 'I can't just sit back and let you people accuse him of something he hasn't done.'

'We haven't accused him of anything he hasn't done, Mr Foster. Jack has admitted to losing the torch in the Dragon Forest, and he's admitted to finding a body there.'

'Yes, but he didn't mean any harm.'

'Didn't mean any harm?' said Norman. 'He had a feel of the body and took a photograph! Are you saying he did that by accident?'

'Of course not, but he's not like that. He's—'

'Are you aware your son uses your login details to watch pornography?' asked Southall.

Foster stared at Southall, momentarily thrown, but he soon regained his composure.

'Far as I know there's no law against adults watching it.'

'Are you saying you know he's doing it?' asked Southall.

'Yes, of course I know. I'm not an idiot.'

'That's interesting. Jack thinks you have no idea.'

'Well, I'm afraid Jack's wrong. I've known for ages. Besides, there's nothing wrong in it. As you were so quick to point out, Jack's an adult. He can watch whatever he likes. And at least this way I know what he's watching.'

'Does that mean you're aware he's into necrophilia?'

Foster's face turned red, as if he'd been caught with his hand in the till.

'That, er, that's not one of the sites he watches.'

'It would explain why he thought it was okay to grope the corpse he found,' said Norman.

'Well, I'm sure it would suit your purposes to think that, but I know what Jack watches, and it's not that kind of stuff.'

Norman raised his eyebrows. 'So necrophilia's your thing, is it?' he asked. 'Jeez, you must be so proud of yourself. There's another site called "Young Asian Girls". Which of you watches that one?'

'It's our business what we do in the privacy of our own home,' snapped Foster.

'Is that a yes for you, or a yes for Jack?' asked Norman. 'Or maybe it's a shared passion.'

Foster glared at Southall. 'Is this going to take much longer?'

'No, I think we've heard more than enough,' said Southall. 'You can go whenever you want.'

'What about Jack?'

'I'm afraid Jack is staying here to help us with our investigation,' said Southall.

'You seem to think we're going to fit him up,' said Norman. 'But don't worry, the duty solicitor will look out for him. He'll have to forgo the porn sites for a while, but that won't do him any harm.'

* * *

It was late afternoon when Acting Superintendent Evans crashed through the doors and stalked across the incident room to Southall's office, where Norman was just confirming Tom Foster's alibi.

'Why have I just had someone called Tom Foster bending my ear about you harassing him and his son, Jack?' he demanded.

'It's all in the report I sent up to you,' said Southall.

'I haven't had time to read that,' snapped Evans. 'And you should have sent it before this lunatic called me.'

'I sent it as soon as I could,' said Southall. 'It's a bit difficult to send a report before it's been written.'

'Don't get funny with me, Inspector. What's this man's beef?'

'He doesn't like us asking him where he was on Friday night, and that we're holding his son.'

'Is this the boy who murdered the girl you still haven't identified?'

'We have nothing to prove he murdered her, and neither I nor Norm think he's capable of murder.'

'We're all capable of murder,' said Evans.

'I'm not sure I can agree with that,' said Norman. 'Because while there are definitely one or two people I'd like to murder, so far I've managed to control the urge, so I've come to the conclusion that I'm probably not capable of it.'

Evans looked sharply at Norman, who smiled back innocently. Evans frowned and turned back to Southall.

'I thought we had agreed that the boy was to be charged with murder.'

'We agreed to no such thing,' said Southall. 'All we know for sure is that Jack Foster was in the forest, and he fell into the freshly dug grave and landed on the body.'

'As you know from the reports, we have six witnesses who saw him trip and fall,' added Norman.

'He's admitted to accidentally touching the body as he was trying to get up,' continued Southall. 'And he's admitted to taking at least one photograph, which he's also admitted to sending.'

'Well there you are then. What more do you want?'

'What more do we want?' echoed Norman. 'Well, for a start, if it's a charge of murder, we want some evidence. The Criminal Prosecution Service tend to get a bit pissed off if we send them a case with no evidence to support it. They call it a waste of their time and, frankly, we can only agree with them. And, of course, in the meantime the real murderer gets away scot-free.'

'Even if you're right, and I don't for a second think you are,' said Evans. 'If you're not going to charge the boy, it strikes me the real bloody murderer has already got away scot-free.'

Southall winced. 'It's not for want of trying, but witho—'

'Well, Detective Inspector, I suggest you stop coming up with excuses and try a bit harder,' snarled Evans. 'Or do I need to call in some real detectives to show you how it's done?'

By now, Southall would willingly have torn Evans's head off. 'No, sir,' she said evenly. 'There's no need to do that. I'm confident we can solve this case. We've missed something somewhere, and starting at eight o'clock tomorrow morning, I intend to take the team back through every scrap of information we have until we find it.'

'You've got until the end of the week,' said Evans. 'If you're still getting nowhere, you'll leave me with no choice.'

He turned, stomped back through the incident room and battered his way through the doors.

'Jeez, do we really have to put up with this crap from him every five minutes?' said Norman.

'I keep telling myself it's not worth fighting him because he's only here for a few weeks while Superintendent Bain is away.'

'Well, I hope you're right, because if he takes over permanently, I'll be bringing my retirement forward.'

'That's not going to happen,' said Southall.

'I mean, he doesn't want much, does he?' said Norman. 'And has he ever been involved in a murder investigation? It's not unknown for them to take months, or even years.'

'It makes you wonder, doesn't it?' said Southall. 'But I meant what I said. We do need to go back to the beginning and start again.'

CHAPTER ELEVEN

Tuesday, 12 November, 08.00

Much to Southall's dismay, Evans had arrived, unannounced, just before eight to lead the morning briefing and offer the team what he called a "gee up". The team appeared just as dismayed to see him as Southall, but if Evans noticed all the glum faces before him, he chose to ignore it.

'Right, team,' said Evans, rubbing his hands together. 'I've called you all together this morning because, "A", I need updating, and, "B", I'm not happy with the current lack of progress.' He looked from face to face. No one offered a comment, even Southall and Norman were keeping quiet. 'So, let's have a recap of where we are and what we have.'

Norman felt the "where we are" was a bit rich. So far, Evans had contributed precisely nothing constructive to the enquiry, and if he had read any of the reports Southall had sent him, the information clearly hadn't registered.

He cleared his throat. 'So, obviously, we have the victim.' He turned to the board and seemed to have trouble identifying the correct photograph.

'Majhul, sir,' said Judy Lane. 'She's the one in the middle of the board. We always put the victim in the middle of the board as they're at the centre of the investigation.'

Evans glanced sharply at Lane. 'Yes, of course. I knew that. I'm pleased to see that at least now you've identified her.'

'Er, no, sir,' said Southall. 'As I told you before—'

'Ah. Yes, of course, I remember,' said Evans through gritted teeth. 'When are you going to properly identify her?'

'DNA profiling has suggested that she's from the Middle East, probably Syria.'

'DNA profiling?' said Evans. 'How much has that cost us?'

'I'm not sure,' said Southall. 'It's not cheap, but at least now we can contact the Syrian authorities—'

'I suggest you hold fire on that before you fritter away the entire year's budget,' said Evans.

'If we're going to identify her—'

'If she's Syrian, there's a good chance she's here illegally,' said Evans.

'Are you saying illegals don't count, and don't deserve justice?' asked Norman.

'Of course not,' said Evans. 'But we don't have unlimited funds.' He turned to Southall. 'Reaching out beyond the UK is a last resort, and only if I sanction it. Is that understood?'

'Yes, sir,' said Southall. 'Of course.'

They all waited patiently for Evans to continue, but if he ever had the thread, he'd lost it now.

'Er, as I'm a bit behind, perhaps it would be better if you run us through the case so far, Southall.'

Southall stepped forward to the board. 'Okay, so we know Majhul was buried in the forest, but we believe she was murdered elsewhere, and up to twenty-four hours before she was taken to the forest.

'We have evidence, both actual and circumstantial, which could implicate the Pagans, Jack Foster and Tom Foster as murder suspects. But, despite all the evidence we've managed to gather so far, we don't have sufficient to confirm without doubt that any of these potential suspects is the actual culprit.' She pointed to the photos of each of the suspects in turn. 'Jack Foster is guilty of one or two lesser crimes, but there's nothing to suggest he's a murderer. His father has an alibi for the Friday night, with more than a dozen witnesses willing to vouch for him.

'The Pagans also seem to be in the clear. Although they frequent the site after dark, and there are over a dozen of them, we have absolutely zero physical evidence to link any of them to the crime, and as we have also been unable to identify a plausible motive, I think we can rule them out.'

'I don't think you should exclude them yet,' said Evans.

'Jeez, not this again,' muttered Norman.

'I'm sorry, DS Norman?' snapped Evans. 'Did you say something?'

'He was just saying none of the suspects are being completely excluded,' said Southall quickly. 'But in light of the forensic reports and follow-up enquiries, they have been relegated to the back-burner for now.'

'What forensic reports?' asked Evans.

'The forensic reports I forwarded to you,' said Southall.

'Oh, right. Those forensic reports,' said Evans, who it was clear had no idea what she was talking about. 'Just refresh my memory, would you?'

Suppressing a sigh, Southall turned back to the board. 'Okay, so from the forensic reports, we know the footprints running from the scene to the small car park were made by a size twelve running shoe, and we know from the tread that it's a brand called "Marathon".'

'It's not a well-known shoe,' said Morgan, who had been researching the brand. 'It's designed for long-distance running, rather than everyday use, hence the name.'

'Thank you, Catren,' said Southall. 'We also know that the spade found near the shallow grave had no fingerprints on it. However, the torch that was also found nearby had two sets of fingerprints on it. These belong to Jack Foster and his father, Tom.' She pointed to the photos for Evans's benefit.

'Have they been interviewed?' demanded Evans.

Southall rolled her eyes. 'Yes, sir. If you recall, that's why you had Tom Foster on the phone yesterday making a complaint.'

'Oh yes, that's right,' said Evans. 'And what about their interviews?'

'I'll get to that in a second,' said Southall. 'We also have DNA extracted from the blood found on Majhul's body. It's not her DNA, and it doesn't match anyone on the database, but we now know—'

'So who does it belong to?' asked Evans.

'It's Jack Foster's blood,' said Southall. 'We took samples from him for comparison, but he's already admitted that it's his blood.'

'It sounds like you've got your killer right there,' said Evans.

Southall looked at Norman, who was staring at the floor shaking his head. He couldn't believe it either.

'As I told you yesterday, sir, Jack admits he found the body but claims it was uncovered when he found it. He's not confessing to the murder, nor to burying the body. The most we can charge him with is interfering with a body, sending an image, and failing to inform us that he had found a body.'

'I still think you should be charging him with murder, and unlawful disposing of a body,' said Evans.

'But we have no evidence—'

'Then, make sure you find some, Detective Inspector,' snapped Evans. 'I don't want any more excuses, I want action, and I want results.'

He banged his fist down on the nearest desk and marched out, the doors crashing shut in his wake.

'Do you think he's all there?' asked Morgan. 'And is it that he can't read, or that he can't be arsed to read the reports you send him?'

'Yeah, and he's full of helpful ideas, isn't he?' said Norman. 'I don't think.'

'Let's just focus on the case, shall we?' said Southall. 'I'm sure we must be missing something.'

'Yeah, I think you're right,' said Norman.

'And it's probably staring us in the face,' said Southall.

'We mustn't forget the footprints that were found leading away from the burial site at a run,' said Norman. 'That adds the possibility of another, so far unidentified, suspect.'

'Thanks for reminding us, Norm,' said Southall. 'That's a further complication we could do without.'

'So how are we going to do this?' asked Norman.

'We need to review everything we've done so far,' said Southall. 'I would like you and Catren to revisit the crime scene, while Judy, Frosty and I start working our way through the statements.'

'That sounds like a plan,' said Norman. 'Come on, Catren, let's go.'

* * *

The sun lit up the clearing in the centre of the Dragon Forest as Norman and Morgan made their way to where the body had lain. It had been removed from the shallow grave and the scene-of-crime officers had long finished their work, but the site was still cordoned off with blue and white police tape. They ducked under the tape and stopped by the pile of soil that had been carefully scraped off the body.

'So, what exactly are we looking for, Norm?' asked Morgan.

'Well, if we knew that, we wouldn't be here now. Someone would have found it the first time we came out here,' said Norman.

'Are you even sure there's anything to find?' asked Morgan.

'Heck, no,' said Norman. 'This could well be a waste of time, but I figure it will be better than getting myself suspended for punching a senior officer who appears to have no idea how to solve a crime.'

Morgan smiled. 'Yeah, I know what you mean. He assumes that every new name that comes up must be the killer, regardless of whether or not there's any evidence. It makes you wonder how he ever got so high up the ladder.'

'Oh, I can tell you how he managed that,' said Norman. 'Haven't you noticed the brown stain on the end of his nose? Anyway, let's not talk about him, we came here to breathe in some fresh air and see if we missed anything.'

Morgan cast her eyes around the vicinity. 'I can't imagine we're going to find anything here that the SOCOs didn't.'

'Yeah, I'm sure you're right about this particular patch,' said Norman. 'But I'm wondering if we missed anything further off, in the actual clearing itself.'

'Now that sounds as if you think there is something to find,' said Morgan.

'I don't know about that,' said Norman.

'But you agree with the boss that we've missed something.'

Norman nodded. 'When you feel you're getting nowhere, or going around in circles, there's always a good chance that's the reason why.'

'There is something that's been bothering me about this case,' said Morgan.

'Go on.'

'Don't you think it's a bit weird that someone would choose to dig a grave right here in the clearing, out in the open? I mean, there's a whole forest to choose from, and some of it's quite dense, so why not bury her in the denser part of the forest where she might never be found?'

'Yeah, but wouldn't that mean more tree roots, which would make it more difficult to dig?' reasoned Norman. 'When I was talking to the forest manager, he said trees won't grow here in the clearing, so there aren't any roots to speak of.'

Morgan sighed. 'Yeah, there is that. The soil's pretty sandy here too, so I suppose it's an easier place to dig if you're in a hurry.'

'Yeah. However, I also think there could be another reason.'

'Such as what?' said Morgan.

'Well, let's think about this,' said Norman. 'It's a really shallow grave, and the soil is really sandy.' He looked expectantly at Morgan.

'Which means there's a good chance a fox, or someone's dog would soon have found it,' she said after a moment's thought. 'But surely that's just another reason to dig the grave somewhere else, or to make it a lot deeper.'

'You'd think so, right?' said Norman. 'But what if our gravedigger was aware of the possibility that an animal might sniff out the body? And perhaps he might also have seen the weather forecast, and realised that heavy rain would wash away the loose sand. Now do you see what I'm getting at?'

Morgan frowned in concentration, and then broke into a smile. 'You think she was meant to be found!'

'That's occurred to me as a possibility,' said Norman. 'But then you have to ask yourself why you would want her to be found.'

'You think it was a warning?' asked Morgan. 'But who for?'

'Now that's the million-dollar question, isn't it?'

'If we're right that she's here illegally—'

'The fact that we can't identify her, nor where she comes from, more or less confirms that,' Norman said.

'Then we're talking people smugglers, right?'

'That's how someone like that usually gets here,' said Norman.

'So, what are you thinking? A war between rival gangs? Really?'

'Maybe,' said Norman.

'But what are the chances of that?' asked Morgan. 'I've seen no intelligence to suggest that this part of Wales is a haven for people smugglers.'

'I'm not saying it is,' said Norman. 'But if you think about it, we are on the coast, and we know it's getting harder to get through the main UK ports.'

'But you'd have a hard job bringing large numbers of immigrants to this place without being noticed,' said Morgan. 'They'd outnumber the locals!'

'Not if they arrived in ones and twos, and doing it that way means they'd be much harder to find.'

'Does the boss know about this wild theory of yours?'

'Nah, not yet,' said Norman. 'I'm not even sure I believe it myself. Besides, she's got enough on her plate trying to deal with the idiot-in-chief.'

'So, how do we prove it?' asked Morgan.

'As I said, so far it's just an idea,' said Norman. 'Maybe it is just a wild theory, and there isn't anything to prove. It wouldn't be the first time I've got something completely wrong. One thing's for sure, standing here talking won't prove anything.'

'Right, so what do you want to do now?'

Putting a hand over his eyes to shield them from the glare of the sun, Norman looked around. 'It's a nice sunny day. Why don't we take a walk around the perimeter of the clearing.'

'Wouldn't it be better going to the car parks?' said Morgan. 'Why the perimeter? Are you really saying you think our grave digger walked all the way around the outside of the clearing?'

'I'm saying the SOCOs have already covered the foot-paths to the car parks, and the public will have walked all over anything they missed. So I think we should try something different. We know there seem to be far more paths coming in and out of the forest than are shown on the park map, so who's to say there isn't an unmarked path that leads straight into this clearing? Maybe that was the escape route, and we missed it because we didn't look hard enough.'

'You really think so?' asked Morgan.

Norman shrugged. 'All I'm saying is that it won't hurt to take a look. If we don't find anything, at least we'll have had a nice stroll in the sunshine before we call it a day.'

'Okay,' said Morgan. 'Is there anything else we should be looking for besides a hidden path?'

'I dunno. Something that doesn't look right, I guess. You're a farmer's daughter, you must know a lot more than me about soil and plants and stuff, so maybe you'll notice something that doesn't look right.'

'Are you keeping it vague to test me?' asked Morgan.

'No, I'm keeping it vague because it is vague,' said Norman. 'Basically, as far as what we're looking for goes, your guess is as good as mine.'

'If I'm honest, I don't think it's one of your better ideas, but as you said, it's a nice sunny day, so why not?'

'I should have brought my dog,' said Norman as they set off. 'She'd love it out here. You remember my dog? You know, the one you said I'd have to give back to the family? The dog the family didn't want and that would have ended up in a rescue centre if I hadn't got involved, even though you told me not to.'

Norman's dog had previously belonged to a murder victim. He and the dog had bonded the moment they set eyes on each other, and despite Morgan and Southall telling him he shouldn't get involved, he had taken her home with him. When it became clear that the murder victim's family had no interest in keeping the dog, Norman had set about officially adopting her. She had lived with Norman and his partner, Faye, ever since.

Morgan smiled. 'Yes, of course I remember your dog. I wasn't against you keeping her, I just didn't want you to get attached to her and then have to give her back. At that stage we didn't know the family wouldn't want her, did we? Now I'm pleased for you, because she obviously makes you happy.'

'That's because she's always pleased to see me when I get home, and all that walking sure keeps me fit.'

'Isn't Faye pleased to see you when you get home?' asked Morgan.

'Well, yeah, of course, but not in the same way. You must know what dogs are like, they go crazy when you come home.'

'That's true,' said Morgan. 'When I lived at home with my parents, I always used to look forward to the dog rushing up to greet me.'

'Of course I love living with Faye, but there's nothing like coming home to a dog,' said Norman. 'Besides, if Faye started whizzing around, jumping all over me and licking me like a maniac, I'd think there was something wrong with her. I honestly think dogs are great for your mental health, they're an escape from the stresses of the world.'

'I can't argue with that,' said Morgan.

The clearing was carpeted in scrubby grass, nettles and brambles, none of which seemed to be growing particularly well, interspersed with random patches of bare soil.

'There's a distinct path across the middle of this clearing, but it doesn't look as if anyone walks around the perimeter,' said Norman. 'Is that odd, or is it just me?'

'Yeah, but that path is the shortest route from the main car park to the small one,' said Morgan. 'And there are notices in the car parks asking people to keep to the paths.'

'Yeah, I saw the signs,' said Norman. 'But how many people actually follow those rules when they're walking their dogs?'

'I take your point,' said Morgan. 'But it seems they do here for whatever reason.'

They were diagonally opposite the crime scene when Morgan stopped and pointed to the ground. 'Here you go, Norm. You were talking about things that looked odd, well, here's one for a start.'

Norman stared down at the piece of ground she was pointing at and then looked up with a shrug. 'Okay, I give up. What am I looking at?'

Morgan waved her arm around the clearing. 'There are odd-shaped, bare patches all over, right? But none of them are very big.' She indicated the patch of ground before them. 'And then, suddenly, there's this bit. Yes, there are a few blades of grass, and the odd nettle, but if you compare this patch with the rest of the clearing, you can see it's out of keeping. I'm guessing it hasn't been here very long.'

Norman's eyes followed Morgan's pointing finger. 'If you ignore the new growth, you can see there's a patch that's what, six or seven feet long and—'

'Two or three feet wide,' finished Norman. 'Jeez, Catren, I think you could have found another grave.'

'Bloody hell,' said Morgan. 'You think so?'

172

'We can't be sure of anything without digging it up,' said Norman. 'But can you think of any other reason we would find a patch of ground that size out here?'

'We're not going to dig it up, are we?'

'No way,' said Norman. 'If this is a grave, it needs to be excavated properly, by the experts.' He fished his mobile phone from his pocket. 'I'd better call Sarah and see how she wants to play this.'

Two or three minutes later, Norman ended the call and put the phone back in his pocket. Meanwhile, Morgan had wandered off and was standing some fifty or sixty yards further on. She waved at him and pointed to the ground in front of her.

'Holy crap,' muttered Norman. 'Please don't let that be another one.'

He hurried towards her and stopped when he saw what she was pointing at.

'It's not quite as clear,' she said, 'but I think it could be another one.'

Norman stared at the ground for a few seconds then fished his phone from his pocket again.

'I think Catren's found another one. We need to call in the cadaver dogs to go over this whole site.'

* * *

Shortly after lunch, Southall and Norman were in Superintendent Bain's office facing Evans across the desk.

'I've just been informed by HQ that you have requested cadaver dogs. Is that right?'

'Yes, sir, it is,' said Southall.

He glared at her, already red in the face. 'Have you any idea how much using those dogs costs?'

'It was my idea,' said Norman.

Evans stared at Norman.

'I might have known you'd be involved. You seem to enjoy wasting time and money, right, left and centre.'

'Norm made the request after going back over the original crime scene and widening the search area. I authorised it,' said Southall. 'In the circumstances, it was the sensible thing to do.'

'It was a bloody reckless thing to do,' said Evans. 'What on earth were you thinking? And why wasn't I consulted?'

'I can't consult with someone I can't find,' said Southall. 'I had no idea where you were, and as you don't answer your mobile phone, I had to make the decision on my own. Superintendent Bain would have—'

'What Superintendent Bain might or might not have done is hardly the point. Superintendent Bain isn't here,' snapped Evans.

'In similar circumstances, Superintendent Bain would expect me to make a decision, and he would have my back, even if that decision was wrong.'

'That's all well and good for Superintendent Bain, but I'm not him, so don't expect me to carry the can when this goes tits up and the shit comes pouring down from Headquarters.'

'I can assure you I wouldn't expect you to carry a can full of shit, or anything else, on my behalf,' said Southall. 'Sir.'

Evans snorted angrily, clearly unsure how to respond. 'I've already had to stop you blowing the entire year's budget on the remote possibility we have a dead Syrian woman on our hands—'

'There's nothing remote about it,' said Southall. 'As you well know, DNA profiling has already proved beyond reasonable doubt that she's almost certainly from Syria, or at least from that region.'

'In which case she's almost certainly here illegally, so there's more chance of finding Lord Lucan than finding her real identity. And as if that wasn't bad enough, you've now gone over my head and wasted a fortune on cadaver dogs!'

'I'd hardly say it was wasted,' said Norman.

'Oh, wouldn't you?'

'The dogs have already indicated that there is a body at the site DC Morgan identified first, and I'm told there are at least two more probable sites,' said Norman. 'If you ask me, that sounds like money well spent.' Before he could stop it, a "told you so" smirk rose to his lips.

'You think this is funny, do you, Norman?'

'I've never found murder remotely funny,' said Norman. 'And multiple murders are definitely nothing to laugh about. Sir.'

Evans was silent for a moment or two as the implications of what Norman had said began to dawn on him.

'Multiple murders, you say.'

'As in three more than the one we were already dealing with, at the last count,' said Norman. 'And the dogs haven't finished yet.'

Evans turned his attention to Southall. 'Those Pagans visit the site several times a year. Didn't I tell you they were responsible for this mess?'

'Yes, you did tell us, several times,' said Southall. 'But, as I've told you several times, we have no evidence to suggest they have anything to do with the original victim, and we're not going to jump to any conclusions regarding any new victims we might uncover. We don't even have any bodies out of the ground yet.'

'So, what do you think, then?' said Evans. 'Are we dealing with a serial killer?'

'Jeez, she just said we're not jumping to conclusions,' said Norman.

'Are you saying it's not a serial killer?' demanded Evans.

'We're not saying anything at this stage,' said Norman. 'If these three possible bodies turn out to be human remains—'

'What do you mean "if they turn out to be human remains"?'

'What Norm means is that until the graves are excavated and we know for sure, we can't rule out the possibility that these might be pet graves,' said Southall.

Evans looked bewildered.

'Pet graves?'

'Like dogs, buried by their owners in their favourite walking spots,' said Norman.

'Dogs? Buried in the forest? Do people do that sort of thing?'

'I understand scattering their ashes is the usual thing,' said Norman. 'But not everyone likes to cremate their pet.'

'Yes, but is that likely?' asked Evans.

'I'd say probably not,' said Norman. 'But there's no point in assuming they're human remains until we know for sure. I mean, we wouldn't want to waste the budget setting up a murder investigation for a bunch of spaniels, right?'

Evans didn't seem to know how to respond to this and stared balefully at the two detectives, who stared defiantly back at him. Eventually, Evans chose to back down.

'Just remember, Southall, if I see a load of shit heading this way, it's all yours, not mine.'

'Yes, sir,' said Southall. 'You're going to duck any shit coming this way, so it hits me first. I'd already worked that one out and, to be honest, I'd expect nothing less of you. Sir.'

Evans's jaw worked, but he chose to ignore the slight. 'Good. Because you won't be surprised when it happens.'

Evans started to shuffle the papers on his desk while the two detectives exchanged a glance, unsure as to whether the meeting was over. After a while, Evans waved a hand at them, shooing them off.

'Well go on,' he said. 'You'd better go and see what your precious cadaver dogs have found, and I'd rather you didn't waste any more of my budget without my permission.'

As Evans returned to his paperwork, Norman opened his mouth to respond. Mouthing, 'Don't,' Southall shook her head vehemently and made for the door, leaving Norman with little option but to follow.

'Thank you for keeping quiet,' she said as they made their way back down the stairs. 'It's really not worth wasting your energy arguing with him.'

'I can't promise I'll be able to keep my mouth shut much longer,' said Norman. 'I mean, did you hear that? He called it "his" budget. He seems to think he's taken over already.'

'Yes, and did you see his eyes light up when he thought we might have a serial killer on our hands?'

'Yeah, he's not going to complain about costs if we solve that, is he? He'll be too busy basking in the glory.'

'If this is as big as it looks, Norm, we're going to need a lot more staff if we're going to have any chance of solving it.'

Norman guffawed. 'Well, good luck with that. I can't see Superintendent Tight Arse sanctioning that sort of spend. You heard him — it's his budget and we mustn't waste it. He'll be expecting us to solve it on our own, so he can take the credit.'

'It's becoming even more of a "damned if we do and damned if we don't" scenario, isn't it?' said Southall.

As they pushed through the doors into the incident room, Judy Lane called out from her desk. 'It's just been confirmed that they've uncovered a body at the first site. And it's definitely human remains.'

'Right,' said Southall. 'Catren, Frosty, best if we all get out there. Can you hold the fort, Judy?'

'No problem, boss. You get over to that forest. I can handle things here,' said Lane.

* * *

Bill Bridger and his forensic team were already on site by the time the detectives were making their way towards the clearing. Two dog vans were parked at the end of the path, and further ahead cordon tape marked off the crime scene. A uniformed PC waited in front of it with a clipboard and a pile of forensic suits.

As they stopped to sign the clipboard and climb into the suits, they looked across the clearing. Towards the edge, about fifty yards from where the original body was found, they could see Bridger and two of his team working under an open-sided pop-up tent. A second tent was being erected fifty or sixty yards further on. A red and white pole had been stuck into the ground further on and a third tent was just about to be erected above it.

'Looks as if they're pretty evenly spaced over there,' said Morgan, pointing to where the tents were going up.

'Jeez, let's hope that's not a pattern that continues all the way around,' said Norman. 'Because if it is, they're going to find half a dozen more bodies by the time they've finished.'

'I think you can relax on that score,' said Morgan. She nodded to where the two handlers were leading their dogs back to their vans.

Southall lifted the tape and led the team into the clearing. 'Can you have a word with the dog handlers and make sure they're happy they've found all there is to find, Norm?'

'Yeah, sure. I'll catch you up.'

* * *

Southall led the way across to the first tent where Bridger and a technician, both wearing masks, were bent over the grave, painstakingly brushing loose soil away from what were obviously human remains.

As they approached, Bridger looked up at them and raised his mask. 'I'd stop there if I were you. There's a good reason those dogs can find buried bodies.'

'I know,' said Southall with a grimace. 'We can smell it from here.'

'I take it that means this one's still quite fresh,' said Winter.

Bridger managed a faint smile. 'I can see why they say you're an ace detective, Frosty.'

'Sorry,' Winter said sheepishly. 'I suppose it was a bit obvious, wasn't it?'

'I know it's early . . .' began Southall.

'If you're going to ask me to name the cause of death, you haven't got a chance,' said Bridger.

'Actually, I was just going to ask if the body is male or female, and if you have any idea how long it's been there.'

'Going by the height and what remains of the clothes, I'd say female. She's not a child, but neither is she an older

178

person. My best guess at this stage would be mid-teens to late twenties.'

'That's a big window,' said Southall.

'Take it or leave it,' said Bridger. 'I did say it was my best guess, and you know very well you'll get nothing more out of me until she's in the lab.'

Southall poked her tongue out at him. 'Helpful as always, Dr Bridger.'

Bridger grinned in return. 'There you are, impatient as always, Detective Inspector Southall.'

'Are you going to hazard a guess as to how long she's been in the ground?' she asked.

Bridger ruminated for a minute. 'Between two and four months, but that could change once I've taken the weather conditions into consideration.'

'I take it there's no ID?'

'Not so far,' said Bridger. 'Now, I must get on, we've got two more of these to do this afternoon, and I'm sure you'd at least like some preliminary findings sooner rather than later.'

'I'm not going to say no, am I?' said Southall.

'Then you'll be pleased to hear I have called for rein-forcements. But even if they manage to raise a small army of forensic pathologists, don't expect me home for tea.'

'Ha!' said Southall. 'You and me both. I think it could be a long night.'

As she led them away towards the second tent, Norman caught up with them.

'They say there are no more bodies out here, apart from these three,' he said.

'How can they be so sure?' asked Winter.

'Trust me, Frosty, I've seen cadaver dogs at work. They're incredible,' said Norman. 'They never miss a thing.'

'Norm's right,' said Southall. 'If there were any more bodies out here, you can be sure those dogs would have found them.'

'I can't quite see what we're supposed to be doing here,' said Catren Morgan. 'I mean, if there are any clues, they'll be buried along with the bodies, won't they?'

Southall sighed. 'Good question, Catren. I was hoping you'd get to see the dogs in action, but we've got here too late for that. There's not really much we can do until the bodies are out of the ground and we get the pathology and forensic reports. Why don't you and Frosty head back to the office?'

'Fair enough,' said Morgan. 'We can start a search of missing persons and see if anyone matches.'

As they headed back to their cars, Southall turned to Norman.

'I don't know why I brought them out here really,' she said. 'I should have known there wasn't going to be much we could do.'

'Pity they missed seeing the dogs,' said Norman. 'It's not something you see every day. Anyway, what about us, what are we going to do?'

'Let's take a walk, shall we?'

'Anywhere in particular?' asked Norman.

'I'd quite like to see that small car park again.'

Norman couldn't quite see what could be gained by revisiting the smaller car park, but Southall must have had her reasons, so he didn't object. Walking side by side they set off, looking for all the world like two friends out for a stroll rather than detectives on the lookout for clues to multiple murders.

Norman cast a sideways look at his boss, who appeared to be in no hurry to get to the car park. She looked distracted, as if she had something to say but wasn't sure where to begin. It was unlike her to be so reticent, and he found it rather disconcerting.

They continued across the clearing in silence, but by the time they reached the far side, Norman's curiosity had got the better of him. 'Would I be right in thinking the reason for this little stroll isn't strictly case related?'

'What makes you think that?' asked Southall, her gaze on the line of trees just ahead.

'If you have something on your mind,' said Norman, 'you know you can always talk to me — whatever the problem is, even if it's something I've done.'

Finally, Southall turned and looked at him. She was smiling.

'I promise you haven't done anything wrong, Norm. Nor has anyone else.'

'So what is it?'

'I'll tell you in a minute.'

A uniformed PC stood at the end of the path leading to the smaller car park. They ducked under the crime scene tape and continued on for a few more yards before Norman glanced back to where the PC was standing, idly shuffling his feet in the sandy soil.

'Okay. We're far enough away, he can't hear us now,' Norman said. 'So, what's the problem?'

Southall looked at the ground. 'A while back I applied to go on a chief inspectors' course, and I've been accepted.'

'Oh, wow, well done, you! Mind you I'm not surprised. You deserve an opportunity like this after all this time.' He glanced at her again, and saw she was frowning. 'Aren't you happy about it?'

Southall slipped her arm through his and heaved a sigh.

'You're a great friend, Norm. You're always so supportive, no matter what.'

Norman shrugged. 'It works both ways. You do the same for me.'

'I'm not sure I do to the same degree.'

'Are you kidding?' said Norman. 'Just look at my life. I've never been so happy. Me and Faye would never have happened for a start. If it wasn't for you, I'd still be dithering about on my own, frightened to ask her out in case she said no.'

'I suppose that's true,' she said. 'Although I seem to recall Faye didn't take much persuading.'

'Yeah, well, she was clearly overwhelmed by my charisma and sex appeal,' said Norman. 'Let's face it, she didn't stand a chance.'

Southall laughed. 'Are you sure it was that? She told me it was because you were cuddly.'

Norman smiled. 'Yeah, well, it amounts to the same thing, doesn't it?'

They walked on in silence for a minute or two, until they came to a bench at the side of the path.

'Have we got time to share a pew?' asked Southall.

'You're the boss.'

'Come on then. I think we're allowed a few minutes while we're waiting on forensics.'

'Okay,' said Norman, taking his seat beside her. 'Getting back to this course. Surely, career-wise, DCI is the next step, right?'

'Yes, it is, and in different circumstances I'd probably jump at the chance, but the invitation hasn't come from here, it's come from my old boss. I can only do the course if I go back to England.'

'Ah,' said Norman. 'And you don't know if that's what you want to do, right?'

'Would you?'

'Come on, Sarah, no one's going to invite me back, are they? I mean, why would they when they couldn't wait to get rid of me before? Besides, listening to Nathan and following him here was the best decision I ever made. Why would I want to walk away from what I have now?'

'That's more or less what I thought you'd say,' said Southall.

'Hey, wait a minute, my situation has nothing to do with it. You can't possibly compare it to yours. I'm just about ready to retire. You've got years ahead of you yet.'

'Yes, I know all that, and when I took this job, I had every intention of using it to prove a point.'

Norman waited for a few moments. 'I could have sworn there was a "but" coming next.'

Southall sighed.

'Come on then, let's hear it,' said Norman.

'You already know what it is.'

'Do I?'

'Remember you once told me that the first time you crossed the bridge into Wales, you felt like you'd come home.'

Norman smiled at the memory. 'Yeah, that's right. It was weird feeling that way when I'd never been to Wales before, even on a day trip. The thing is, I still feel like that. How long have we been here now? What is it? Three years?'

'It's actually coming up to five,' said Southall.

'Jeez, five years, and I thought it was three. They say time flies when you're enjoying yourself, right? Anyway, my point is this: in those five years I've not been back over that bridge once, and I've not even thought about doing so. In fact, I don't think I ever will. I don't miss it. Not one little bit.'

'Well, that's the thing, see,' said Southall. 'I didn't realise just how happy I am with my job, the team and my home life until I was faced with the prospect of going back and having to give it all up.'

'Yeah, I can relate to that,' said Norman. 'There's something about living here, isn't there. I can't even tell you exactly what it is. I suppose that's because it's a whole bunch of things that come together and kind of creep up on you, and before you know it this place has taken over your heart.'

'You make it sound like a love story,' said Southall.

'But that's exactly what it is,' said Norman. 'I am in love with this place. I wouldn't go back if you paid me.'

They sat in silence for a minute or two.

'Have you discussed this with Bill?' asked Norman.

'You know Bill. He says I should think of my career.'

Norman nodded. 'And what do you think about that?'

'Up until five years ago, I would have agreed with him,' said Southall. 'But now I'm not so sure. Since we've been here, I've got used to having a career and having time for a life as well. The reason my marriage ended in England was because I was always at work. I was never at home when my husband was, and when I was there, I was usually tired and grumpy. We lived separate lives.'

'Been there, done that, got the T-shirt, and the divorce,' said Norman. 'Never again.'

'It certainly helps that Bill's in the same line of business. The fact is, for the first time in my life, I've actually got a pretty good work/life balance.'

Norman smiled. 'Yeah, that's another T-shirt we both have. And I have no intention of losing mine.'

'I don't think I want to lose mine either,' said Southall.

'I sympathise with your dilemma, Sarah, but I can't tell you what you should do, we're too different. I was never interested in climbing ladders. All I ever wanted was to do my job and catch the bad guys.'

'I'm not asking you to tell me what to do, Norm. I just needed to speak to someone in order to help get things clear in my head. And I knew that if I shared it with you, you'd offer your thoughts but wouldn't try to push me in one direction or the other.'

'I like to think that listening is partly what I'm here for,' said Norman. 'But did it actually help?'

'Yes, you've been a great help, far more than you realise.' She leaned over and lightly kissed his cheek. 'Thank you. Now, we'd better get back to the office.'

Norman raised a hand to his cheek. 'Jeez, I hope none of the uniforms saw you do that. We'll be the talk of the town.'

'Ha! We should be so lucky.'

CHAPTER TWELVE

The sun had not yet risen when the team gathered in the incident room for a briefing.

'As you know, living with the district pathologist does give me a certain amount of leverage when it comes to getting quick results,' said Southall. 'Dr Bridger, bless him, has been working all night so I haven't seen him, but we have spoken on the phone. We're meeting at the lab in an hour, but he's been good enough to give us a little preliminary information to be going on with. So, I can tell you that we have three bodies, all female, and all in the same age group — late teens to mid-thirties.'

'We set up a missing persons search late yesterday afternoon,' said Lane. 'We set a radius of fifty miles, missing within six months. There are two women who would have met the criteria, but they're both alive, their whereabouts known, so they're no longer missing.'

'Dr Bridger thinks the bodies were buried at different times,' Southall said. 'He's suggesting the first body they uncovered was buried around two months ago, and the other two at between three- and six-month intervals before that.

185

So, I think we should probably be looking back through mispers as long ago as eighteen months or even two years.'

'Right,' said Lane. 'Consider it done.'

* * *

Bill Bridger, looking utterly exhausted, was waiting for Southall and Norman when they were shown into his lab.

'On your own?' asked Norman. 'I thought you were calling for help.'

'Spending twelve hours poring over bodies in various stages of decay is more than enough for anyone,' said Bridger. 'They've booked into a hotel to get some food and sleep. They'll be back here later today.'

'Does that mean you haven't finished yet?' asked Southall.

'Not completely, no,' said Bridger. 'But I think we've done enough, so far, to give you a good start.'

'Okay,' said Southall. 'So, what have we got?'

'As we have no idea who these three young women are, for the time being we've called them A, B and C, in the order in which they were excavated. Not very imaginative, but then we're scientists, not novelists.

'So, let's start with woman A, found by DC Morgan. We estimate that she was in the ground no more than four to five weeks. Age, between eighteen and twenty-one. Slim build, blonde hair, five feet seven inches tall. We have managed to salvage some clothing, which suggest she was wearing a white T-shirt and blue jeans, but no underwear, along with red and white trainers, size six.' He handed a small, clear evidence bag to Southall. 'We also found these on her.'

Southall held the bag up to the light. 'Gold earrings, and a gold hair clip.'

'I didn't realise it at first,' said Bridger, 'but the grip is actually in the shape of the letter "A".'

'Ah, that could be useful,' said Norman. 'Maybe it's her initial.'

'It could be,' Southall said, and turned back to Bridger. 'Do you have a cause of death?'

'Nothing immediately obvious, but I can tell you it wasn't blunt trauma to the head. Obviously, the body is a little decomposed, so it's difficult to identify bruising or defensive wounds to her hands or arms, but she did sustain two cracked ribs.'

'And what do you conclude from that?' asked Southall.

'It raises the possibility that someone could have been kneeling on her torso, pinning her down while she was being suffocated with a pillow or something similar.'

'Was she raped?' asked Norman.

'Her state of decomposition makes it difficult to determine,' said Bridger. 'But as far as we can tell, no, she wasn't. However, she was sexually active. There again, with no evidence of rape, we can't say if that's relevant to her death.'

'How sure are you that she was suffocated?' asked Norman. 'Only that's quite a specific way of killing someone.'

'That's true,' said Bridger. 'It's what you might call a "softly" violent way of killing someone in that although a certain degree of force is involved, it doesn't always leave obvious traces, unlike strangulation, which usually results in a broken hyoid bone and bruising to the neck. In this case, because she has the damaged ribs and she seems to have been young and fit, and because there are no other signs of damage, it seems the most likely cause of death.'

'So, you think she died in the same way as our first victim?' asked Southall.

'If you mean your mysterious young Syrian woman, I'd say there are definite similarities,' said Bridger.

'This is beginning to look more and more like we have a serial killer at work,' said Norman.

'And I'm afraid the evidence from the other two only adds to that assumption,' said Bridger. 'While victim B's ribs are intact, like victim A she shows no signs of an assault of any kind so, once again, suffocation is a distinct possibility.

Victim C has cracked ribs but no other signs to suggest a violent death.'

'Holy shit!' said Norman. 'I thought I'd left that sort of crap behind when I moved here from England.'

'Can you tell us anything else about the other two victims?' asked Southall.

'Victim B is slightly older. We think she was between twenty-five and thirty, slim build, five feet six inches tall, brown hair, probably buried between six and nine months ago. Her clothing is decayed, but the remnants suggest a blue T-shirt, black trousers and again no underwear. She was also wearing black trainers, size six.

'We think victim C had been in the ground the longest, probably as much as twelve or even eighteen months. Age twenty-one to twenty-five, slim build, five feet eight inches tall. Her hair was fair but shows signs of having been dyed pink.'

'Pink?' said Norman. 'That should help identify her.'

'It might,' said Bridger, 'and another thing that might help is that she was wearing a tracksuit. She had no underwear on, but she was wearing the sort of vest an athlete might wear.'

'You mean like jogging stuff?' asked Southall.

'I'd say she was a bit more serious than that,' said Bridger. 'More like a competitive athlete. I'm not saying she was in the Olympics, but she was possibly serious enough to be a member of an athletic club.'

'That might be useful,' said Norman, 'if only we knew where she came from.'

'I've included photographs of all the clothing and shoe labels in the initial report,' said Bridger. 'I'm hoping we can be of more help when we've done further tests and the DNA samples are analysed. I've told them this is top priority, so hopefully they won't take too long.'

'So, to summarise,' said Norman. 'We have three young women, all aged between eighteen and thirty, all missing their underwear, all killed by suffocation, and all buried in the same area.'

Bridger nodded. 'That's about the size of it.'

'In that case, there's only one conclusion,' said Southall. 'We've got a serial killer on the loose.'

Bridger, who had been shuffling papers around on his desk, finally found what he was looking for. 'I've got one other piece of news for you. This relates to the first body found in the Dragon Forest.'

'Ah, Majhul,' said Southall.

'Yes, that's the one. Remember I said I had found some tears on the sheet? Well, I've got the results back.' He read from the sheet of paper. 'Unfortunately, the tears found on the sheet were not of good enough quality to provide a DNA sample that could be used in a court of law.'

'Oh well, you did say it was a long shot,' said Norman.

'Hold on, I haven't finished yet,' said Bridger. 'The sample wasn't good enough to be used as evidence in court, but it was good enough to suggest that the person who cried onto the sheet wasn't the one who left their blood on the body.'

'So, there was someone else involved,' said Southall.

'That doesn't exactly confirm Jack Foster had nothing to do with her death, or her burial,' said Norman, 'but it definitely backs up his version of events.'

* * *

Southall and Norman had just finished giving Acting Superintendent Evans a summary of the preliminary post-mortem results.

'So, there we are,' said Southall. 'Three more victims in the Dragon Forest.'

'And all disturbingly similar to your original victim,' said Evans. 'I can hardly believe it of a teenager, but there it is.'

'You can't be serious,' said Norman. 'We already told you we don't think Jack Foster killed Majhul, and he certainly didn't seduce these three women, murder them, and bury them.'

'How can you be so sure?' demanded Evans. 'What are the chances that the boy would choose to bury a body where there are already other women buried unless he knew it was a safe hiding place?'

'What? And then takes his friends to his safe hiding place, falls over the body he hasn't yet finished burying and then sends a photograph?' Norman shook his head. 'I mean, if he is a cold-blooded serial killer, like you seem to think, why would he do something as dumb as that?'

'I've already suggested they could all be in it together,' said Evans. 'Or maybe he wanted to show off to his friends. Whatever, it's obvious these women are all victims of the same deranged maniac.'

'Not necessarily,' said Norman.

'Don't tell me you think these crimes aren't related!'

'Not all of them,' said Norman. 'If we just look at the three victims the dogs found, it looks as if the killer likes his victims to be white, young and slim. They all seem to have been sexually active, but there are no signs of rape. They are all dressed, but none have any underwear on. So, what if he seduces them, suffocates them, dresses them again and then buries them?'

'That's exactly what I'm saying,' said Evans. 'And with the original body, that means there are four victims.'

'Yeah, but not all victims of the same killer.'

'Give me one good reason why that should be the case,' said Evans.

'Okay. If the profile of this guy's victims is tall, slim and white, where does a tiny Syrian woman fit in?'

'I'm not convinced these people have a preferred type,' said Evans. 'That's just psychobabble, isn't it? And, even if they do, what if he felt the urge and he couldn't find anyone who was his type? Perhaps this Syrian girl was just in the wrong place at the wrong time.'

'No way,' Norman said. 'It's a fact that most serial killers don't act randomly.'

'And you've investigated so many serial killers you're qualified as an expert, are you?' asked Evans, his voice rising.

'No, I'm not claiming to be an expert,' said Norman. 'But I've read enough books and papers on the subject to know what the consensus is among people who are experts. And this particular guy seems to select victims that he's confident are going to be up for it.'

'And your point is?' said Evans.

'Apart from being the wrong skin colour and having the wrong body type, Majhul was still a virgin,' said Norman. 'She wouldn't have been willing to be seduced.'

'You can't possibly know that,' said Evans. 'Maybe she was all for it, then changed her mind, and that's why he killed her. Perhaps she resisted and he lost it.'

'She wasn't even close to being his type, and there is no evidence to suggest she was subjected to a frenzied attack,' said Norman. 'I just can't see it happening that way.'

'Perhaps you just don't want to see it that way because I suggested it,' said Evans.

Norman looked at Southall. 'Did he really just say that?' Turning back to Evans, he said, 'Four young women are dead, and you want to make this about me not liking you? Are you serious?'

Evans looked distinctly uncomfortable. 'Of course that's not what I want. Nevertheless, I think you're making this more complicated than it needs to be. You need to stop ignoring the obvious link between the four victims.'

For a moment Norman looked as though he was going to explode.

'If you mean the Dragon Forest, that's not the link, it's a coincidence,' said Norman tightly. 'The link is that the guy picks victims he knows he can seduce.'

'Well, I'm afraid I disagree,' said Evans. 'What about you, Southall? Don't you have an opinion?'

'I think Norm's theory makes a lot of sense and shouldn't be ignored,' said Southall, diplomatically. 'And as it's his theory, I think he should be allowed to explain it himself, without my interference.'

'This guy is a smooth operator who seduces young women,' said Norman. 'They trust him enough that they're willing to get naked for him and have sex with him. But once he's had the sex, things change, and he suffocates them.'

'But didn't the pathologist say there was no indication of any violent assault? How do you explain that if he turns on them after sex?'

'I think there's no sign of a violent struggle for two possible reasons. First, because the bodies have been dead for so long, decomposition has removed any bruising from the skin. Second, because the victims trust this guy so much, they end up sleeping next to him. He smothers them with a pillow while they're asleep. Yeah, they'll wake up, but if he's already got them pinned down there's nothing they can do.'

'Well, there you are then,' said Evans in exasperation. 'The Syrian girl was naked when she was found, wasn't she?'

'But that's what I'm saying,' said Norman. 'He gets his victims naked, has sex with them, kills them while they're asleep, then dresses them, keeping their underwear as a trophy. So, if the same guy killed all four, why didn't he dress Majhul? Why alter his ritual in her case?'

'Ritual? What makes you think it's a ritual?'

'Because, for people like him, the whole thing is about ritual,' said Norman. 'Dressing a dead body is bloody hard work. He wouldn't do it if it wasn't important to him, and that means it would be too important to not do it. Likewise, choosing victims he believes he can seduce is another part of the ritual. Jeez, the whole seduction probably follows some sort of ritual. A random Syrian teenager who is a virgin just doesn't fit that profile.'

'You're convinced this is just a one-man operation, are you?' said Evans.

'It would be easier for two people to dress and dispose of a body,' said Norman, 'but our man wants to be in control. This whole thing is about control. Involving another person would mean losing that control.'

'So, you're suggesting it's all about rituals,' said Evans.

'For this guy, definitely.'

'In that case I'd like to remind you that we have a whole group of people who, we know for a fact, love a good ritual.'

Norman rolled his eyes. 'Oh, no. You're not going to start banging that Pagan drum again, are you?'

'Why not?' said Evans.

'Because the rituals they follow are a whole different type of ritual. They're nothing like the compulsions of a psychopath.'

'But look at the burial dates. They seem to be between three and six months apart, and those Pagans celebrate every three months. It must be them. It's obvious!'

'You can't say the burials happened every three months on the dot,' said Norman. 'The pathologist says there's a three-month window around each of the burial dates. Anyway, the other day you said it was obvious that Jack Foster was the murderer. Or are you now going to suggest he's in league with the Pagans?'

'Never mind Jack Foster. You check those burial dates against the Pagan celebrations,' said Evans. 'You'll see I'm right.'

Becoming more and more frustrated with Evans's refusal to let go of his Pagans theory, Norman knew that if he didn't walk away now, he was going to blow a fuse. He made a show of checking his wristwatch.

'I need to be somewhere,' he said.

'Oh yes, you'd better be off, or you'll be late,' said Southall, who had detected Norman's mounting anger. 'Tell Faye good luck from me.'

Norman just about managed to hide his surprise as he turned and walked away.

Evans turned to Southall. 'What was that all about? He can't start an argument with me and then just walk out like that.'

'DS Norman's partner has a hospital appointment, and she requested that he be there to support her, sir,' lied Southall. 'I think he should be there for her. I think it's important we look after our families, don't you?'

'Er, yes, I see. Well, in that case I suppose—'

193

'Norm works very hard, sir,' said Southall. 'And he rarely takes time off. Besides I know he'll make up for any lost time, and then some.'

'Yes, well, just make sure he does,' said Evans. 'And perhaps you could point out to him that I am the senior officer around here now, and I would appreciate it if he showed me the respect my position and experience deserves.'

'I'm sure Norm didn't mean any disrespect, sir. He's just very passionate about catching the killer.'

'And you think I'm not?' said Evans. 'At the moment DS Norman is pushing his luck, and I suggest you make it clear to him that I won't stand for it. Is that clear?'

'Crystal clear, sir,' said Southall.

Evans looked at the clock on the wall. 'Now, I'm afraid I must go too. I have an appointment at HQ.'

'Is this about our staffing level?' asked Southall. 'We'll need a lot more bodies if we're going to find a serial killer.'

'Er, right, I'll see what I can do,' said Evans, gathering bits of paperwork and stuffing them into his briefcase. 'It's not the main reason I'm going, but I'll certainly bring it to their attention. I'll probably be out for the rest of the day, and while I'm away, I suggest you follow up about the Pagans and those dates. And make sure you speak to DS Norman when he comes back.'

'Yes, sir, of course, sir,' said Southall.

* * *

Southall closed the door to Evans's office and made her way slowly down to the incident room, wondering how she was going to manage the friction between Norman and Evans. She understood perfectly just how annoying Evans was, but it wasn't her job to be playing peacemaker all the time. Somehow, Norm was just going to have to find a way to deal with it.

'Right,' she said as she pushed her way through the doors into the incident room, 'I'm sure you've all had time to read the preliminary forensic report, so you'll be aware it appears we have a serial killer burying bodies in the Dragon Forest.'

'What about Majhul?' asked Judy Lane. 'Is she one of his victims?'

'Norm thinks not, and I agree with him,' said Southall.

'Is it someone we've already spoken to?' asked Winter.

'Of course, anything's possible at this stage, but there's nothing to suggest that's the case. In fact, it seems likely that the cases are not linked.'

'Really?' asked Morgan. 'You think it's a coincidence that four victims have been killed in the same way, their bodies buried within yards of each other, and they're not connected? I thought you guys didn't believe in coincidences.'

'Well, in this case we have compelling reasons for making an exception to that rule,' said Southall. 'We think Majhul is not connected to the other three, but they are linked to one another.'

'Why not all four?' asked Winter.

'Think about it,' said Southall. 'Three bodies have lain there for months without anyone noticing, but Majhul is found within a couple of days of being buried. Three victims are white, tall and slim. Majhul is none of those things.'

'Norm did mention that he thought the intention may have been for Majhul to be found,' said Morgan.

'Which rather proves the point,' said Southall. 'There was no way the other three bodies would have been found if it wasn't for a sharp-eyed detective and a pair of cadaver dogs.'

Morgan beamed at the compliment. 'It was Norm's idea to walk the clearing.'

'Yes, but he tells me he didn't think he'd have spotted the grave,' said Southall. 'That was down to you, so well done, Catren.'

'So, what are we looking for?' asked Winter.

'Okay, based on one or two assumptions, we think the man we are looking for is a bit of a charmer who seduces his victims, sleeps with them and then smothers them while they're asleep. Then he dresses them minus their underwear and buries them.'

'What's with the underwear?' asked Morgan. 'Trophies?'

'That's my guess,' said Southall. 'And wherever he's doing this, it must be somewhere private where a body can be moved without anyone noticing.'

'So, we could be looking for someone with his own pad,' said Winter. 'Somewhere warm and cosy.'

'Yes, that's a strong possibility,' said Southall.

'So where do we start looking?' asked Winter.

'That's a good question,' said Southall. 'And to be honest, I'm not sure. If the girls haven't been reported missing within fifty miles, it suggests they're not from around here, but the killer is, and brings them back here. But if the girls are from miles away, how does he persuade them to come here with him?'

'Perhaps he plays a long game,' suggested Lane. 'Maybe he spends weeks gaining their confidence before he strikes.'

'An HGV driver might be in a position to do something like that,' suggested Winter. 'Especially if he had a regular run. You know, if you were going to the same places every week, you could easily strike up a relationship along the way. It wouldn't be the first time, would it?'

'That's a definite possibility,' said Southall, 'but it would help if we could identify at least one of the victims. Judy? I take it you've had no luck with missing persons?'

'Sorry. Even with the additional details from the report, I've still got nothing,' said Lane. 'We'll have to go wider, but how far do you want me to go?'

'I think you should try the entire UK,' said Southall.

'I'll set it up now,' said Lane.

'Before we get into anything, I need one of you to do something for me,' said Southall.

'I'll do it,' said Morgan.

'It's to humour Superintendent Evans,' said Southall.

Morgan's face fell. 'Oh. Really?'

'It'll get him off my back for a few days,' said Southall.

'Oh, I see. In that case, what do you need me to do?' said Morgan.

'He has a theory that the deaths are linked to the Pagans. So, I need you to see if the burial dates coincide with the dates of the Pagan ceremonies.'

'I can do it, but the trouble is they're bound to coincide,' said Morgan. 'The burial dates have three-month windows so it would be almost impossible for them not to.'

'Yes, I know,' said Southall. 'The thing is, Superintendent Evans isn't going to stop going on about the Pagans being there each time one of the victims was buried until he understands how unlikely it is, so I want your comparison to make it very clear.'

'Ah, I see what you mean. That shouldn't be too hard to do,' said Morgan. 'I'll get onto it now.'

'Frosty,' said Southall. 'As you were the first one to mention HGV drivers, can you check the list of Pagans to see if that's what any of them does for a living? That should pre-empt the next instruction from above.'

'Sure,' said Winter.

Once everyone was busy, Southall went to her office and called Norman.

'Yo,' said Norman. 'What's up, boss?'

'Are you okay?'

'I'm sorry, I just had to get out before I lost it with that idiot.'

'Just in case he asks, I told him you had to take Faye to the hospital.'

'You didn't need to do that, Sarah.'

'Yes, I did,' said Southall. 'But I won't do it again. You must find a way of dealing with him, Norm. You're going to push it too far if you're not careful.'

'So, what's he going to do, fire me? I'm close to retiring anyway.'

'It's not just about you,' said Southall. 'I'm not prepared to keep on being piggy-in-the-middle while you two argue all the time. Remember that offer I told you about? If this is how it's going to be working here, I might be persuaded to accept it.'

'No, please don't do that,' said Norman in alarm. 'I'll find a way. I'll fix it. I promise.'

'Where are you?'

'In the car park. I'm just coming in.'

CHAPTER THIRTEEN

Thursday, 14 November, 08.00

'I think we've got an ID for one of our victims,' said Lane, studying her computer screen. 'Her name is Abigail Ross, aged nineteen, from Nottingham. Five feet seven inches tall, slim, blue eyes, long blonde hair.'

'That sounds like a possible,' said Norman.

'I think she's better than a possible,' said Lane. 'According to this description, she was wearing a gold hairgrip in the shape of the letter "A". It was given to her by her grandmother before she died, and she always wore it.'

'That's too much of a coincidence,' said Southall. 'It must be our victim A. What else does it say?'

'Her father last saw her when he dropped her off near the Victoria Embankment in Nottingham at seven a.m. on Saturday, twenty-eighth September. She was wearing her running gear, but was carrying a brown bag with a change of clothes.'

'Does it say what the clothes in the bag were?'

'Her mother thinks it was jeans and a T-shirt.'

'Isn't that an early start for a teenager on a Saturday?' said Norman. 'Or am I even more out of touch than I thought?'

'She was going to run in the Robin Hood Half Marathon,' said Lane. 'It starts at nine thirty. She was running to raise money for a local cancer charity which had looked after her grandmother before she died.'

'Sounds as though she was close to her grandmother,' said Norman. 'That'll explain why she always wore the hair grip.'

'We know she finished the race at twelve fifty-five, but after that it gets a bit vague. A witness thinks he might have seen her talking to one of the male runners, but he's not sure and couldn't describe the man. Someone else thinks they may have seen a young woman with long blonde hair walking off with a man, but he only saw their backs.'

'That's not really much help,' said Norman. 'It could have been any young blonde walking off with a guy.'

'As I said, it all gets a bit vague,' said Lane. 'I mean, just think how many runners must have been milling around after that race.'

'In fact there were twelve thousand runners at this year's race, raising close to half a million pounds for various charities,' said Morgan. 'I just looked it up.'

'Yeah, you could get lost in that big a crowd all right,' said Norman.

'Or disappear in it,' said Southall. 'If we're thinking this man has spent weeks winning her trust, maybe she was planning to run off with him.'

'That's a good point,' said Norman. 'And it could explain why her body showed no signs of a struggle.'

'Dr Bridger thinks she was buried four or five weeks ago,' said Morgan. 'So, if she disappeared on the twenty-eighth of September, that means she could have been brought back here and buried that same weekend.'

Southall turned to Winter. 'Frosty, see if you can find any haulage companies based within twenty miles of the Dragon Forest that travel to and from Nottingham on a regular basis, or might have been in that area at the right time.'

Winter nodded and turned to his computer.

'Norm, can you keep the wheels turning in here?' said Southall. 'I'd better phone our colleagues in Nottingham and tell them we think we've found Abigail Ross. Maybe they'll have made some progress since the possible last sightings.'

Southall had just gone into her office when Lane called out, 'I think I might have found another one.'

'In Nottingham?' Norman asked.

'No, this one disappeared from Hastings on the South Coast. Her name is Jessica Jordan, twenty-eight years old, slim build, five feet six inches tall.'

'Anything else?' asked Norman.

'That's about it,' said Lane.

'That's it?' asked Norman. 'We get all that detail from Nottingham, and zilch from Sussex. Jeez, talk about inconsistencies in the system!'

'It seems Sussex police aren't so keen for everyone to know how their missing persons cases are going,' Lane said.

'Is there a contact number for whoever is in charge of the case?' Norman asked.

'It's being printed right now,' said Lane.

Norman collected the printout, settled at his desk and dialled the number.

'DS Alisson.'

'Hi, this is DS Norman from Llangwelli station in Wales. I understand you're running a missing person case for a Jessica Jordan.'

'Ah, she's turned up, has she?' asked Alisson. 'I had a feeling she was just a runaway trying to get away from her parents.'

'She may well have been a runaway,' said Norman, 'but I'm afraid she won't be running anywhere again.'

'What's that mean?'

'It means we've found a body,' said Norman.

There was a muffled curse. 'She hasn't topped herself, has she?'

'Our pathologist thinks not,' said Norman. 'It looks as if she was smothered with a pillow or something, and then buried in a shallow grave.'

'How long had she been in Wales?'

'Forensics are saying she was buried not long after you first posted her missing.'

'And you've sat on her body all this time?'

'Of course not,' said Norman. 'We've only just found her grave. There was no ID on her, and after six months or so underground, her face wasn't exactly recognisable. So, we've resorted to going through mispers, and Jessica's description fits the bill. We'll need a DNA sample to confirm it, of course, but we think it's her.'

'We've got a sample here, just in case,' said Alisson. 'But I never thought we'd have to use it. My theory was that she came down here to college to get away from her parents, and having tasted a bit of freedom, she decided she wanted more. Even though she's a bit older than the average runaway, I really thought that's what she had done. If you met her parents, you'd understand why. I'm sure they mean well, but Christ, talk about overprotective! If they were my parents, I think I'd be doing life by now.'

'Is that right?' said Norman. 'Well, whatever they're like, I hope you're going to be a little more sympathetic when you tell them their daughter's dead.'

'What? Well, yeah, of course. I didn't mean . . . they're nice enough in their way, I suppose. It's not as if they knocked her around or anything.'

'Look, I'm sorry. That was way out of line,' said Norman. 'I have no right to—'

'No, you're right, mate, it's me who's out of line. I'm sure her parents were doing their best to keep her safe, and it's not very respectful of me, is it? I'm just disappointed to hear she's dead. After all this time I was hoping she'd settled somewhere and made a new life for herself.'

'So, what can you tell me about her,' asked Norman, 'and when she disappeared?'

'Hang on a tick. Let me get the report.' There was a crackle as Alisson put down the receiver, followed by the sound of fingers tapping a keyboard, then he was back on the line. 'Right, here we are. Jessica Jordan, twenty-eight years old, slim build, five feet six inches tall. Was studying for a Higher National Diploma at Sussex Coast College in Hastings. Went missing sometime between seventeenth and thirty-first March this year.'

'So, seven months ago, and our pathologist reckons she had been between six and nine months in the ground,' said Norman. 'That's why we think she's a good fit. Your date for when she went missing isn't very precise, though. Is there a reason for having such a big window?'

'Let me see now, what's the report say . . . ah, here we are. She was a student, bit of a loner, no close friends, lived alone in a bedsit. Last seen at college during week ending seventeenth March. Wasn't missed at college after that because it was closed for the Easter break. She also had a part-time job in a cafe, but she only worked there during term time. The owner said she was a good worker, got on well with the customers but kept herself to herself and didn't share anything about her private life. Everyone assumed she had gone home to Cambridge for Easter until her parents contacted us just after Easter to say they had been expecting her, but she hadn't turned up and they hadn't heard from her.'

'It's always easier when people have friends,' said Norman. 'They can usually give some sort of insight into where a missing person might be, or what their state of mind was, so at least you have somewhere to start. You don't get that with a loner, unless they leave a clue for you to find.'

'I'm afraid Jessica didn't leave a single clue for us to find,' Alisson said, 'unless you count taking nothing with her as a clue.'

'Now that, in itself, could be a clue to one of two things,' began Norman.

'Yeah, we know,' said Alisson. 'Either she was abducted, or she was intending to commit suicide. Except there was nothing to suggest she had been abducted, and there was no evidence that pointed to her being depressed, although having said that, no one seems to have known her very well, so the chances are we wouldn't have known anyway.'

'I'm guessing it's no longer an active case,' said Norman.

'It's not closed officially, but it's more or less gone cold by now, so we've scaled it right down. You know what it's like — too many cases, not enough staff and no money to spend on something as insignificant as a missing person. Especially a missing adult who we suspect doesn't want to be found. She's still on file as missing, but presumed to have either run away, or committed suicide.'

'Could I have a copy of that file?' asked Norman. 'Or are you not allowed to share stuff with other forces?'

'I don't go in for all that political bollocks,' said Alisson. 'If you ask me, solving crimes is much more important than that kind of crap. I'll email a copy to you. I'll sort out that DNA sample too.'

'That would be great,' said Norman. 'Being a DS yourself, you'll know it's a decision that's way above my pay grade, but I think you're probably going to have to bring that case out of cold storage, warm it up, and change it to a murder investigation.'

'Is that going to be ours, yours, or shared?' asked Alisson.

'I'm guessing it will be ours as we've got the body,' said Norman. 'But again, that decision—'

'Is way beyond your pay grade,' finished Alisson. 'Yeah, mine too. I'd like to know what happened, though. I spent months looking for her before we gave up. If that DNA sample proves you're right, I hope that means the parents won't have to go through the agony of formally identifying her.'

'I don't think there would be much point in them coming to look at her,' said Norman. 'As you can imagine, she's not going to be in any recognisable kind of state. I mean I haven't got one, but if I had, I wouldn't want to see my daughter after she'd been decomposing for six months.'

'If it needs doing, maybe I could,' said Alisson. 'Or there's a sister. She's made of much sterner stuff than the parents. I'll see if I can persuade her to do the identification.'

'I'm pretty sure the coroner would accept the DNA evidence as proof enough,' said Norman. 'There again, if she and the parents want to come, we can't stop them. I just wouldn't advise it.'

'I'll do my best to put them off,' said Alisson. 'I might come down myself if I can persuade my boss. Just to see the burial site like. Try to find some closure for the parents. That sort of thing.'

'Let me know if you do,' said Norman. 'I'll be happy to share what we know if it'll help them deal with it.'

* * *

'Right, then.'

Back from her call to Nottingham, Southall was standing at the board pointing to the photographs of the two newly identified victims. 'We can see they're both young, fit and attractive, which gives them something in common, but Abigail was last seen in Nottingham—' she pointed to the map Judy Lane had put up — 'and Jessica was last seen in Hastings. These places are two hundred miles apart. We know they're linked by the burial site, but what enabled our killer to meet them both?'

'Are we assuming they weren't abducted, but came here willingly?' asked Morgan.

'We can't rule it out, but we have no evidence to suggest they were forcibly abducted,' said Southall.

'So, what are we saying?' asked Morgan. 'That these young women were desperate to come to Wales? And why not come on a train like everyone else?'

'I don't think it's quite that black and white,' said Norman. 'And, much as I can understand why people want to come here, I doubt they were coming on a visit.'

'So why come here, then?' asked Morgan.

'I think if we focus on the fact that they end up here, we're missing the point,' said Norman. 'The reason he brings them back here is because he knows he can hide the bodies in the forest and they won't be found.'

'I'm confused,' said Lane. 'Didn't you say you thought Majhul was supposed to be found?'

'That's right,' said Norman. 'But remember, I also said I think her death has nothing to do with the others. It was an unfortunate coincidence that led us to discover the three other bodies.'

'I think what Norm is suggesting is that our killer is an opportunist,' said Southall. 'He kills his victims where he finds them and then brings them down here to bury them.'

'You think he seduces them?' asked Morgan.

'Could be,' said Southall. 'Or at least he befriends them and offers them something they find hard to resist. That could be sex, or an escape from a dull life . . . There could be any number of reasons.'

'There we are then,' said Winter, decisively. 'It's an HGV driver, it's got to be. Or, at the very least, someone working for a delivery service.'

'If you're talking parcels, they tend to be mostly local,' said Morgan.

'Yeah, but they have central hubs, don't they?' said Winter. 'Someone has to collect the parcels from there.'

'Okay, so that would need an HGV,' agreed Morgan. 'But don't those guys tend to do the same routes?'

'Yeah, true,' said Winter. 'But there must be spare drivers who cover holidays. One of them would be doing different routes all the time.'

'That's all very well,' said Norman. 'But how does an HGV driver meet them both? I can see how he might meet Jessica if he stopped for a meal in the cafe where she worked, but what about Abigail?' He turned to Southall. 'Didn't you say she was a nurse?'

Southall nodded. 'Yes, that's right. Nottingham City Hospital.'

'Maybe he had to go to A & E, and he met her there,' said Winter.

'Good theory, Frosty,' said Southall. 'But I'm afraid Abigail worked in the Maternity Unit.'

'Maybe someone he knew had a baby,' said Winter, sounding slightly desperate.

'You keep clutching at those straws, don't you, Frosty,' said Morgan.

Lane gave Winter a sympathetic smile. 'Never mind, you can't win them all.'

'Yeah, I know you're right really,' said Winter. 'When I was checking out the haulage companies, the one thing I noticed was that nearly all the drivers seemed to have set routes every week and, from what I could see none of them goes all over the UK.'

'It can't be a random thing, can it?' asked Morgan.

'With them all being buried in the same place? No chance,' said Norman. 'I reckon we're looking at a one-man operation, and it's one man who either lives in this area or knows it really well. But my money is on someone local. This is the place he always comes back to, and he brings his victims' bodies with him.'

'How local?' asked Winter.

'I'm thinking within fifty miles,' said Norman, 'but probably even closer.'

'Oh, that's all right, then,' said Morgan. 'That means we've only got about a hundred thousand men to choose from.'

'Only if all of them like to travel up and down the UK,' said Norman. 'We're looking for someone who has reason to travel around, and it doesn't have to be for business. Don't forget, people travel to shows, events and all sorts.'

'And remember, we think this guy travels alone, but sometimes comes home with a body,' said Southall.

After another hour of discussion, they were getting nowhere fast.

'I think we're going about this whole thing arse about face,' said Norman. 'Wouldn't it be better to try and find something that links Abigail and Jessica?'

'You're right,' said Southall. 'Start with social media.'

'But won't that have been done when they went missing?' asked Winter.

'Yes,' said Southall, 'but they would have been looking at each one of them separately.'

CHAPTER FOURTEEN

Friday, 15 November, 07.30

Southall pulled up alongside Norman in the car park.

'Early start for you too, Norm? They say great minds think alike.'

'I don't feel like I have a great mind,' said Norman wearily. 'I hardly slept at all for thinking about those missing links. In the end I thought I might as well get up and come in a bit earlier.' He looked at the other cars parked nearby. 'Looks as if the rest of the team had the same idea.'

Southall had noticed them too. 'They were still here when we left last night. You'd think they hadn't gone home at all.'

As they pushed through the doors into the incident room, Judy Lane was adding information to the board, while Winter and Morgan were comparing notes.

'Have you three been here all night?' asked Southall.

Lane smiled. 'Not quite, but we did stay long enough to achieve what we think is a breakthrough.'

'Tell me more,' said Southall.

'Catren spotted it first,' said Lane, 'so I think she should explain it.'

Southall and Norman turned to Morgan.

'Frosty and I were looking at social media,' explained Morgan. 'As you'd expect, both Abigail and Jessica are on all the usual channels, and it was no surprise to find they have no common friends since they live two hundred miles apart. They do follow some of the same people on TikTok, YouTube and Instagram, but these are the type of well-known stars that thousands of others follow, and who are unlikely to be a serial killer. We figured it was more likely to be someone a bit more niche, but we were still getting nowhere, until Frosty started to look at podcasts—'

'Podcasts?' said Norman.

'Yeah, you know, it's where people talk, and listeners subscribe to hear more and become followers.'

'I know how podcasts work,' said Norman. 'I just didn't think you would find a common link there.'

'Well, there's this guy who's on TikTok and YouTube, and each of the women follows him on one or the other of those, but it's the podcast that links them both.'

'Who is this man, and what's the podcast?' asked Southall.

'He calls himself the "Half Harrier," and the podcast is called *Cool Running*,' said Morgan. 'Basically, it's just a guy talking about running.'

'And people actually listen to that?' asked Norman.

'He's got a couple of thousand followers,' said Morgan. 'It's not mega, but then he's not a big star, and it is a bit of a niche topic.'

'I listened to a couple of episodes last night,' said Winter. 'It's probably quite good if you're into that sort of thing.'

'And the guy has the sort of voice your average woman could listen to all night,' said Morgan. 'I reckon if he hit on me, I'd be hard pushed to resist.'

'Yeah, but then you are the adventurous type,' said Winter.

'There's nothing wrong with being adventurous, Frosty,' said Morgan.

'Actually, Catren's right,' said Lane. 'The guy has the sort of dreamy voice that might be irresistible, especially if you were a bit lonely.'

Winter looked shocked. 'Really? You too?'

'I said "if I was a bit lonely", but I'm not, am I?' said Lane pointedly.

Winter suddenly found something terribly important in his notes.

'Let's not get off topic,' said Southall. 'Tell me more about this man.'

'From what I can see, the reason he calls himself the Halfway Harrier is because he specialises in half marathons, and he travels all over the UK to compete in them. According to his blurb, he does it to raise money for various charities. But — get this — he also encourages other runners to team up with him at events!'

'Do we know his real name and where he's based?' asked Southall.

'Not yet,' said Morgan. 'He's a bit vague about that stuff, but we're working on it.'

'Do we know how he hooks up with other runners?' asked Norman.

'At the end of every podcast he mentions a website where you can send him a message.'

'Abigail was last seen at the Robin Hood Half Marathon on the twenty-eighth September,' Lane reminded them all. 'And there's a possible sighting of her speaking to one of the runners after the event.'

'Was he there?' asked Norman.

'He has a calendar of events on his website, and it's listed on there,' said Lane. 'But the list has been copied from another website, so there's no guarantee it's his personal event list.'

'That's great work,' said Southall, 'but I don't think it's enough, unless we can prove he was at that event, and that he met Abigail there.'

'And at best it's a tenuous link to Jessica,' said Norman. 'There was no mention of her being into running.'

'Maybe she was, but the Hastings police just didn't think it was relevant,' said Southall. 'Don't forget they didn't know what we now know, and she did follow this Harrier person.'

'Now that is a very good point,' said Norman. 'And it wouldn't hurt to give them a call and ask, would it?'

* * *

'DS Alisson.'

'Oh, hi, it's DS Norman down at Llangwelli.'

'Have you called to tell me you know who killed Jessica?'

'I wish,' said Norman. 'I was hoping you might be able to fill a couple of gaps for me.'

'Of course, if I can. Have you got a lead?'

'We think we're making progress, but you know what it's like — you think you've got a good lead, you spend days and weeks following it and then it fizzles out to nothing and you're back where you started.'

'Tell me about it,' said Alisson. 'Anyway, what can I help you with?'

'Do you know if Jessica was into sports?'

'Was she into sports?'

'Yeah. To be more specific, was she into running?'

'You mean was she an athlete, as in taking part in races?'

'Not necessarily competitively,' said Norman. 'We're thinking more sort of fun run for charity type events. You know the sort of thing, five K, ten K, half marathons . . .'

'I can tell you for a fact that she didn't do anything like that. Her mother said she was asthmatic when she was little and never got into sports. And we didn't find any sports gear when we searched her rooms.'

'Crap,' said Norman. 'That's another bright idea crushed before it even got off the ground.'

'Hang on a minute,' said Alisson. 'She didn't participate, but she could have been a spectator.'

'You reckon?'

'Well, put it this way, we found leaflets for several events like the ones you mentioned. They were all in this part of Sussex. I'm sure there were a couple of programmes from athletic meetings too. Is that any help?'

'You know, it just might be,' said Norman.

'But you're not going to tell me why, are you?' asked Alisson.

'You know how it works,' said Norman. 'It's just a theory right now, but I promise, you'll be the first to know if it does turn out to be something concrete.'

'Yeah, right,' said Alisson. 'As you said, I know how it works.'

Norman was just going to thank him again when Alisson put the phone down.

'Suit yourself,' muttered Norman.

'Any help?' asked Southall.

'I think we might have a winner,' said Norman. 'Jessica wasn't a runner, but she was a keen spectator, or perhaps a wannabe runner. Apparently, she had leaflets for fun runs in the local area.'

'I'm sure I saw something about a Hastings Half Marathon on that events calendar,' said Lane. She consulted her notes. 'Here we are. Hastings Half Marathon, twenty-fourth March 2024.'

'And Jessica disappeared between the seventeenth and the thirty-first,' said Morgan. 'What if she had been in touch with this half marathon guy and they arranged to meet?'

'It makes sense,' said Norman. 'And it would explain why she never made it home for Easter.'

CHAPTER FIFTEEN

Friday, 15 November, 10.30

Lane raced back to her desk and grabbed the phone before it stopped ringing.

'DC Lane.'

'This is DS Carragher from Formby police station, near Liverpool.'

'How can I help?' asked Lane.

'I'd like to speak to the person who sent out a bulletin about an unidentified body.'

'You're speaking to her,' said Lane.

'Ah, right. Well, I think I might know who your body is. To be honest, it nearly passed us by, but a sharp-eyed sergeant was reading through the daily bulletins and saw the part about pink hair. We had a young woman go missing in May 2023 who liked to dye her hair bright pink.'

Lane nearly squealed in excitement. She had posted the bulletin more in hope than expectation. 'Does she fit the rest of the description?'

'Twenty-three years old, five feet eight inches tall, blue eyes and fair hair dyed a lurid shade of pink. I'd say that was close enough, wouldn't you, DC Lane?'

'Let me put you through to DI Southall, she's leading this case.'

* * *

Fifteen minutes later, Southall called everyone together again.

'I believe we now know the identity of the third victim recovered from the clearing.' She pinned a photograph to the board. 'This is Ruby Hunter from Formby, near Liverpool. Her description fits the profile put together by Dr Bridger, and she was last seen on the seventh of May 2023. That's eighteen months ago, which is a perfect fit for when Dr Bridger estimates she was buried.'

'Do we know where she was when she was last seen?' asked Norman.

'The Aintree Half Marathon took place on Sunday, seventh May 2023,' said Southall. 'Ruby's finish was officially timed at twelve fifty-eight. After that she seems to have vanished.'

'That's too many coincidences to be anything but a match,' said Norman.

'They're sending a DNA sample to confirm it, but as you say, everything points to this being our third victim.'

'Unless there are more victims we don't know about,' said Morgan.

'That's a possibility I'd rather not consider at the moment, so let's not go there,' said Southall. 'We can only deal with those victims we know about.'

'There is one thing we do know for sure,' said Norman. 'Evans will have to stop insisting that Jack Foster is our serial killer. He wasn't even driving eighteen months ago, so there's no way he could have abducted someone from Liverpool.'

'What's the betting he's still gunning for the Pagans,' said Morgan.

'Yes, well, let me worry about that,' said Southall. 'Right now, I want you guys to concentrate on identifying the man in the podcast. Yes, we may be able to link all three victims to our killer, but if we can't identify him, we're still nowhere.'

'What about Majhul?' asked Lane.

'If you can link her too, all well and good,' said Southall, 'but I would focus on finding that man first.'

'No, I meant what about her?' said Lane. 'It seems as if she's been forgotten, now that we have three white victims.'

Southall's face darkened. 'I'll pretend I didn't hear that, Judy. I haven't forgotten Majhul at all, but perhaps you have forgotten that we were getting nowhere with her investigation. Every avenue we explored led us to a dead end, and unless we can get permission to take our search beyond the UK, I suspect that's how it will stay. Whereas we know the identities of the other three victims, we know when they were last seen, and we think we know why they're dead. So, until Acting Superintendent Evans produces the additional staff I've requested, I have to use our meagre resources in the best and most effective way I can. Bearing that lack of manpower in mind, if you were wearing my shoes, where would you focus our attention?'

The icy silence that followed seemed to last an age.

'I'm sorry,' said Lane. 'I didn't mean to speak out of turn—'

'But you did speak out of turn,' said Southall. 'And, frankly, I'm disappointed that you thought it necessary.'

Southall stared hard at Lane for a moment, and then turned and headed back to her office.

* * *

A while later, Norman peered into Southall's office.

'Knock, knock.'

Southall looked up.

'Can I come in?' asked Norman.

'The door is open,' said Southall.

'Yeah, I can see that, but if you're still in the mood for a fight, I'll come back later.'

Southall tried to look stern, but the corners of her mouth twitched upward.

'That was an hour ago,' she said. 'And anyway, that's not fair. Judy was way out of line—'

'Yeah, and doesn't she know it,' said Norman.

'Well, I'm sorry if she's upset, but I'm not having my integrity questioned like that.'

Norman raised his hands in surrender. 'Hey, look, I'm on your side. I've had a quiet word with her, and I can assure you she's mortified at the thought of having upset you.'

'I hope you haven't come in here to try to smooth things over—'

'It's not my argument, and I'm not getting involved,' said Norman. 'I'm just telling you she didn't mean it to come out the way it did, and she's truly sorry, and she's desperate to make it up to you.'

'Well, that's not going to happen just because she wants it,' said Southall. 'She can stew on it for a while, and I'll see about moving on when I'm good and ready.'

'You're not going to hold a grudge, are you?'

'You know me better than that, Norm, but I do intend to make sure she gets the message.'

'Okay,' said Norman. 'You're the boss.'

'Is that what you came in here for?'

'Yes and no,' said Norman. 'Ever since we heard about this runner guy, something started nagging at me in my head, and I couldn't for the life of me think what it was. I had a feeling it was something from the very beginning, so I went back through the early evidence.'

'Did you find it?'

Norman shook his head. 'Nothing doing, but going back to the beginning did seem to jog my memory, and then I got it. The very first time we went to the crime scene, as I was walking across the clearing, I recall seeing a guy in running gear talking to the PC doling out the forensic suits. At the time I wondered how the guy had managed to get so close to the crime scene, and then when you arrived, you said you hadn't seen him heading back to the car park.'

'That's right, I remember now,' said Southall. 'You said there must have been a side path he had used.'

'I'm glad you remember too,' said Norman. 'That means I didn't imagine it, and the guy really was there. Yet there's no record of him being at the scene. Everyone connected with the team had instructions to send the public away, but get their name and address, just in case. There are about a dozen dog walkers listed, but no runner.'

'Do we know who the PC was?'

'Yeah, I've just requested his sergeant to tell him to call in here. I'm hoping he got the address, and just forgot to add it to the list.'

'It could be nothing,' said Southall.

'Yeah, I know,' said Norman. 'But if running is involved in these murders, it won't hurt to check the guy out. After all, it's not unheard of for a murderer to revisit the scene, is it? What if he runs there on a regular basis to monitor his handiwork and make sure it hasn't been discovered?'

'If that's the case, he may well have fled the area by now,' said Southall.

'Not necessarily. Remember, Majhul's grave was the only one we knew about at that stage. So, if he didn't kill her, he would have known it wasn't the site of one of his graves. He might have lain low for a while, but with any luck, he'll think he's got nothing to worry about. I mean, his bodies were buried on the other side of the clearing, and the oldest one hadn't been discovered in eighteen months. On that basis, he would have good reason to be confident that his bodies were hidden well enough.'

'Your theory only works if he has nothing to do with Majhul's death, and even then, we can't be sure he won't have been spooked when he saw us excavating out there.'

'If we're saying he's finding his victims at half marathon events, I can't see how Majhul can be one of them. And the way she was buried was just too careless—'

'Hey, Norm,' called Catren Morgan. 'There's a PC Williams downstairs to see you.'

217

'On my way,' Norman called back. 'That must be my guy,' he said to Southall. 'Fingers crossed he's got what we want.'

'Good luck,' said Southall.

* * *

Norman recognised PC Williams straight away.

'I got a message saying you wanted to speak to me. Have I done something wrong?'

'Yes, you have,' said Norman. 'But I'm giving you the chance to put it right.'

Williams looked blankly at him.

'Okay, remember the body that was found in the Dragon Forest?' asked Norman. 'You were on duty issuing forensic suits and keeping access records, right?'

'Oh, that, yeah,' said Williams. 'I'm hardly going to forget that in a hurry.'

'Good,' said Norman. 'In which case you'll recall being asked to keep the public away but take the personal details of anyone who was there, right?'

'Yes, that's right.'

'So, you remember I collected my suit from you, put it on and set off across the clearing?'

Williams nodded. 'Yeah, that's right.'

'And when I got near to where the pathologist was working on the body, I stopped in the middle of the clearing and did a three-sixty-degree turn to get the lie of the land,' said Norman. 'And when I did that, I saw you speaking to a guy in running gear.'

'Yes, that's right.'

'But you didn't take his name and address,' said Norman. 'Or, if you did write it down, you didn't add it to the list we have. I must tell you, I'm really not happy about that, because it could be important, but if you have the information in your notebook, I'm prepared to turn a blind eye. After all, we all make mistakes, right?'

Williams bristled. 'Of course I added . . . Oh.' He stopped speaking, his face red.

'You do have it written in your notebook, right?' asked Norman.

Williams shook his head. 'Er, no, I didn't write it down.'

Norman erupted. 'You what? Jesus, this was a murder scene, and it was a simple enough instruction!'

'All right, sir, calm down,' said Williams. 'I can tell you his name and address if it's so important.'

'Of course it's bloody well important,' snapped Norman. 'I wouldn't be asking for it if it wasn't. Why didn't you add it to the evidence list at the time?'

'But he's a mate, sir. I thought we only needed to add the names of people who looked a bit suspicious, or had no reason to be there.'

'I ought to kick your arse for this, Williams. It's not up to you to decide who is or isn't suspicious.'

'But I know him, sir. His name is Dan Maddison. He's an all-round good guy.'

'Oh yeah? You know this for a fact, do you?'

'Yeah, he raises loads of money for charity. Runs all over the UK, he does.'

Norman's antenna was twitching.

'Hang on a minute,' he said. 'Does this guy have a podcast?'

'That's right. I believe it's called *Cool Runner*, or something like that.'

'Does he call himself the Half Harrier?'

'I think that's it. Because he runs half marathons,' said Williams.

'You said he was a mate. Just how well do you know him?' asked Norman.

'Not that well, I suppose. He was in the year above me at school.'

'So, you're not bosom buddies or anything like that?'

'Heck, no, he's more what you'd call an acquaintance than a friend, if you see what I mean. He lives not far from here, so I bump into him now and again. We say hello, but we don't socialise or anything like that.'

'Is he married?'

Williams nodded. 'His wife's called Megan.'

'Family?'

'Not sure. I don't think they have any kids.'

'And you know where he lives, right?'

'I'll write it down for you,' said Williams.

'Yeah, you do that,' said Norman. 'And next time you're asked to do a job, make sure you do it properly.'

'What's he done exactly?' asked Williams.

'I can't tell you that,' said Norman. 'But I hope I can trust you not to say anything to him about this.'

'Don't worry about that,' said Williams. 'I'm not looking for another bollocking. Chances are I won't see the guy, and even if I do, it'll only be a passing "hello".'

* * *

It was one p.m. by the time they finally set out for the small cul-de-sac where Dan and Megan Maddison lived.

'I can't believe it takes so many phone calls to get an operation like this organised,' fumed Southall.

'I guess that's the problem with us being such a small outfit,' said Norman. 'It's good that we have a small tight-knit team, but the downside is we have to go begging when we need backup.'

'It wouldn't have been such a big deal if our acting super-intendent had been available to make the call,' said Southall. 'Being just a lowly DI, and a woman at that, I don't have the necessary clout to grab people's attention. I had to go to the chief constable for God's sake!'

'Yeah, well, I've said from the start that Evans is a waste of space. Where the hell is he anyway?'

'I don't know,' said Southall.

'What about your new buddy, the chief constable?' said Norman. 'Doesn't he know where Evans is?'

'That wasn't a conversation we had. It doesn't look good to show disloyalty to your boss.'

'Are you sure about that? I mean, do you think Evans would cover for you? I think not. Besides, he's not your boss, is he?' said Norman. 'He's just some temporary, jumped-up freeloader, who knows which arses to lick to get him higher up the ladder.'

'We don't know that for sure,' said Southall.

'You can let those blinkers of yours obscure the truth all you want,' said Norman, 'but you know I'm right.'

'Let's keep our minds on the job at hand,' said Southall as she pulled over and turned off the engine. 'We can argue about Evans another time.'

They were parked just a few yards before the turning into the cul-de-sac. Ahead of them on the other side of the cul-de-sac, a police van was waiting. Southall glanced in her mirror to make sure Morgan and Winter were behind them. Further back, a white van carried a forensic team.

Speaking into her radio, Southall made sure everyone was in place, and ready, then gave the word.

'Okay. Let's do this!'

The police van was first around the corner, followed by the two unmarked cars carrying the four detectives. The van screeched to a halt at the end of the driveway to the Maddison's house, and six black-clad officers from the backup team poured from the back, one carrying a heavy-duty battering ram for use on the front door.

The detectives ran up the drive behind the backup team, and gathered on either side of the front door. The officer carrying the battering ram looked to Southall, who had a quick look around and gave him the nod. He ran up to the front door and took a mighty swing.

Norman braced himself for the crash of metal on uPVC, then watched, fascinated, as the door opened at the critical moment and the officer was carried through the open door by the momentum of the heavy battering ram. There was a loud crash from inside the house as the battering ram found a target.

'Did you see that?' said Morgan, who'd been watching over Norman's shoulder. 'The door flew open like magic. He didn't even have to—'

The rest of her words were drowned by a high-pitched scream from inside the house.

Norman rolled his eyes. 'Thank goodness we called in the professionals to get us into the house.'

Taken aback by what had just happened, the backup squad hesitated. Southall, who had no such qualms, was first through the door, and began calming the hysterical woman.

'It's okay,' said Southall. 'We're police officers.'

'In what way does that make it okay?' demanded the woman, pointing to the figure struggling to extricate his battering ram from a shattered internal wall. 'Would you say it was okay if he'd just smashed a wall in your hallway?'

'Well, no, I suppose not,' said Southall. 'I'm sorry about that.'

'You're sorry, are you? Oh, well, that's all right then,' said the woman. 'Why on earth didn't you just knock on the door like normal people do?'

The backup team suddenly swarmed through the front door and began tramping from room to room searching the house.

'Now what's going on?' demanded the woman. 'What are they doing?'

'Are you Megan Maddison?' asked Southall, determined to keep control of the situation.

'Yes, of course I am. Who were you expecting to find in my house?'

Southall turned to Norman, who produced the search warrant with a theatrical flourish and announced, 'We have a warrant to search your house.'

Megan hefted two suitcases from the floor. 'Go ahead. Do what you like. I'm leaving.'

Southall stepped in front of her, blocking her exit. 'I'm afraid that won't be possible, Mrs Maddison. We need to ask you some questions.'

'Why? What am I supposed to have done?'

Just then the backup team leader appeared. 'The house is empty,' he said. 'We'll be on our way unless you want us to stay.'

'No, that's fine, you get off,' said Southall. 'Thank you for your help.'

Megan glared at Norman. 'What about my bloody wall?'

Norman shrugged. 'Yeah, sorry about that. It's usually the front door that gets smashed to bits.'

'But why would you want to smash my front door?'

'We're actually looking for your husband, Dan,' said Southall.

'Well, you're wasting your time, he's not here. But when you do find him, you can tell the cheating bastard from me that I've had enough, and I've gone.'

'I take it he's not here then.'

Megan looked at Southall as if she were a halfwit.

'Well, obviously. I just said he's not, didn't I? But I'll tell you this, if he was here, I'd be only too glad to show him to you.'

'Well, if he's not here, can you tell us where we can find him?' asked Southall patiently.

'He'll be off running somewhere,' Megan said.

'That's a regular thing, is it?' asked Norman.

'You've heard of golf widows, right? Women whose husbands spend all weekend at the golf club. Well, I'm a half marathon widow, but my husband doesn't go to the same club, he goes all over the country.'

'He makes a habit of going away, does he?' asked Norman.

'That's an understatement if ever I heard one,' said Megan.

'So, it would be fair to say he takes his running seriously?' asked Southall.

By now, Megan had set down the suitcases. 'It wasn't so bad when he first started and it was just the odd weekend, but these days he's away more than he's at home. And if that's not bad enough, the cheating swine likes to embellish his trips with a bit on the side.'

Norman and Southall exchanged a look.

'You already know all this, don't you?' Megan said.

'Do you know what brand of running shoe he uses?' asked Norman.

'You think I care about his shoes?'

'Look, I can understand why you don't, and why you might think it's a stupid question,' said Norman, 'but it's actually really important.'

'What has he done exactly?' asked Megan. 'Has one of his fancy women accused him of rape?'

'Not that I'm aware of,' said Southall. 'The type of shoe?'

Megan thought for a moment. 'Well, I can tell you it's not just a bog-standard trainer, it's a proper running shoe. I think it's called Marathon or something like that.'

'Do you know what shoe size he is?'

'This is serious, isn't it?' asked Megan. 'Jesus. What has he done?'

'We can't tell you that,' said Norman. 'But you can tell us Dan's shoe size.'

Megan shrugged. 'I can't swear to it, but I think he's a size twelve. You'll find his shoes upstairs anyway.'

Southall turned to Morgan and Winter. 'Call the forensic team in and start upstairs. Make sure to check the shoe size.'

'Dan must do a lot of training,' said Norman.

'Every day,' said Megan. 'He never stops. He even cut his work hours down so he can spend more time running. I wouldn't mind, but that means I have to work extra hours to make up the shortfall. How fair is that? With the cheating on top of that, you can see why I've had enough, can't you?'

'Does he run in the Dragon Forest?'

'Look, I'm not into his stupid running, so I can't say for sure where he goes, or how often, but I believe it's one of the routes he uses.'

'If it's so bad, why have you put up with it so long?' asked Southall.

'He raises money for charity, so I put up with it because I thought he was at least doing something worthwhile with his time. But when I found out about the women, I realised he was taking me for an idiot. I mean, what would you do?'

'Do you know where he is at the moment?'

'As I said, he's running somewhere. All I can say is it'll be in the UK, but I don't know where exactly.'

'I take it he has a mobile phone?' asked Norman.

'Are you from the Dark Ages, or what?' said Megan. 'Of course he has a bloody mobile. Doesn't everyone?'

'We'd like the number,' said Southall. 'We might be able to track him.'

Megan gave them the number.

'Are you sure he didn't say where he was going?' asked Southall.

'We're not speaking. We fell out, and we haven't spoken in weeks.'

'Do you mind if I ask why you fell out?'

'We fell out when I finally found out for sure that he'd been with another woman at one of these running events. He'd always denied it before, but I had proof this time.'

'How did you find out?'

'I found female underwear in his camper van. As far as I was concerned, that was the final straw.'

'Can I ask when this was?'

'If you let me get his diary, I can tell you exactly when it was,' said Megan.

'Do you know where the diary is?' asked Southall.

'Follow me,' said Megan.

She led them through a door into what was originally the garage, but had been converted into a home office with what looked like a DIY sound recording booth. Norman peered inside and noticed what he took to be a high-tech microphone.

'Does he use this stuff?' he asked.

Megan rolled her eyes. 'He likes to think he's so special people want to hear about his running exploits. I can't imagine anyone does, but what do I know?'

'The diary?' asked Southall.

'It should be in here,' said Megan, sitting down at the desk and opening the top drawer. She lifted a calendar from the drawer.

'That's a calendar, not a diary,' said Norman.

'You don't miss much, do you?' said Megan. 'Anyway, it's the same sort of thing.'

'It's a bit old-fashioned for a guy who uses all that tech,' said Norman.

'The diary proper will be on his laptop, but he always takes that with him. He used to keep this old calendar up to date, so I'd know where he was. But, as you can see, he stopped updating it after I confronted him about his extra-curricular affairs. That's why it's still open at September.' She slid a finger down the page. 'Here we are. September twenty-eight, the Robin Hood Half Marathon.'

Norman and Southall exchanged that look again.

'Are you going to tell me what he's done? asked Megan. 'Has this girl made a complaint about him? Oh God, he didn't rape her, did he?'

'I already told you we have no evidence to suggest he has raped anyone,' said Southall. 'Do you have reason to think he has?'

'He's what you might call a charmer,' said Megan. 'He's always been a flirt, and I reckon he can pull women easily enough without resorting to that.'

'Are you sure you don't know where he is now?' asked Southall.

'I don't know, and I don't care,' said Megan.

'I appreciate how you must feel about your husband, Megan, but we wouldn't be asking if it wasn't important,' said Southall.

Megan heaved a huge, exasperated sigh. She turned the calendar to November. 'Like I said, he stopped filling this in after I caught him out.' She pointed to a pile of paperwork on the desk. 'There might be something in there.'

Norman began sorting through the papers. 'There are entry forms for events here,' he said. 'Oh, hang on, what's this?' He picked up a flyer, scanned through it and handed it to Southall. 'This looks promising.'

'Conwy Half Marathon, Sunday, seventeenth November,' Southall said.

'Day after tomorrow,' said Norman. Then, turning to Megan, he added, 'Does that sound right? Would he be there already, do you think?'

'It's not unusual for him to arrive as much as a week before an event. He claims he wants to familiarise himself with the course before the actual race.'

'Yeah, but when did he leave this time?'

'He left first thing on Wednesday morning in his camper van.'

'He uses a camper van, does he? Does he always go in that?' said Norman.

'He says hotels cost too much.'

'Did he seem any different to normal?' asked Norman. 'Did he take more stuff than he usually does?'

'Like I said, we're not speaking, but as far as I could tell, he wasn't acting any differently,' said Megan.

'Do you know the registration number of his camper van?'

Megan wrote it down, and Norman immediately hurried from the room.

'What's the big deal with the camper van?' Megan asked Southall. 'I might have been blind to my husband's cheating but I'm not stupid. I didn't have to be a genius to see your ears prick up when I mentioned the camper van. And you asked about the Dragon Forest as well . . .' She stared wide-eyed at Southall. 'Oh. My. God! You're investigating that dead woman who was found in the forest, aren't you?'

'All I can say is that we need to speak to Dan with regard to an ongoing investigation. I can't say any more than that, I'm afraid.'

'You don't need to. Was it her underwear I found in his van?'

'You said the underwear proved he was cheating. Do you still have it?'

'It is her, isn't it?'

'Mrs Maddison. Do you still have the underwear?' Southall said.

'Yes. I kept it as evidence to confront him with.'

'Right,' said Southall. 'I need you to show me where it is. Then, if you would come to Llangwelli with us and make a statement, I'll tell you what I can.'

'What do you mean, make a statement?' said Megan.

'To help us with our investigation.'

'But I haven't done anything. And I was just on my way out of here when you barged in.'

'Where were you going to in such a hurry?' asked Southall.

'I'm going to stay with my sister while I sort out my divorce. You can't say that's a surprise, surely?'

'No, I suppose not,' said Southall. 'Look, I'm not arresting you, Megan, nor am I accusing you of anything. We'd just like you to help us with some background information about Dan and his running. We'll bring you back here afterwards, and you can head off to wherever you want. Is that all right?'

'Why can't I drive to Llangwelli, make a statement and then be on my way?'

Southall thought for a moment. 'Well, yes, I suppose that would work, but I'll travel with you.'

'What for? You think I'll abscond?'

'I need to split my team, and we've only got two cars,' said Southall.

Megan shrugged. 'Okay. But I don't want you complaining about my driving.'

'Fine,' agreed Southall. 'I won't say a word. But before we go, I need that underwear.'

Megan led Southall back through the office to a second room in the converted garage. 'I hid it here in the laundry room.' She reached behind the washing machine and produced a small plastic bag, which she handed to Southall. 'I knew Dan would never think of looking in here.'

Southall took the bag. 'Give me a minute to talk to my team and I'll be with you.'

She found Morgan and Winter upstairs.

'Catren, Norm's outside talking to Conwy police. As soon as he's finished, I want you to come back to Llangwelli with him. Frosty, I'd like you to stay here with the forensic team until they've finished.' She handed him the bag. 'Make sure they understand we need DNA from this. I'm hoping it will confirm that the victim from Nottingham was definitely in his camper van.'

'Right. Got it,' said Winter.

'I'm going back with Megan Maddison. She's going to give us a statement. We'll catch up back at Llangwelli.'

* * *

Back at Llangwelli, Southall settled Megan in the interview room with a coffee, and went to see if Norman and Morgan were back.

'What's the situation, Norm?'

'I've been in touch with Conwy police and explained the situation, and that we think it's possible another young woman could be in danger. Our contact is DS Terry Nelson. He tells me they always open a special campsite for the week running up to the event. I've given him the registration number of the camper van and he's going to go down there, have a wander around and see if he can spot our man.'

'Do you think he'll be there?'

'I dunno,' said Norman. 'He could have taken off and we may never see him again, but my gut feeling is that he would have disappeared straight away if he'd been spooked by seeing us at the clearing. Megan says he didn't leave until Wednesday and he was behaving as normal.'

Southall pulled a face.

'Yeah, I know she's probably not the best judge of his behaviour right now,' said Norman, 'but her word is all we've got. If she's wrong, we're probably not going to find him anyway.'

'If he is there, are Conwy going to arrest him?'

'I've told DS Nelson we don't think there's any need until after the event, but to jump in if anything looks suspicious.'

'What about us making the arrest?'

'He says we'll need to consult with the higher ups if we want to make an arrest on their home turf.'

'That's fair enough, I suppose,' said Southall. 'What about if you and Catren take the statement from Megan Maddison while I bring Superintendent Evans up to speed and get him to make the necessary arrangements.'

Norman looked at his watch. 'It's nearly four on a Friday afternoon. D'you think he'll still be around?'

'There's only one way to find out,' said Southall.

'You're not going to let him make us wait until Sunday to make the arrest, are you?'

'No, that's far too risky. I intend to get Evans to make the arrangements right now. Then, as soon as DS Nelson confirms Maddison is there, we go and grab him.'

Norman nodded. 'Decisive,' he said. 'Now that's the sort of plan I like.'

* * *

It was six p.m. by the time they were all back in the incident room.

'How did you get on with Megan?'

Norman pulled a face. 'There's something about her that seems a bit off.'

'But then we did arrive unannounced, smash up her house, and go rampaging through it,' said Morgan. 'It's not the best way to introduce ourselves and make friends, is it?'

'I get that,' said Norman. 'I just think there's more to it than that. My gut tells me she knows more than she's letting on, but it's just a hunch and not a good enough reason to hold her.'

'So, you've let her go?' Southall asked Norman.

'Yeah, but not before we got her sister's address in Tenby.'

'Good, although I expect she complained about that,' said Southall.

'She did, until I explained we needed to know where she was so we could let her know what's happening with her husband. She seemed to like that idea. I had Catren make sure the name and address checked out before Megan left.'

'It's there on the electoral role, just as she said,' added Morgan.

'Fair enough,' said Southall. 'Has the camper van been found yet?'

'DS Nelson called it in half an hour ago,' said Lane. 'It's definitely there at the campsite and has been since Wednesday afternoon.'

'What about Dan Maddison?'

'He hasn't seen him, so he can't confirm if he's there.'

'The van couldn't have driven itself,' said Norman. 'He must be there. What's the deal with the arrest?'

'First thing in the morning,' said Southall.

'What does that mean?'

'A Conwy squad car has been arranged to meet us at six a.m.'

'Holy crap. That early?' muttered Norman.

'Superintendent Evans insisted we make the arrest as we worked the case. He doesn't want anyone else to get the credit for what he calls "our brilliant work".'

'Ha. "Our brilliant work". Meanwhile, he's going to be snoring his head off in bed,' said Norman. 'You know it's over four hours from here, right? We'll have to leave at two a.m.'

'We'll leave at three,' said Southall. 'There'll be no traffic, and we can blue light it all the way.'

'Oh, great,' said Norman. 'You know what Welsh roads are like. So we'll be spending three hours rattling around on a rollercoaster, while the person who'll claim all the credit is sleeping in his pit.'

'It'll be fine, Norm,' said Southall. 'I suggest we all go home now, and we can meet up again just before three a.m. Of course, if you'd rather not come . . .'

'That's a cheap shot,' said Norman. 'You know I'll be here. In fact, I bet I'll be the first to arrive.'

CHAPTER SIXTEEN

'Holy crap!' said Norman, squeezing in through the sliding door on the side of the camper van. 'This isn't quite what I was expecting. Is that just a single stab wound?'

'It looks that way,' said Southall. 'But let's leave it to Forensics to make sure. I don't want to mess with the scene.'

'No sign of a struggle,' said Norman, casting a look around the cramped interior of the camper van.

'He was either asleep, or he was expecting the perpetrator,' said Southall. 'Which means it was planned. And I'm guessing that whoever did it wouldn't have left the knife if there were any fingerprints on it.'

'So we needn't have set off quite so early,' said Norman. 'We rushed all that way for nothing.'

'Is there a problem?' The speaker was DS Terry Nelson, who was standing behind Southall and Norman and so was unable to see inside the van.

Norman stepped back to allow Nelson to take a look. 'That's something of an understatement, Terry. It seems our murder suspect has now become a murder victim!'

'What, on our patch? Right under my bloody nose?'

233

'I'm afraid so,' said Norman.

Nelson shook his head. 'Jesus. My boss is going to go apeshit when he finds out what's happened.'

'There's no way anyone could have stopped it from happening,' said Norman. 'I mean, we hadn't even considered the possibility that . . . this would be waiting for us.'

'Tell your boss it's our fault,' said Southall.

'Oh, don't you worry, I intend to,' said Nelson.

'Fine,' said Southall, stepping out of the van. 'In that case I'm sure your boss won't mind us handling the investigation.'

'Oh, now, I'm not sure about that. I'll have to ask him.'

'At this time of the morning?' said Norman. 'I don't want to stop you, but if he's anything like our boss, he'll just love getting a call this early on a Saturday.'

'You're right,' said Nelson. 'It'll only make him twice as mad.'

'You can wait until later if you want,' said Southall, 'but we can't just leave the body unattended, especially since he's obviously the victim of foul play. As the senior local officer here, it's your call.'

'Oh, shit. Really? I'm not sure I know what to do. You might have plenty of murders in your neck of the woods, but this sort of thing just doesn't happen round here.'

'It does now,' said Norman, sagely.

'Do I need to call a doctor first, do you think?' asked Nelson.

'I think it's a bit late for a doctor,' said Norman. 'A forensic pathologist might be better.'

'Oh, you're kidding me. I don't even know who we use!'

'Jeez, you really are out of your depth,' said Norman. 'Looks like it's probably a good job we're here. We do this sort of thing all the time.'

Nelson looked around him helplessly, as if he wished the earth would open and swallow him up, but when this didn't happen, he began to panic.

'Come on now, Terry, pull yourself together,' said Norman.

'I don't know what to do first.'

234

'Hey, look, we've all been there,' said Norman. 'Just take a few deep breaths, remember procedure, and then act on it.'

Sadly, this did nothing for Nelson's vanished confidence.

'Can I give you some advice, Terry?' asked Southall.

'I wouldn't say no.'

'Okay. Why don't you let us make a start and handle finding a pathologist. You hang on for a while before you call your boss.'

'I don't know about that. He won't like it.'

'You just agreed he won't like being woken early,' said Norman. 'He can't have it both ways.'

'Remind him that as the senior officer on site you had to make a decision, and you were trying to cover all bases,' said Southall. 'Tell him you're calling to hand control over to him, but in the meantime, as we were already here, you thought we should make a start. We'll share whatever we find, obviously.'

Nelson regarded Southall and Norman dubiously. 'Well, all right. I suppose I'm just going to have to trust you, aren't I?'

'Aw come on, Terry. Haven't we shared everything so far?' said Norman. 'And we're only going to look. Trust me, the first few hours are the most important, and you wouldn't want to be the guy who hindered a murder investigation, would you?'

'What should I do now?' asked Nelson.

Norman looked around. There were a handful of similar vans parked nearby, and a sea of assorted tents. 'You could wake some of these people and see if you can find any witnesses. That would be a great help.'

Reluctantly, Nelson turned and made his way slowly to the tents.

'You're taking a chance, aren't you?' Norman said quietly to Southall.

'Yes, but you know what it's like, Norm. If we let them start the investigation, it'll probably be days before we get access to any evidence. We can't afford that.'

Norman smiled at her. 'Oh, I agree it's the right thing to do, I was just a bit surprised at how easily you misled the poor guy.'

'It's not my fault he doesn't know his arse from his elbow, is it?' said Southall.

'That's true enough,' said Norman.

Southall beckoned to Winter and Morgan who were hovering in the background.

'Cover the door for a minute, guys, would you?' she said.

'What have you got?' asked Norman.

'There's a mobile phone on the floor.'

'Any sign of the laptop?'

'I can't see it,' said Southall. 'Maybe that was the booty that cost him his life.' She slipped the mobile phone into an evidence bag and then turned to Winter. 'Frosty, take this and see if you can get it working.'

'I thought we were sharing everything with them,' said Winter. 'I don't think DS Nelson is going to be very happy about me walking off with a key piece of evidence.'

'Don't worry about him,' said Norman. 'What he doesn't know about can't make him unhappy. And we don't know if it is key evidence yet, do we? For all we know it might be totally irrelevant.'

'We'll almost certainly get the case because we have the experience,' said Southall. 'But if there's an argument over jurisdiction it could take a while to sort out, which will be time wasted. So before that happens, we might as well try to make the most of it. As Norm said to Nelson, the first few hours are the most important.'

CHAPTER SEVENTEEN

Sunday, 17 November, 08.00

Back at Llangwelli, Southall was holding an impromptu briefing. 'Dr Bridger is carrying out the post-mortem this morning, so this is not yet confirmed, but he estimates the time of death to have been between eight p.m. and midnight on Wednesday evening,' announced Southall. 'Cause of death, a single stab wound to the heart.'

'Jeez, so he was killed within a few hours of arriving at the campsite,' said Norman.

'So it seems,' said Southall. 'I believe Frosty has made a breakthrough with the mobile phone we found, so over to you, Frosty.' She stepped back to allow Winter to come to the front of the room.

'I was lucky,' admitted Winter. 'I don't know why, but Maddison had only the most basic security on the phone, so it was easy to get in.'

'Maybe he thought because he always had it on him no one else was ever going to get their hands on it,' suggested Morgan.

'Or perhaps he was just lazy,' said Winter. 'Whatever, I'm in.'

'And what have you found?' asked Southall.

'Text messages and images that go back months. Reading through the messages, I think they demonstrate how he operated. It seems that once he got the victims' mobile numbers, he started sending them text messages with advice on basic training for first-time marathon runners.'

'How did he get the victims' numbers?' asked Southall.

'I've been looking at his podcasts and website,' said Judy Lane. 'There's a contact form on the website. If you want, you can request personal training, and to do that you have to submit a mobile number. After that it's all done by text.'

'So, it all seems very innocent at first,' said Southall. 'Clever.'

'He keeps sending the "training" texts until he persuades his victim to enter an event, on the understanding that he will meet them there and run with them.'

'So, basically, he's grooming them,' said Norman.

'Right from day one,' said Winter. 'He even gets them to send a selfie, so he knows what they look like.'

'Have you got that sort of evidence for all three victims?' asked Southall.

'For sure,' said Winter. 'Better still, I've even got a photograph of the girl who would have been his fourth victim were he still alive. Well, actually there are several photos.'

'You mean he was going to meet someone at today's race in Conwy?' asked Southall.

'They had actually arranged to meet before that,' said Winter. 'And it wasn't so they could go training.' He handed the mobile phone to Southall. 'Her name is Jilly Jones, and you can see why I said she's a girl. From her pictures, she looks about fourteen, but if the messages and photos she was sending in the weeks leading up to the race are for real, she's obviously a well-developed woman. Maddison would have thought he was in for a good time.'

'Wow!' said Norman, peering over Southall's shoulder. 'That explains why he was naked in bed. Having to defend himself would have been the last thing on his mind.'

'But did she kill him?' said Southall. 'There's no message to say she was coming to see him on Wednesday.'

'So why was he stark naked, if he wasn't waiting for her?' asked Norman.

'I think I may be able to help you there,' said Winter. 'As part of his patter he mentions that he always sleeps naked. I guess if they don't take offence, and from what I've seen they don't, he knows he's in with a good chance.'

'You think he really did sleep naked?' asked Southall.

Winter shrugged. 'Why not? Lots of people do.'

'So, if he wasn't expecting a visitor, he could just have been asleep when he was attacked,' said Norman. 'That would explain a lot.'

'If we can get Jilly Jones picked up at the race, she'll be able to confirm how she first made contact, and how the whole grooming thing proceeded,' said Winter.

'There's just one problem with that idea,' said Norman. 'If she did kill him, I don't think she'll be waiting around to run a half marathon.'

'And, just in case you've all forgotten, our murderer is now dead,' said Morgan. 'She can't be a witness if there's no trial.'

'We still need to find her in connection with Maddison's murder,' said Southall. 'And we need to know how he worked, even if there isn't going to be a trial. We think we know it all, but we can't leave a case like this with any doubts about who the killer really was.'

Much to everyone's surprise, Evans had made the effort to come in. He had been sitting at the back listening in, but now he spoke.

'I think we have more than enough evidence to prove what he was doing and how he found his victims, just from that mobile phone.'

'We still need to find this girl to question her about his death,' said Southall.

'Yes, yes, I understand that,' said Evans. 'But isn't it a burner phone he was using?'

Southall nodded. 'That's right.'

'That means the mobile he used normally, and his laptop, are still missing. My bet is that whoever stabbed him took those.'

Norman was tempted to congratulate him for stating the obvious, but realised that now wasn't the right time to rouse his ire.

'We keep trying to call the mobile number Megan gave us, but all we get is an out of service message,' he said. 'It's either switched off, or it's been disposed of.'

'Wasn't there another mobile phone found at the Maddison house?' asked Evans.

Southall could barely hide her surprise. It seemed Evans was finally up to date with the reports she had submitted. 'That's right,' she said. 'Unfortunately, that's gone to the Forensic tech department. I understand they're going to fast-track it, but we're waiting to hear from them.'

'So, if Dan Maddison owned the burner Frosty's got, whose is the one Forensics have got?' asked Morgan.

'That's exactly my point, DC Morgan,' said Evans.

'Maybe it's a spare,' said Norman. 'Or, maybe he was planning to replace the one we found.'

'Or maybe there are more victims on that second phone,' said Winter.

'Don't say that, Frosty,' said Southall. 'We don't want to spend months looking for more bodies.'

'I'm afraid I have to go now,' said Evans. 'But well done, everyone. You've all done a great job, and as I said, find the person who has the laptop, and you'll find Maddison's killer.'

'You have a nice day,' said Norman. 'Don't worry about us guys working our arses off.'

Evans stared at Norman, but bit back his retort. Smiling broadly, he pushed through the doors and was gone, satisfied in the knowledge that he had plans for Norman.

Norman turned to Southall. 'How long was he here? Twenty minutes?'

'At least he made the effort to show his face,' said Southall.

'Yeah, right,' said Norman. 'Anyway, what about Jilly Jones? Do you want me to contact Terry Nelson and ask him if he can find her?'

'After the sneaky way I stole their thunder yesterday, I don't think his boss is going to be keen to allow anyone from there to help us,' said Southall. 'Why not try the race organisers first? They'll have her entry form.'

'Do you really think I'll be able to find anyone with time to help on the day of the race?' asked Norman.

'You can probably find a list of entrants online,' said Morgan, turning to her computer. 'Let's have a look . . .'

Half an hour later, Norman went to find Southall in her office. 'We have a problem. Jilly Jones never submitted an entry form for the race.'

'What? Are you sure?' asked Southall.

'There are about three thousand names listed online, but there's no Jilly Jones among them,' Norman said. 'Catren can't find any trace of her online, either. Judy's trying to get hold of the race organisers, but I'm beginning to think we're looking for someone who doesn't exist.'

'What are you thinking, Norm?'

'What if someone worked out what Maddison was doing? Maybe they think the police aren't doing anything to stop him, so they've decided to step in and do it vigilante style. They create this fake persona, throw in a few saucy photos when Maddison shows an interest and then, when he swallows the bait, they lead him to Conwy, agree to meet, and wallop, he's a goner.'

'And when she arrives, he's waiting for her to slip into bed next to him,' said Southall.

'Or, if he's not expecting her, he might even be asleep,' said Norman. 'Either way, it would explain why there was no sign of a struggle. I can even suggest a prime suspect.'

'Megan Maddison,' said Southall. 'She wasn't happy about him cheating on her, was she?'

'And I reckon she knew a lot more about his running activities than she let on,' said Norman. 'Even if I'm wrong about that, she admitted she knew he was cheating, and she didn't strike me as the sort of woman who would be able to let it rest—'

'Without doing something to stop it,' said Southall.

Norman rushed to the office door and called out. 'Can someone try to get hold of Megan Maddison? Try her mobile or call her sister.'

Southall looked distinctly sick, and for the first time since they had started working together, Norman heard her use a four-letter word.

'Jeez, I've never heard you say that word before,' said Norman.

'I can't believe I've been such a fool,' said Southall. 'I should have seen it. She even had her suitcases packed and ready to go when we got there.'

'Not just you. I can put my hand up to that, too,' said Norman.

'Yes, but I even helped her escape by allowing her to drive her own car here, and then telling you to let her go.'

'That's crazy,' said Norman. 'At that point we had no reason for holding her. Jeez, we didn't even know for sure that the guy was in Conwy, and we certainly had no way of knowing she'd murdered him.'

Judy Lane poked her head through the door. 'Megan's mobile phone is out of service, so we tried her sister. She says Megan's not there, and she hasn't spoken to her in months. They don't get on, apparently.'

Southall looked at the clock and swore again. 'It's been forty hours since we let her go. She could be halfway across the planet by now!'

'I'll set up an alert,' said Norman. 'Ports, airports, you name it. I'll get Catren on the ANPR cameras. We'll find her, you'll see.'

CHAPTER EIGHTEEN

Monday, 18 November, 08.00

'How can Megan Maddison have just vanished?' asked Southall. 'Her car hasn't shown up on a single ANPR camera since the time she left here.'

'She hasn't triggered any of my alerts either,' said Norman.

'But how can that be?' asked Southall.

'She put a lot of thought into how she was going to kill her husband,' said Norman. 'I mean, creating a fake persona and following it up like that takes some planning, right? I can't believe she wouldn't have put an equal amount of thought into what she was going to do afterwards.'

'Don't forget, you can travel a long way without passing any ANPR cameras if you know your way around,' said Morgan. 'And what if she had arranged a rendezvous with an accomplice?'

'Now that would make sense,' agreed Norman. 'I wouldn't mind betting we'll find her car abandoned in a car park miles from here, but she'll be long gone.'

'Sorry to interrupt,' called Judy Lane. 'I've just had the prelim report from digital forensics.'

'What does it say?' asked Southall.

Lane scanned the email. 'The phone found in the house was unregistered, pay-as-you-go—'

'No surprise there,' said Norman.

'Ah, but here's the good bit,' said Lane. 'There are texts on it between Jilly Jones and Dan Maddison. So, you were right, boss, she did lure him into a trap.'

'That doesn't prove she killed him though, does it?' said Southall. 'If we're right about her having help, then it could have been the accomplice who did it.'

'But she's still complicit,' said Norman. 'Even if she didn't actually stab him, that phone proves her guilty of conspiracy to murder. That'll be fifteen years at the very least.'

'Only if we can find her,' said Southall. 'And that's getting more unlikely by the minute. I'm not suggesting we should give up, but I think we must face up to the fact that we got it wrong.'

'Yeah, but did we?' said Norman. 'We were looking for the person who killed three women, and we identified him. How were we to know his wife was going to bump him off before we got there?'

'It doesn't matter how we dress it up, Norm, the fact is we've been well and truly led up the garden path.' She sighed. 'And now I suppose I'd better go upstairs and face the music.'

'Not without me,' said Norman. 'You're not taking all the blame for this.'

* * *

As Southall finished explaining the situation they now found themselves in, Acting Superintendent Evans sat back in his chair, gazed up at the ceiling and twiddled his thumbs. After a few seconds he looked at the two detectives and let out a huge sigh.

'So, in a nutshell, what you're saying is we could have solved four murders and captured one killer, but instead we now have five victims and no killer. Is that right?'

'Er, yes, I suppose you could look at it like that, sir,' said Southall. 'In our defence—'

244

'I think it's up to me to decide if your incompetence is defensible, don't you, Detective Inspector? Just think how this looks, not just for you, but for all of us.'

'Can I say something?' asked Norman.

'Ah, Detective Sergeant Norman, sharing your many years of experience with the younger members of the team but still coming up with diddly-squat. Please, go ahead. I can't wait to hear your words of wisdom.'

Norman bristled, but did his best to keep his cool.

'Okay, so we may have temporarily lost the chief suspect in Dan Maddison's murder, but we have enough evidence to prove he groomed and then killed the three victims he met via his running.'

'That's all very well, but we can't charge a dead man, can we? And, even if we could, I suggest the Criminal Prosecution Service would be reluctant to prosecute a corpse, even one that used to be a serial killer.'

'But isn't it our job to solve crime?' said Norman. 'Dan Maddison wouldn't be the first murderer to die before he was proven guilty. The way I see it, whether Maddison is alive or dead, technically the crimes are still solved.'

'Oh, I see,' said Evans. 'So, "the way you see it" is all that matters, is it?'

Norman shrugged. 'You could argue we've solved Maddison's murder too. We know it was either his wife or her accomplice that stabbed him.'

'But you don't know for sure, do you?' said Evans. 'That's just a hypothesis.'

'But it's based on very strong evidence,' said Southall.

'I agree you have evidence of a possible, or even proba-ble, conspiracy to murder, but there is no evidence, forensic or otherwise, to prove who actually stabbed the man. His wife may have intended to kill him, or she may have arranged for this supposed accomplice to do it, but for all we know a complete stranger could have done it.'

'Yeah, but how likely is that?' said Norman.

'It's likely enough to be used as reasonable doubt in court, or at least it would be if the woman in question hadn't morphed into Houdini over the weekend. No, I'm sorry, but that's just not good enough. We'll have to come up with something better than that if we're going to save face here.'

'Save face?' said Norman. 'I got the impression you were holding us responsible.'

'Which you are,' said Evans. 'But I've got to think of my own career. A cock-up on this scale won't look good. It won't look good at all.'

'Ah. Now we're really starting to see what you're about,' said Norman. 'And it turns out you're exactly what I thought.'

Evans stared at Norman, his lip curling in a sneer. 'Do you really want to see your DI's career come to a halt and her chances of promotion evaporate because of you?'

'Who, Sarah? She's one of the best officers I've ever worked with,' said Norman. 'And what do you mean "because of me"?'

'Well, think about it, Sergeant,' said Evans. 'Who let the prisoner go?'

'Megan Maddison wasn't a prisoner. She was a witness making a statement!'

'Be realistic, man,' said Evans. 'If I go down, DI Southall goes down with me. It won't hurt you to take the blame since I've recommended that you be pensioned off anyway, whereas Southall has years ahead of her.'

'Pensioned off?' said Norman. 'That's not up to you to decide.'

'Sadly, no, or you would be gone already, but I am able to make recommendations as part of cost-cutting measures.'

Southall, who had been struggling to get a word in, finally managed to intervene. 'Are you threatening us?'

'Come now,' said Evans. 'As if I would do such a thing. I'm just trying to make sure we don't lose face over this.'

'Oh, yes?' said Southall. 'And how do you suggest we do that?'

'Well, DS Norman takes responsibility for letting a killer get away—'

'That was my decision,' said Southall.

'I'm sure your loyalty to a colleague is admirable, Detective Inspector, but it's not going to look good for you either. I don't like to think what the chief constable will say when I tell him you set the woman free without bothering to consult with your senior officer.'

'But I was the senior officer on duty,' said Southall.

Evans shrugged. 'Yes, but wouldn't you have consulted with Superintendent Bain over such a decision?'

'Possibly, if I felt I needed advice, but in this case, we had no grounds to keep Megan Maddison here once she had given her statement.'

'But hadn't she murdered her husband two days earlier?'

'Give me strength,' said Norman. 'Yes, we believe she did now, but as we've already said more than once, we didn't know that at the time.'

'You can argue the finer details all you want,' said Evans. 'The fact is, Norman, you let the woman go without consulting a senior officer.'

'That's total bullshit, and you know it!' said Norman. 'We've done nothing wrong, we were just unlucky. And the case is far from being closed, we're still looking for her.'

'Yes, well, perhaps you'll be able to explain your bad luck to the chief constable when the time comes.'

'With pleasure,' said Norman. 'I'll look forward to it.'

Evans shuffled the papers on his desk with the air of a man with places to go, things to do. 'Of course, on the plus side, we have solved the murders of four young women.'

'I think you'll find it's three,' said Norman.

'Not if we say Dan Maddison murdered all of them.'

'Jesus!' said Norman, unable to stop his voice from rising. 'How many more times do we have to tell you? Dan Maddison didn't kill Majhul!'

Evans looked at Southall. 'I think this discussion would go much more smoothly if your sergeant didn't keep interrupting—'

'I'm only interrupting because you're too stupid to admit we still don't know what happened to the Syrian girl!' said Norman.

'Right, that's it. I've had enough of your insolence,' said Evans. 'DS Norman, please leave my office.'

'Yeah, but—'

'Would you rather I ordered you to get out?' said Evans.

'Sir, I think you're being a bit harsh,' said Southall.

'It's okay, Sarah,' said Norman. 'It's best if I leave, or who knows what might happen. You can manage just fine without me being here.'

With a final angry glare at Evans, Norman let himself out, closing the door very quietly behind him. Evans watched him go, and then turned to Southall with a smile.

'Anyway,' he said, 'now we're no longer being constantly interrupted, perhaps you and I can come to an understanding.'

'Sir?'

'How best to wrap up this case in a satisfactory manner.'

'But Norm's right. There were only three victims that can be attributed to Maddison. The original victim, Majhul, has nothing to do with him.'

'That's not even her real name, is it?'

'No, as you well know.'

'And where has giving her a name got you? Are you any more likely to find her killer by doing that?'

'That's not the point. Anyway, we do have evidence, just that none of it points to Maddison.'

'There's enough circumstantial evidence to make her one of his victims,' said Evans. 'She was buried less than one hundred yards from the other bodies, for God's sake! She was murdered in the same way.'

'I'm afraid I can't agree that that makes her one of Maddison's victims,' said Southall. 'For a start, the other victims were all in contact with Maddison before they were killed. Majhul wasn't.'

'As far as you know,' said Evans. 'He could have had another phone we don't know about.'

'We have no evidence to suggest she had a mobile phone, and the pathologist's report says she wasn't an athlete.'

'Perhaps she had plans to become one. We all have to start somewhere.'

'What about the tears found on the sheet she was buried in? They're not a DNA match for Maddison.'

'Is that all you've got?' asked Evans. 'If the girl slept around, they could be anyone's tears.'

Southall rolled her eyes. 'If you read the pathologist's reports, you'll see that far from sleeping around, she was still a virgin.'

'Virgin or not, like most of the evidence concerning her, those tears lead nowhere.'

'If you tried to use all that contradictory and dubious evidence to link her death to Maddison, the Criminal Prosecution Service would throw it out,' said Southall.

'You seem to be forgetting something, Southall. As the murderer is dead, the CPS aren't going to be involved, so what they might, or might not say is irrelevant.'

'So, you're saying we should forget about finding out who killed Majhul, and blame Maddison, even though we know he didn't kill her. Is that right?' asked Southall.

'Ah, but think of how the numbers will look. We can either say we've solved three murders, but failed to solve two, or we can say we've solved four murders and have one ongoing enquiry. Which do you think the CC would prefer to hear?'

'You're distorting the facts,' said Southall. 'Which are that we've solved three, and have two ongoing enquiries.'

Evans waved away her protests. 'And then there's the budget. You won't have to waste money contacting the Syrian authorities. It'll be a feather in both our caps.'

'Even if I agreed with you about the number of murders we've solved,' said Southall. 'I have to ask what about the one I let get away?'

'Don't you worry about that. As I said before, we can make it look better for us if I say DS Norman acted on his

249

own initiative but got it badly wrong. It'll add weight to my recommendation that he should retire.'

'You can forget that idea,' said Southall. 'There's no way I'm going to hang Norm out to dry. And I won't pretend that Majhul was one of Maddison's victims.'

'But think of your career,' argued Evans.

'I'm more interested in my integrity,' said Southall. 'I like to be able to sleep at night. I will report the facts as they are, and I will not adjust them to fit your version of events. And I most definitely will not make DS Norman a scapegoat just to suit your stupid agenda.'

Evans's eyes narrowed, his face took on a look of sly cunning. He had never been averse to using a little leverage to get his own way, and now he played what he thought would be his trump card.

'Lane and Winter,' he said with a smile. 'They're living together, aren't they? Do you think you should be allowing that sort of thing to go on under your watch?'

'What's this, more threats?' said Southall. 'I'm afraid you'll have to do better than that.'

Disconcerted, Evans began, 'Yes, but—'

'I think you'll find the rule is specific to higher ranks and subordinates,' said Southall. 'As both Lane and Winter are DCs, it doesn't apply, not that anyone gives a damn these days anyway.'

'This isn't a request, Southall,' said Evans.

'As I said, I'll report the facts. Twist them as much as you like, but bear in mind that I won't be holding the ladder if it begins to wobble while you climb it.'

'What's that supposed to mean?'

'I think you know exactly what I mean. Sir. Now, if there's nothing else, I have a fugitive to find.'

Southall turned, marched to the door and opened it.

'Come back here,' said Evans. 'I'm not finished yet.'

'Well, sorry, sir, but I am,' said Southall. She went out through the door, pulled it closed behind her and made her way back down the stairs.

As soon as she got back to the office, she asked where Norman was.

'He said something about needing some air,' said Lane. 'But he took his car keys, so I think he's gone home. Shall I call him?'

'No, it's okay,' said Southall. 'It won't hurt for him to take a bit of time out.' She made her way to her office and stopped at the door. 'If anyone wants me, I'm on the phone to head office.'

CHAPTER NINETEEN

Monday, 2 December

'Any news on Megan Maddison?' asked Southall, as she pushed her way in through the office doors.

Judy Lane looked up from her desk and shook her head. 'Sorry. I live in hope, but there's still no sign.'

They had launched a public appeal for any sightings of Megan Maddison, and another for information on Majhul. It had become Southall's daily ritual to ask the question when she first came through the doors, but she was beginning to think they were wasting their time.

Norman followed Southall into her office. 'Let's look on the bright side, maybe Megan wasn't the killer and we got it wrong.'

'Then why escape?'

'Perhaps she disappeared because she knew we'd have her down as our chief suspect.'

'You can keep telling yourself that if you want to, Norm, but you don't believe it any more than I do,' said Southall.

'You're right there,' agreed Norman glumly. 'I hate to admit it, but I can't help thinking we've been privy to a near perfect crime.'

'She'll slip up sooner or later.'

'You think?' said Norman. 'She doesn't seem to have put a foot wrong so far.'

Out in the main office, Judy Lane had just ended a phone call. She tore a sheet of paper from her notepad and rushed to Southall's office.

'We've got a hit,' she said. 'A Mr Jessop thinks he may have seen Majhul in Llangwelli on the night she died!'

'And he's only decided to come forward now?' asked Norman.

'He's been away,' said Lane. 'He wouldn't even have thought of it if it hadn't been for our notice.'

'How sure is he?' asked Southall.

'He's got footage from a doorbell camera,' said Lane. 'He's bringing it in right now.'

* * *

An hour later, they gathered around Lane's desk to watch the footage.

'It's ten twenty p.m., so it's dark, and it's not exactly UHD quality, but see what you think anyway,' said Lane, as she started to run the footage.

They watched an empty road, until what appeared to be a tiny woman rushed in from the left of the screen and stopped in front of the house. She looked up into the camera lens, and then reached forward to press the doorbell.

'It's Majhul,' said Lane.

As Majhul waited at the door, a large black SUV pulled up on the road behind her. The passenger window of the car was down, and the occupant leaned out and spoke to her. Majhul turned and backed up against the door, raising her hands to her face.

A figure wearing a huge coat and a baseball cap got out of the car, approached Majhul and began speaking to her. After about a minute, this individual took Majhul's arm, led her to the car and opened the passenger door for her to get in.

She did so very slowly. The figure appeared to give Majhul a final push into the car, closed the door, ran round to the driver's side, climbed in and drove off.

'Right,' said Southall, as the video ended. 'Do we know where this is?'

'It's at the far end of the High Street,' said Lane, 'those small, terraced houses with front doors that open right onto the street.'

'I don't think there's any doubt that it's Majhul,' said Norman. 'In which case, what is she doing in Llangwelli, how did she get here, and why was she ringing that particular doorbell?'

'We've got to check it out, but I think it's just luck she chose that particular house,' said Lane. 'The homeowner is a pensioner who says he doesn't recognise her and wasn't expecting anyone. He also said he hasn't been well, and he's been staying with his son for a few weeks, convalescing, so he wasn't there the night she rang the bell. He was also adamant he wouldn't have answered the door at that time of night even if he had been there.'

'Maybe she was trying to get away from the car, was looking for somewhere to hide and just rang the nearest bell in desperation,' suggested Winter. 'I mean, if the door had opened, would that car have stopped?'

'That would depend on how desperate they were to catch Majhul,' said Norman.

'Is the driver a man?' asked Southall. 'That coat is so huge, it's difficult to make out one way or the other. And the baseball cap obscures the face.'

'Yeah, it looks like someone didn't want to be recognised,' said Norman.

'Poor little Majhul seems to know who it is,' said Lane.

'And she's scared of them,' said Southall. 'Look at her body language, and how reluctant she is to get into the car.'

'So, what's going on?' asked Morgan.

'I'll hazard a guess,' said Norman. 'Remember she had that number tattooed on her foot? My guess is we're looking at people trafficking, and if someone is trying to keep hold of her, there's a good chance she has been procured for sex.'

'Is that a thing around here?' asked Morgan.

'Why not?' asked Norman. 'Trust me, there are perverts and weirdos everywhere, even here in Wales.'

'Have we come across that car before?' asked Southall. 'Any CCTV footage?'

'I certainly don't recall seeing it before,' said Winter, 'but we were looking at footage near the Dragon Forest on Friday the first, not in Llangwelli on the night before.'

'Right then, Frosty—'

'Don't tell me — check CCTV and ANPR around Llangwelli for Thursday thirty-first and Friday first,' said Winter. 'I'll get onto it right away.'

'Do we know what car it is?' asked Southall.

'Could be a Merc,' said Winter. 'One of those G-wagon things that Norm hates so much.'

'Wait a minute,' said Norman. 'Don't we know someone who drives one of those?'

'We do. And we've spoken to him about this case,' said Morgan.

'If you mean Tom Foster, I think you're forgetting he has an alibi,' said Southall.

'Yeah, but that was for the night Majhul was buried,' said Norman. 'What about the night she died?'

'Good point,' said Southall. 'I think we should get him in and ask him where he was that night.'

* * *

'Where was I on the night of Thursday, thirty-first October?' repeated Tom Foster. 'Why do you need to know that?'

Norman smiled at him across the interview room table. 'As we said on the phone, we're just tying up some loose ends in the Dragon Forest case.'

'I thought that happened on Friday the first.'

'We've since discovered an incident that occurred in Llangwelli on the night before that we think may be connected,' said Southall.

'That was Halloween, wasn't it?' asked Foster.

'Thirty-first October usually is,' said Norman.

'I was at home,' said Foster.

'Can anyone verify that?'

'I'm afraid not. My wife's mother has been ill, and she was staying with her for a couple of nights.'

'What about Jack?' asked Southall.

'He was out.'

'What, all night?' asked Norman.

'Look, why are you so interested in Jack's whereabouts? I thought it was me you wanted to question.'

'That's right,' said Southall. 'We were only asking about Jack because we thought he might be able to corroborate your story.'

'What story? And why are you asking me about the Thursday night? The incident you're investigating happened on the Friday, didn't it?'

'It's true the body of a young woman was buried in the Dragon Forest on the night of Friday the first,' said Southall. 'But she died on the night of Thursday thirty-first October.'

'What? You think I have something to do with her death?'

'Do you?' asked Norman.

Foster licked his lips, staring first at Norman and then at Southall. He didn't speak for a long time.

Finally, he shook his head. 'I can't believe this, it's ridiculous. I'm not saying another word without my solicitor.'

'That's your right,' said Southall. 'We'll take a break, and resume when your solicitor arrives.'

* * *

'Wow! He lawyered up quick, didn't he?' said Norman, as he and Southall made their way to the office.

'Makes me think he's got something to worry about,' said Southall.

'Well, if his wife was away and Jack was out, he's got no alibi,' said Norman. 'What if he let Jack take the car, though?'

'That's the first thing we need to find out,' said Southall. 'Frosty should have the telematic data for the car about now. That will tell us where the car was.'

'And whether Foster's lying,' said Norman.

* * *

It was almost two hours before Tom Foster's solicitor arrived, spoke with his client and decided he was ready to allow the interview to proceed.

'You told us earlier that Jack was out that Thursday night. Can you tell us where he was?' asked Southall.

'He had a ticket to some Halloween gig in Carmarthen. I think there was a band playing or something.'

'Was he driving your car?'

Foster looked horrified. 'My Mercedes? You must be kidding. I know he's my son and all that, but have you seen his driving? Normally he uses his mother's hatchback, or he takes the van.'

'Normally? What does that mean?'

'On this occasion I thought it would be safer if I took him.'

'Why is that? He told us he doesn't drink,' said Norman.

'That's what he tells me too,' said Foster.

'You think he lies to you about it?'

'He's a teenager and he does what most teenagers do. I know for a fact that he drinks occasionally, and I worry he dabbles in drugs. The gig in Carmarthen seemed just the sort of event where that might happen. I don't want him driving if he's off his head, I'd rather be his personal taxi driver for the night.'

'What time did he come home?' Norman asked.

'He called me at around ten forty-five, and I went and picked him up.'

257

'That was an early finish, wasn't it?'

'He wasn't enjoying it, apparently. He didn't say, but I think he may have got into a fight.'

'Right,' said Southall. 'So, when you say you were at home all night, you actually weren't.'

'I dropped Jack in Carmarthen at about eight p.m., drove back home, watched some TV and then when he called later, I went to pick him up,' said Foster.

'So, the first time, you would have been back home between eight thirty and eight forty-five,' said Southall.

'About then,' said Foster.

'And you're sure you went straight home and didn't go anywhere else?'

The solicitor cleared his throat. 'Mr Foster has already stated that he went to Carmarthen and then came straight home. So, unless you have some reason to keep labouring the point . . .'

'Actually, I have,' said Southall. She opened her laptop and swung it round so Foster could see it.

Norman made a brief announcement for the record, and Southall pressed play. Foster stared at the screen with an expression of mounting horror. As the video clip finished playing, he turned to his solicitor.

'Could I have five minutes with my client?' asked the solicitor.

'Be my guest,' said Southall.

* * *

Five minutes later they were back at the table.

'I think we can wrap this up pretty quickly,' said the solicitor as the two detectives sat down. 'My client's car has telematics. If you bother to check, you'll see exactly where the car was on the night in question.'

'Yes, we know about telematics,' said Southall. 'We'll come to that in a minute.'

Foster's eyes widened in alarm, and he turned to the solicitor.

'Just remember my advice,' the solicitor murmured.

'Okay, let's cut to the chase,' said Southall. 'Are you the driver in the video we showed you a few minutes ago?'

Foster shifted awkwardly in his chair. 'You heard what he just said about telematics.'

'We were a bit surprised you wanted to bring that up,' said Norman.

'What do you mean?' asked Foster.

'According to the records, your car's telematics don't work, and they've been like that for about six months.'

'But that can't be,' said Foster.

'Yet it is,' said Norman.

'You've rigged this,' said Foster.

'Don't be absurd, Mr Foster,' said Southall. 'Are you suggesting we set you up six months ago? For a murder we didn't know was going to happen?'

'But I don't understand . . .'

'What you need to understand, Tom, is that you can't prove that isn't your car in the video,' said Norman.

Ignoring Foster's apparent confusion, Southall pushed a photograph across the table. It showed Majhul's body lying in the shallow grave. Foster's eyes widened as he looked at the photograph and then up at Southall.

'Recognise her?' asked Southall.

Foster shook his head. 'No comment.'

'She's the girl in the video we just showed you. We believe she was trying to hide from you, and she rang the bell in the hope that someone would open their door and let her in.'

Foster kept shaking his head. 'No comment.'

'We found carpet fibres on the sheet the body was wrapped in,' said Norman. 'They match the sort of carpet used in cars like yours. We have a warrant to impound your car. In fact, our forensic team are swarming all over it right now. Do you think they'll find traces of the dead woman?'

Foster swallowed hard. 'No comment.'

'Just so you know, we've also got a forensic team at your house,' continued Norman. 'Do you want to tell us what they're going to find?'

'No comment.'

Norman pointed to the photograph. 'We call her Majhul,' he said. 'It means unknown in Arabic. We call her that because we don't know what the poor kid's real name was. You can see she looks just like a kid, right? We believe she's about eighteen, but she'd pass for much younger, don't you think?'

Foster licked his lips. 'No comment.'

Norman smiled his fakest smile. 'There's no need to be coy, Tom. We all know you like them young, and Asian. You've even got a subscription to a "Young Asian Girl" porn site, remember?' He paused for just a moment. 'You don't need to "no comment" that one. You should remember we already spoke about this in a previous interview, where you admitted it.'

Foster stared at Norman, his eyes wide, apparently mesmerised.

'Here's what we think happened,' said Norman. 'Somewhere along the line, you procured a young Asian virgin, whom someone had been holding for you. On Thursday, thirty-first October, your wife was away and Jack was out, so you thought you'd go and collect your goods. Or maybe the supplier got fed up with holding her for you. Either way you went to collect her. Only the girl figured out what was going to happen and she somehow escaped. That's why you're on video chasing her and "persuading" her to get into the car. How am I doing so far?'

Foster's voice was almost a whisper. 'No comment.'

There was a knock on the door. Norman slipped from his seat, padded across and opened it a crack. Judy Lane slipped a note into his hand, and he returned to the table. He handed the note to Southall.

'Apparently the forensic team checking your car have found some oil on the carpet,' she told Foster. 'There was an oil stain on the sheet the body was wrapped in. What are the chances they're going to be a match, Tom?'

'No comment.'

'Only you know what happened next, Tom,' Norman said to Foster. 'Perhaps she just wouldn't play ball. Or maybe she tried to put up a fight. Whatever, we reckon you must have lost it and murdered her.'

'No! That's not how it happened. I did not murder her! I just wanted to look after her, to love her.'

The admission was so abrupt and unexpected it took everyone by surprise. Even Foster himself seemed startled. It seemed an age before anyone spoke.

'So, why don't you tell us what did happen, Tom?' said Southall.

* * *

'How weird was that!' said Southall an hour later, after Foster had been led away and locked in a cell for the night. 'I really didn't think he'd confess so readily, and I don't get why he brought the telematics into it when he knew they'd been disconnected. He had no defence after that.'

'Yeah, but did he know they weren't working?' said Norman.

'I suppose it could have happened by accident while the car was being serviced,' said Southall. 'It's not the sort of thing you normally use, is it?'

'Young Jack's a slippery character who knows a thing or two about electronics,' said Norman. 'What if he disconnected the telematics so he could use the car without his father knowing?'

'Do you really think so?'

'Honestly? I don't know, but as you said, why would Tom mention it if he knew they didn't work?' Norman said.

'That was a master stroke, accusing him of murdering her,' said Southall.

'When the defence see the pathology report, I reckon they're going to plead manslaughter,' said Norman. 'And they might even get away with it if he sticks to his story.'

'I hope not,' said Southall. 'He covered her in blankets and locked her in the boot of his car while he went to collect his son in the van, for God's sake. It's no surprise the poor girl was scared literally to death.'

'I know what you mean, but I suppose he couldn't exactly have sat her in the passenger seat while he was picking up Jack, could he? I mean, how would that conversation go? "Hi, Jack, this is my new Asian girl, don't tell your mum." Just a tad awkward, don't you think?'

'And then when he found her dead, he left her in the back of his car for twenty-four hours,' said Southall. 'Do you really believe he managed to arrange for someone to take the body from his car in that hotel car park and dispose of it for him?'

'He's got an alibi that says he didn't bury her, and we know someone did. Maybe he made a deal with the people who supplied the girl. In fact, thinking about it, perhaps they made sure we found it so they could use it as some sort of warning to the rest of their clients.'

'I wonder if we'll ever find out who provides the girls,' said Southall. 'I was hoping Foster would tell us. After all, he's going away for long time, so he's got nothing to lose, has he?'

'The sort of people who run an operation like that don't pussyfoot around,' said Norman. 'I wouldn't be at all surprised if they've threatened to harm his wife, or Jack.'

'You mean like, one word to the police and they die?'

'Yeah, exactly that,' said Norman. 'And in my experience people like that don't make idle threats. It's how they manage to stay under the radar.'

'You should get off home,' said Southall. 'We can catch up with all the paperwork tomorrow.'

'Now that sounds like a plan I can work with,' said Norman.

CHAPTER TWENTY

Tuesday, 3 December, 15.00

Hand in hand, Norman and Faye ambled along the path that led up the side of the hill overlooking the sea. Their small dog scampered ahead, turning back every so often to make sure they were still there. Norman was gazing out to sea, taking in the view, which wasn't unusual, but he hadn't said a word for at least five minutes, which was.

'Do you want to talk about it?' Faye asked, giving his hand a squeeze.

Almost reluctantly, he tore his eyes away from the view and turned to her. 'What's that?'

'I can't recall the last time you came home so early, Norm, and you're never this quiet. It doesn't take a degree in psychology to know you have something on your mind. So, I wondered if you wanted to talk about it.'

Norman managed a wry smile. 'You don't miss much, do you?'

'It'd be hard to miss something so obvious. Is it the case? Is it getting to you?'

'No, it's not the case specifically,' said Norman. 'They all get to me, you know that.'

Years ago, someone had thought to install a bench at the side of the path. Now Norman steered Faye over to it and they sat down. The dog jumped up and settled on Norman's knees, where she could look out to sea and watch the gulls wheeling in the sky.

'So, what is it then?' asked Faye.

Norman sighed. 'D'you think people have a sell-by date?'

'Oh my God,' said Faye in alarm. 'Is it me? Are you telling me we're—'

Norman put his arm around her, pulled her close and gently kissed the top of her head. 'Jesus, Faye, of course it's not you. Come on now, do you seriously think I'd let go of the best thing that's ever happened to me? That's the last thing I would do.'

'Well, I'm glad to hear it. So, what is it with this "sell-by date" thing?'

'I was actually thinking in terms of work, not that I'm past it,' said Norman. 'I'm not in my dotage yet.'

Faye studied his face. 'I'm not sure I understand what you're saying.'

'I don't know, I just feel as if I've lost my spark. I've always relied on my intuition, but it seems to have deserted me lately. I mean, I completely missed Megan Maddison being a killer.'

'But didn't you say Sarah missed it too?'

'Yeah, I suppose that's true. It's not just that, though. I used to enjoy going to work and I was always excited about our cases, but recently it seems like more of a chore.'

'Have you spoken to Sarah about this?'

Norman shook his head. 'No, I haven't. She has her own decision to make. She's been offered a job back in England.'

'D'you think she'll take it?'

'I'm not sure. She says she's not keen on going back to England, but at the same time it's a promotion she's always wanted. I get the feeling she's finding it hard to resist. And if this new guy ends up taking Nathan's job, she'd be a fool to stay.'

'Ah, is that it? D'you think you're going to miss her?' Faye asked.

'Oh, sure I'll miss her if she goes, but it's not just that. Everyone seems to be down in the doldrums, even Catren. There used never to be a dull moment when she was around, but even she's no fun now. It's as if all the joy's been sucked out of the place.'

'Is it because of this new man — what's his name, Evans? Is that it?'

'He's definitely not helping. He seems to think we should make the evidence fit the most convenient suspect, whatever the reality might be. I'm used to coming up against the odd person like him, but there seem to be more and more of them these days, and they're all in senior positions.'

'Maybe you'll feel different when Nathan's back in charge, and Evans has gone back to wherever he came from.'

'I don't think it's going to make a great deal of difference who is in charge,' said Norman. 'I think you always know when it's time for a change, and maybe this is my time.'

Faye waited, but Norman seemed to have run out of steam.

'You'll miss it if you do leave,' she said. 'What would you do with yourself all day?'

'Do you know I've been in Wales nearly five years?'

'Yes, I suppose it must be something like that,' said Faye.

'There are all these fabulous, beautiful places to visit, and I haven't visited any of them, unless at least one dead body was involved. I think it's time I enjoyed everything Wales has to offer. And I'd like to enjoy it with you.'

'But I still have to work,' Faye said.

'Yeah, I know that. But you don't work every day, do you? Besides, I can find plenty to do when you're working.' He patted the dog on the head. 'Me and Trudy can go walking for a start. I could start that vegetable patch I keep going on about, and maybe grow a few fruit bushes. And I quite fancy having a greenhouse.'

Faye laughed. 'You don't know the first thing about growing vegetables.'

'I can learn,' said Norman.

'It sounds as if you've already made your decision,' said Faye.

'You don't mind?'

'Mind? Why would I mind? My only concern is that you'll get bored. Your job is such a big part of you.'

'Yeah, well, maybe I've got it the wrong way around and it's the job that's past its sell-by date, not me.'

She gave him a cheeky grin. 'Well, Mr Norman, take it from me, you are most definitely not past your sell-by date, and you prove it several times a week. I reckon there's a good few years left in you yet.'

'I'd like to think so,' said Norman, still looking slightly despondent.

'So, when are you going to hand in your resignation?'

'Oh, I don't know. I can't go before this current case is solved, that's for sure.'

'You mean the woman who killed her husband and then vanished?'

'Ha! Evans is trying to blame me for that. He seems to think I knew she'd murdered her husband and let her go, like I was her accomplice or something!'

'Is that what's really bothering you? You need to catch her to clear your name?' Faye said.

'I'm not worried about clearing my name. My conscience is clear whatever Evans might say. Anyone else would have done exactly the same in my place. And, I'm not overly worried about her getting away, she'll turn up eventually, whether I retire or not.'

'It's all the fuss over that young Syrian woman, isn't it?' asked Faye. 'I thought you had solved that.'

Norman looked out across the sea, absently stroking the dog. 'Well, yeah, we have, but only because we ignored Evans. A creep like him shouldn't have the right to decide that a victim be denied justice just because he wants to massage the crime figures and make himself look good.'

He turned and looked into her eyes. 'She was just a kid, no more than eighteen years old. We called her Majhul because we had no idea who she really was. She must have a family somewhere who are wondering where she is and they'll have no idea what's happened to her. Can you imagine that?'

Seeing how close he was to tears, Faye took his hand and gave it a squeeze.

'Maybe Evans is right, and we wouldn't have found out who she really was,' said Norman, 'but he refused to even let us try!'

Faye studied Norman's face for a moment. 'I understand how frustrated you are, but don't let it push you into making a hasty decision. I think you need to let the dust settle and give it a bit more thought, or you might come to regret it.'

Norman gave her a sad little smile. 'I don't think any amount of dust settling is going to change my mind.'

'Maybe,' said Faye. 'But it won't hurt, will it? You do know that whatever you decide, I'll be right here with you, don't you?'

Norman pulled her close. 'Jeez, I really struck gold when I found you, didn't I?'

THE END

THE JOFFE BOOKS STORY

We began in 2014 when Jasper agreed to publish his mum's much-rejected romance novel and it became a bestseller.

Since then we've grown into the largest independent publisher in the UK. We're extremely proud to publish some of the very best writers in the world, including Joy Ellis, Faith Martin, Caro Ramsay, Helen Forrester, Simon Brett and Robert Goddard. Everyone at Joffe Books loves reading and we never forget that it all begins with the magic of an author telling a story.

We are proud to publish talented first-time authors, as well as established writers whose books we love introducing to a new generation of readers.

We won Trade Publisher of the Year at the Independent Publishing Awards in 2023 and Best Publisher Award in 2024 at the People's Book Prize. We have been shortlisted for Independent Publisher of the Year at the British Book Awards for the last five years, and were shortlisted for the Diversity and Inclusivity Award at the 2022 Independent Publishing Awards. In 2023 we were shortlisted for Publisher of the Year at the RNA Industry Awards, and in 2024 we were shortlisted at the CWA Daggers for the Best Crime and Mystery Publisher.

We built this company with your help, and we love to hear from you, so please email us about absolutely anything bookish at feedback@joffebooks.com.

If you want to receive free books every Friday and hear about all our new releases, join our mailing list here: www.joffebooks.com/freebooks.

And when you tell your friends about us, just remember: it's pronounced Joffe as in coffee or toffee!

www.ingramcontent.com/pod-product-compliance
Ingram Content Group UK Ltd.
Pitfield, Milton Keynes, MK11 3LW, UK
UKHW010835031125
8727UKWH00043B/452

9 781805 733041